A M.

S. SHANKAR

A MAP OF WHERE I LIVE

HEINEMANN
Portsmouth, NH

Heinemann
A division of Reed Elsevier Inc.
361 Hanover Street
Portsmouth, NH 03801-3912

Offices and agents throughout the world

© 1997 by S. Shankar

All rights reserved. No part of this book may be reproduced in any form or by any electronic or mechanical means, including information storage and retrieval systems, without permission in writing from the publisher, except by a reviewer, who may quote brief passages in a review.

Library of Congress Cataloging-in-Publication Data

Shankar, Subramanian, 1962–
   A map of where I live / S. Shankar.
      p.   cm. — (Asian writers series)
   ISBN 0–435–08143–8 (acid-free paper)
   I. Title. II. Series: Asian writers series (Oxford, England)
PS3569.H332614M37 1997
813'.54—dc21   97-530
                                                              CIP

Editor: Lisa A. Barnett
Production: Vicki Kasabian
Cover design: Jenny Jensen Greenleaf
Cover illustration: Venantius J. Pinto
Author photograph: Anannya Bhattacharjee
Manufacturing: Louise Richardson

Printed in the United States of America on acid-free paper

01 00 99 98 97   DA   1 2 3 4 5

For
Anannya
vazhkai thunaivi

Author's Note

The Madras sections of this book are a work of fiction. All names, characters, incidents, organizations, and places in these sections are either invented or used fictitiously. Any resemblance to actual persons, living or dead, events, organizations, or locales is entirely coincidental.

I wish to acknowledge Hosam Aboul-Ela, Anannya Bhattacharjee, John Zuern, and Louis Mendoza for their invaluable suggestions on the manuscript. Vivek Bahl, Mallika Dutt, and Barbara Harlow had the kindness to read the manuscript at various stages and offer encouragement. I wish also to thank Amitava Bhattacharjee, H. Bruce Franklin, Shona Ramayya, Jael Silliman, Shashi Tharoor, and my father, K. S. Subramanian, for support and advice of various kinds in bringing this book to publication. A very special thanks goes to Lisa Barnett for believing.

Prologue

One October evening in Madras innumerable things were happening at the same time in a street in Krantinagar. In the living room of a second-floor apartment of a building called Anand Vilas, for example, an old woman with white hair was sitting with a steel tumbler of coffee in her right hand and reading the latest issue of *Kalki,* her head cocked strangely over her right shoulder as if she were watching something surreptitiously. Above her, a ceiling fan turned slowly.

In the small kitchen behind her, her daughter-in-law was heating coffee for her son. They were both silent because the son had just returned from the doctor with terrible news. The old woman did not know this yet, and turning a page she thought pleasantly of traveling to Calcutta to visit her daughter in December, after her late husband's death anniversary. In a corner of the living room, behind the TV, unseen and unknown to anybody, a wall lizard had been waiting frozen for over fifteen minutes, since before the son had returned. The fly it had been waiting for in ambush had long since gone elsewhere, but the lizard remained, still trapped in its singlemindedness. The fly was now in the kitchen, circling and whirling over the sugar jar.

These are just a few of the innumerable things that were happening in a single apartment in a street in Madras.

Other people in Ganapathy Kovil Street were engaged otherwise. Ganapathy Kovil Street is a short, straight street in Krantinagar, the treeless expanse of the open maidan separating Krantinagar from Kuppancherry on one side of it and the large compound of Anand Vilas along most of the other side. At six past six in the evening, three hundred and forty-four people were gathered together in various attitudes and moods and circumstances in that street. We are not concerned with all of them. Only a handful of them are of any consequence to us.

Who are they? What were they doing?

Five people were in an Ambassador car with dark, tinted windows that was making its way through Ganapathy Kovil Street. Of them, one was the driver and he is one of those who are not of especial consequence to us, though if another story were being told we might want to inquire into the facts behind a single human finger that lay buried in one corner of his ancestral home in his village and was his chief worry in life. The other four in the car were Bhimanbhai Dwarkanath (the owner of Kuberan A/C Theater in Krantinagar and other business interests in West Madras), Sethuraman (a local politician), Shanthamma (a local union leader), and Vasanthi (Shanthamma's companion).

Sethuraman, Shanthamma, and Vasanthi were seated in the backseat of the car. Vasanthi was sitting in the middle, holding a briefcase in her hand. Shanthamma, a gray-haired woman with bold, firm features that belied her gray hair, was looking out of the window on her side. Her eyes, behind utilitarian, plastic-frame glasses, were studiedly expressionless.

The face of Sethuraman, who was sitting on the other side of Vasanthi, however, was not quite so expressionless. The faintest outline of a smile was lifting the self-indulgent pout of his lips. He was watching Shanthamma, but he was doing this in a covert fashion and it was not clear if Shanthamma had noticed him. He was a lean, elderly man with an aristocratic cast of features which age had molded into gentler but also more self-satisfied lines. When he was standing, he towered over most people around him.

Bhimanbhai Dwarkanath, sitting beside the driver, was, on the other hand, a round man. His face was pudgy and beaded with sweat, although the air conditioner of the car was humming gently. He had just spoken and was looking down at the interlocked fingers in his lap, waiting for a response. On two of the fingers, gold rings stared back at him. The words Dwarkanath had just spoken settled without any immediate response into the persistent hum of the air conditioner. If Dwarkanath was surprised at the lack of response, he did not show it. But the tension in the car between Dwarkanath and Sethuraman on the one hand and Shanthamma and Vasanthi on the other was a solid, tangible thing.

The Ambassador car in which these people were traveling was Bhimanbhai Dwarkanath's. At the moment, it was passing a wayside stall that stood opposite Anand Vilas in Ganapathy Kovil Street. The expanse of the maidan between Krantinagar and Kuppancherry spread out behind the stall. A woman in a blue cloth was sitting on a bench in front. It was at her that Shanthamma was looking from the passing car. Her name was Selvi.

A man was behind the counter of the stall. The name of this man was Joseph. In front of him were eight dirty glass jars with various sorts of candy, biscuits, and nuts in them. Overhead on strings hung bananas, plaintains, a wire basket of eggs, and a collection of cheap cloth caps. To his right, in little compartments against the side of the stall, sat packets of cigarettes, matchboxes, and beedis. Behind him, in an icebox filled with ice, lay bottles of soft drinks in cool darkness, with the lid closed over them. Large vessels of water, milk, coffee, and tea, and smaller containers of sugar, coffee grains, and tea leaves sat on a little table by the side of the icebox. Against the sides of the stall, on the outside, various Tamil and English newspapers and magazines dangled from strings. Joseph, a dark, stocky little man from Kerala with curly graying hair, was himself at that very moment in the act of considering whether to squash an ant climbing obliviously up the side of one of the eight jars in front of him.

Two wooden benches faced each other across six feet of dusty soil in front of the stall. Selvi, at whom Shanthamma was looking, was seated on one of these two benches, cupping one of Joseph's glasses in her hands. In the glass, steam rose from the four inches of warm coffee and fogged the sides. Selvi was small, with a broad face in a head that was too large for her body. Everyone who saw her noted her tidiness. There was a kind of precise neatness about even her skeletal structure. Her body, wrapped in a blue cotton cloth and a blouse of indeterminate color, was bony. The shoulders jutted up through the folds of her garment. This neatness was repeated in the way she had done her hair, in a tidy little bun at the back of her head.

Selvi worked daily, except for Sunday, as a maidservant in two different houses. She worked in Dr. Ranga's house from six to eight in the morning. Then she worked from eight-thirty to eleven-thirty for Accountant Prabhu's family, which lived in Apartment C-10 in Anand Vilas. At one in the afternoon, by which time lunch would have been eaten in Dr. Ranga's house, she went back and worked there until four. She was also involved with Shanthamma's Domestic Workers Union. Now she was sitting on the bench in front of Joseph's stall, holding in her hands a glass of coffee poised in front of her mouth and looking over its curved edge at a cycle-rickshaw. The cycle-rickshaw had just entered the street at the far end and was passing one of the two gates of Anand Vilas.

One of the two people sitting in the rickshaw was a young man in a white shirt. C. Ramakrishnan was his name, but everybody called him RK. Prominent about him just then was a blue stain on his white shirt, right above his heart, where his shirt pocket had held a pen. In his right hand, RK brandished the culprit pen and was attempting to clean it by running it through his untidy long hair. A brown canvas bag lay in his lap. RK kept it from falling out of the jerking rickshaw with his left hand. Two thick tomes, entitled *Indian Constitutional Law* (volumes I and II), nestled in the bag among sundry notepads, pencils, pens, and scraps of paper. There was also a thick notebook that RK had bought many weeks earlier to keep a journal. *Journal* was written on the first page in large untidy letters, but RK had not gotten around to making any entries yet. Many weeks later, one of the entries he would make in the notebook would begin, "What a horrible way to die! Stabbed in the stomach and chest more than thirty times. There was blood everywhere, even in the hair, which had come loose and fallen on the shoulders." At the moment, his lips were pressed together in exasperation at the unsteady bag, the ink stain, and the pen.

A white woman who was clearly a few years older than RK sat next to him in the rickshaw. She had short brown hair that she kept tucking behind her ears. Sunglasses covered half her face. Large earrings dangled against her cheeks. A silver cross rested against the sunburnt skin of her neck. She was wearing sandals and a printed cotton dress that reached below her knees. A large bag with *Esprit* stenciled on it hung from her right shoulder. She was an American and her name was Carol Carby. She was scrunched uncomfortably into a corner of the rickshaw because of RK's vigorous treatment of the pen, but, if she had not been wearing sunglasses, a tolerant amusement would have been visible in her eyes.

Powering the rickshaw were the legs of Kulan, which means "short" in Tamil. His real name was Kanakaraj, but everybody had always called him Kulan because of his height and he did not mind. Because the street was inclined here, Kulan had risen from his seat and was pedaling standing up. His two black legs were hard with tense, corded muscles. His head was bowed over the metal handlebar of the rickshaw and his mouth was open in a slight grimace. His two fists were wrapped tightly around the handlebar. The thumb of his right hand was pressing down on the lever of the bell of the rickshaw, filling the street with a jangling noise, and his quick eyes were following a dog that was rushing to the side of the street. All in all, Kulan seemed at the moment little more than a dark collection of pulsing, pushing, pulling, turning muscles hanging poised between two rubber pedals and a metal rod.

One of the people who had looked up at the sound of the bell of Kulan's rickshaw was Mohan. He had just sat down by the wall of the small Ganapathy temple that stood opposite the second gate of Anand Vilas. Mohan was a man of many trades but mostly he lived by ironing clothes. This he did on a little mobile cart whose usual position was under a tree by the Ganapathy temple. Piles of clothes and a large heavy iron, heated with burning coals, lay on the cart. To this cart, people from the apartments and houses in the area brought him sarees, shirts, blouses, trousers, and other pieces of clothing to be ironed. Sometimes Mohan himself went to collect clothes from houses or apartments, but this he did only for very regular customers. Usually he sat here by the wall of the temple, where the tree cast a shadow most of the day, smoked beedis as he was doing now, and waited for his customers to come to him. Mohan did not know it at this time, but he was sitting right where, in a few weeks, a murder was to take place.

Two people were in the living room of Apartment B-6 in Anand Vilas, where the bustle of the street below was little more than a hum. The living room had white walls, on one of which hung a picture of RK's father with a garland around it. In one corner stood a TV, in another a large radio from many years ago, its wooden cabinet top marked by the white rings left by cups and glasses. One of the persons in the room was RK's mother. The apartment was hers. The other was Chandran, a bald old man in a shirt and veshti. Both the shirt and the veshti were starched and spotlessly white and made a striking contrast to the brownness of his skin. Chandran was a well-known Tamil writer, editor of a journal and a political figure of prominence. "I'm old," he was saying to RK's mother at the moment, as an explanation for a persistent pain that he had begun to feel in his right arm. "I'm old." But the vigor of his manner and his general air of impatience did not bear out his words. He was a close friend of Shanthamma's and was engaged in a political project of some consequence. He could not afford to feel old.

Some way down Ganapathy Kovil Street, beyond Joseph's shop and beyond the far wall of the Anand Vilas compound, a long building with a thatched roof and rough cement walls stood in a little compound of its own. This building was divided into four rooms, each one of them a separate dwelling. The doors of the rooms all opened onto a verandah, which was covered by a tiled roof. Behind the building, not visible from the street, was an outhouse with a bathroom and a toilet.

In the first room of the main building, the room closest to the street, Valur Vishveswaran looked up with annoyance at the sound of Kulan's rickshaw bell. Valur Vishveswaran was a middle-aged man, tall, with long, prematurely white hair that reached below his shoulders. He also had a long beard that spread its white hairs stiffly across his chest. He was wearing a white kurta and a white pyjama. At the moment of his hearing the bell, Valur Vishveswaran was sitting in his chair at his desk. There was little else in the room. A wooden cot stood against a wall and a steel trunk stood in a corner. These were his only possessions. Valur Vishveswaran had appeared quite suddenly in Ganapathy Kovil Street with his trunk a few weeks earlier. He had rented the room, bought the few pieces of furniture that he had, and moved in with no further ado. The curious people of Ganapathy Kovil Street, the loiterers at Joseph's stall, could learn nothing about him. He did not socialize with anybody. Nobody visited him.

On the desk in front of Valur Vishveswaran lay a stack of A-4 paper. He had written *Account of My Journey to Lilliput* at the top of one sheet, crossed it out, rewritten it below, and then put a question mark next to it. The text on the sheet continued, "I, Valur Vishveswaran, in the fortieth year of my life, having ascertained after great research the exact location of Lilliput, traveled thence for a . . ." This much Valur Vishveswaran had accomplished when the sound of Kulan's bell had disturbed him and caused him to look up.

Chapter 1

How should I begin? How do you begin a journal when you have never kept a journal before? What goes into it? What is its purpose? Is it enough to record only the daily happenings of an uneventful life? Or should I aim for something else, perhaps for the satisfaction of a more selective but coherent account of my life?

This is the question that has kept me frozen helplessly for so many weeks before the first page of this notebook.

What is worst is to be rendered impotent by such a banal question. . . .

What is a journal? It is what I make of it. My journal shall be a fresh acquaintance with whom I shall have a conversation. I shall explain to it the events of my life, I shall introduce to it the most familiar, and perhaps unfamiliar, people and places in my life.

So I shall begin at what seems to me both a perfectly arbitrary as well as a perfectly logical place. I shall begin with myself. And I shall begin with my condition as per the moment. One day toward the end of the summer of '92, I shall write, I, RK, returned from the U.S. to Madras with an M.A. in history. I moved back into my old room in Apartment B-6 of Anand Vilas, where my mother had been living alone for a little over two years, ever since I had left for the U.S. I put my books (some of them the same old books, some of them new) back on the bookshelves. I moved my desk back under the window where I like it to be. On the door to my room, I put up some posters and postcards that I like.

I have returned to Madras to pursue a degree in the Law College, but it is too late to join this year. What shall I do in the months that remain before the fresh academic year begins? I have asked myself this question numerous times. The answers seem many. Perhaps I should look for a job. Perhaps I should write—something that I have always wanted to do but for which I have never had the time. Perhaps I should travel. Perhaps I should listen to my mother and get married.

Sometimes the options seem too many and sometimes they seem too few. The decisions seem so hard to make. Especially since my father, when he died, left enough money for there to be no immediate worry about things. In the meantime, I read. I sleep late in the mornings. Sometimes I visit old friends and try, with mixed success, to renew old friendships. This has been the nature of my life for the last few weeks. I did, however, at my mother's repeated suggestion, go to see my father's old and dear friend, Chandran. It's years since my father's death, but Chandran has kept up his friendship with us without change. This is a loyalty that my mother will not let pass unappreciated, even though she does not entirely approve of Chandran because of his outspokenness.

Chandran . . . How strange and scandalously liberating to write the name instead of "Uncle." I could never call the old man "Chandran" to his face.

Chandran is the kind of person who is referred to as "a grand old man." He too refers to himself in this fashion sometimes. "I am a grand old man of Tamil literature and edit a Tamil political journal famous for its independence," I once heard him announce to someone who was being introduced to him (as he himself is being introduced to my journal this very moment). Chandran is only his pen name, but he is universally known as Chandran and this is the name he prefers. He is fond of playing ironically on this pen name in his articles. For example, he sometimes signs his articles "Only Chandran, not Suriyan." If he is only the moon, who is this sun that he alludes to? My father would jokingly ask him this question. Chandran was not forthcoming with an answer. "Not you, certainly" is the only answer that he would make to my father. He has been married three times and when I went to visit him before I left for the U.S., he said to me with mock seriousness, "I have never been able to keep the women I have been married to. Even in their moments of greatest passion they have cried out, 'Only Chandran, not Suriyan.'" Chandran is sixty-eight years old and likes to shock people. He is famous for his cutting sense of humor. In the moribund Tamil society of Madras, he is a veritable force of destruction. At that time, two years ago, I too was appropriately shocked.

When I went to see Chandran after my return from the U.S., he told me of Carol Carby, who has come from the U.S. to do some research on unions in Madras, partly here where I live, in Krantinagar, and in adjoining Kuppancherry. "Isn't that a wonderful coincidence?!" he cried. "Who would have thought such things happened. Of course you must spend time with Carol and help her now. Take her around. Act as a liaison between her and us natives. Keep a watch on the savages that she is studying. What if somebody abducts her? Nobody would understand her cries for help because of her American accent, and that would be too bad." This was Chandran's tiresome way of getting me involved in the local events of Madras. My mother had been talking to him. The plan is to get me interested in "things in Madras." And so I am to chaperone an American professor of anthropology around the city. I only hope she isn't trying to discover the "real India" or something like that.

Actually I am not against the idea at all. I have respect for Chandran's political sensibility and judgment of people. I am sure the experience will be interesting. Chandran is not an easy man to refuse, especially in something as reasonable as this. I consented. A time was set for me to meet Carol on a day convenient for both of us (today) at Krantinagar railway station. I was to go with her at six in the evening to see this woman Selvi, who is a member of the Domestic Workers Union.

Today I was at the station as planned and there was another surprising coincidence—Kulan, who used to take me to school in his cycle-rickshaw many, many years ago when I was a child, was with his rickshaw in front of the station. He approached me. "Are you here to meet the white lady?" he said to me. "Carol Carby," he added with just a moment's hesitation. I nodded and looked at him with surprise; he did not recognize me, but I recognized him. "Kulan," I said to him. "It's me, RK. Don't you remember me?" He looked at me closely for a moment. "Apartment B-6. Anand Vilas," he said. "Krantinagar Primary School."

We looked at each other uneasily. Years before, when I was a child and he was little more than a boy just beginning to run a cycle-rickshaw, we had been great friends. Sometimes he had let me ride on the bar of the rickshaw, in the front, where I was given authority over the bell. He was, in those days, a kind of hero to me. Now he was a man in a dirty white cloth with abnormally developed calf muscles and prematurely graying hair; and I was a young man with a degree in history who had just returned from the U.S. because I felt somehow I had to come back "home" and do something about something, what I wasn't clear.

Kulan, it turned out, knew Chandran and had been asked by him to meet Carol and me at Krantinagar station. In his typical way, Chandran had not bothered to give him my name. He had only told him to watch for an "impatient young man with long hair" who looked as if he was waiting for someone.

Carol arrived a little early. She was a plain but not unattractive woman of the serious American academic type—short hair, no makeup, wearing the cotton dress that is the uniform for a cheap-traveling female First Worlder in the "Third World." I decided I liked my first impression of her. There was a kind of complicated and self-conscious sincerity and eagerness in the way she paid attention to both Kulan and me as she and I climbed into the rickshaw and we set off down the road toward Kuppancherry. She kept trying to speak to Kulan in her very rudimentary Tamil. She was uncertain about traveling in the rickshaw, I could tell. I too became ashamed at having climbed into the rickshaw. I dutifully stopped traveling in rickshaws many years ago, and I could not imagine why I had climbed into the rickshaw in this instance. It seemed the easiest way to resolve the awkward pause in front of the station. Now Carol sat carefully pressing herself into a corner, as if making herself as small as possible would also make her lighter. I wished I hadn't climbed into the rickshaw.

My assignment from Chandran was as follows—I was to go with Carol to Selvi's house, which was in Kuppancherry, to introduce ourselves and make an appointment to see her, so that Carol could interview her for her research; but we found Selvi sitting in

Joseph's coffee stall, right across the street from where I'm writing these words right now. Kulan, who knows Selvi well, pulled up to Joseph's stall when he saw her sitting there. "This is Selvi," he said, sitting back on the seat of the rickshaw and wiping the sweat off his face with a cloth that he had. Selvi, a small woman in a blue cloth, looked up at us from the bench on which she was sitting, wondering what all this was about.

I climbed out of the rickshaw and bought Campa Orange for Carol, Kulan, and myself. Selvi, who was drinking coffee, declined. I knew Joseph, the stall owner, slightly, because I often bought drinks or magazines from him. I had begun to keep an account with him a few weeks earlier. "How are you, RK-sir?" he said to me as he swung the lid of his icebox open and took three bottles of Campa Orange from the ice within. The ice broke and crackled as he lifted the bottles out. "Really cold," he assured me as he maneuvered a bottle into the mouth of the opener on the icebox. It was an old Coca-Cola icebox, from the days before Coca-Cola had been kicked out of the country.

Kulan was already explaining to Selvi the purpose of our coming to see her. Shanthamma, he was telling her, had asked the white woman, who was a professor in America, to interview her for a book that the white woman was writing on unions. Shanthamma, I remembered as I listened to Kulan, is a prominent personality in the trade union movement in Madras. Her chief achievement has been the difficult task of organizing the overwhelmingly female domestic worker population in a few parts of Madras into something resembling a trade union. I have seen her name in newspapers now and then. I know Chandran has some connections with her, but I have never met her.

"Me?" Selvi said to Kulan in response to his explanatory remark. "Why is she going to interview me?"

"Shanthamma is the one who gave her the idea," Kulan replied. "Don't you have experience in the union? She is going to interview many union workers. Why shouldn't she interview you?"

Selvi looked at Carol doubtfully. "How will she interview me? Does she know Tamil?"

Carol understood Selvi's glance and the last words she had spoken. "Little, little," she said in Tamil, much to the delight of Joseph, who made an amused noise.

"I will be there too," I said to Selvi, and Kulan explained to her who I was.

Selvi considered for a moment, her broad face furrowing with thought. "Tomorrow at four-thirty," she said. "Bring her home." And she told me where she lived. On a piece of paper, I jotted down her directions. Selvi lives across the maidan in Kuppancherry.

Carol and I figured out how to meet the next day. I was pleased that the interview with Selvi had been arranged so expeditiously. Matters taken care of, I was about to suggest that I take Carol back to Krantinagar station when things suddenly got a little nasty. Mohan, who irons clothes on his cart under a tree a little down the street, had come up to Joseph's stall to buy some beedis and was standing and watching us with glowering eyes. He lit up a beedi, snorted, spat to one side and spoke. "Selvi is going to be famous it seems," he said. "Will the lady interview me also?" He looked at Carol and me as he said this.

No one responded. Carol looked at me inquiringly.

"What am I?" Mohan continued, taking the beedi from between his teeth. "Am I a union member? I am only a foolish person who irons clothes under a tree. Am I worthy of an interview?"

"You? Foolish?" Kulan retorted with a laugh. Apparently, he knew Mohan.

"Compared to you, I am foolish," Mohan said. "You are a union king. You are a king amongst workers." In the deepening hum of the evening, his voice was sharp with sarcasm.

"Don't look for trouble, Mohan," Selvi said quietly.

In all this, there was an undercurrent of emotion that I was not catching. There was something going on there that I was not quite a part of.

Joseph stirred uneasily on his stool. He leaned over the counter of his stall. "Be quiet," he said to Mohan. "No trouble. Look, that boy Nagesh from A-9 has come looking for you." A small boy was standing by Mohan's cart down the street with a bundle of clothes in his hand.

Mohan looked round sullenly. "No more today," he shouted to the boy. "I have closed everything for today. Come tomorrow." The boy hesitated for a moment and then went away toward Anand Vilas.

"I must get back to the station," Kulan said, putting his empty bottle back on the counter of Joseph's stall and ending what was becoming an unpleasant situation. Carol decided to go back to the station with him. Selvi set off toward Kuppancherry. I remained to find out from Joseph how much my account with him had become.

"Unions," Mohan said bitterly, as Kulan's rickshaw and Selvi disappeared in opposite directions. In a moment, most of his former audience had vanished. He addressed Joseph but meant the words for me. "Because of Selvi's union, my woman couldn't work at Contractor Krishnan's house last year. Selvi wouldn't let her. Contractor Krishnan kept calling her back but Selvi came and threatened her."

Joseph looked at Mohan. "You are a very stupid man," he said to him. "If you don't learn to behave properly, you need not come here. I don't like loud talking."

Mohan glared at Joseph but did not say anything.

It had grown dark all around. The trains from Madras Central were beginning to bring people back from work at the office buildings around Mount Road and Beach. All along the railway tracks, from Madras Central in one direction and Madras Beach in the other, suburban electric trains, I could imagine, were stopping even at that moment to let off commuters at places like Krantinagar railway station. From there, people were dispersing in different directions again. Some of these were moving in a steady stream up Ganapathy Kovil Street. A few turned into Anand Vilas. Others turned into other streets of Krantinagar. Some continued down Ganapathy Kovil Street to the path that led to Kuppancherry. Nine-to-five humanity was on the move.

Lights had come on in Ganapathy Kovil Street. Outside one of the gates of Anand Vilas, three youths were standing and talking and joking with one another about cricket. One of them was demonstrating a square-cut. He made a loud noise with his tongue to indicate the ball hitting the bat—"tock." We could hear the sound at Joseph's stall. The others in the group were laughing and shaking their heads. Their friend nodded his head vigorously, insisting on his point. He repeated the action and the sound—"tock." Another train drummed into Krantinagar station in the distance. Quite suddenly, I thought of this corner that I know on the edge of Harlem where the subway tracks appear above ground for a short distance. On that corner too young men hung around, talking and joking. Graffiti covered the wall behind them—*Just Say Yes to People Power, Suck Cock, The Black Man Is Awake, Hey!* . . .

As I left Joseph's stall and crossed the street to Anand Vilas, a tall man in a white kurta and white pyjamas came out of the compound next to Anand Vilas and stood in the street for a moment before turning toward the station and striding away. This strange man is named Valur Vishveswaran and he lives in one of the rooms that have been built in a row in the little compound adjacent to Anand Vilas. He walked with his head bent. His long, white hair fell down his shoulders and brushed against his chest. "White-Beard Grandfather! White-Beard Grandfather!" some small boys shouted at him, using the nickname they had given him. "White-Beard Grandfather! What do you do in your room all day?" Valur Vishveswaran walked straight ahead, without looking up. The people coming from the station made way for him, stepping aside to let him pass.

By the time I came up to my room here, I was feeling all gloomy. A quiet, solitary man whose only fault is his eccentricity (if that is what it is) cannot walk down the street without being heckled by children. Four persons cannot stand by a wayside stall and talk about unions without a fifth person, who has nothing to do with anything, butting in. What was the use of *anything*? I kept brooding and brooding about this, getting into a bad mood. I am given to such temperament.

Chandran had come by on a rare visit to see my mother. I had just missed him. He had left perhaps a few minutes before, even as we were at Joseph's stall, talking. I changed my clothes and watched some stupid family planning show on TV for some time. My mother was in the kitchen. What to do? It was still too early for dinner. On an impulse, I came in here and started this journal I have been wanting to start for many weeks now. Now it is long after dinner and late at night.

Chapter 2

I, Valur Vishveswaran, in the fortieth year of my life, having ascertained after great research the exact location of Lilliput, traveled thence for a journey of discovery. The wonderful events of that journey, what I saw, heard, recorded, what all these events portend for the community of man, for the community of bandur, which is the name in High and Northern Lilliputian for us and means "giant ones," shall form the text of these my memoirs.

Skepticism I expect. I expect bandur to say, "What! An undiscovered land of tiny dwarfs?! There can be no such thing. This land of Lilliput is but the invention of an Irishman. It is nothing more." Not so, say I. Much is invented in Jonathan Swift's tale of Gulliver's journey to Lilliput. I will not deny this. Swift took the few real details of Mr. Lemuel Gulliver's travels to Lilliput that he knew and surrounded them with the inventions of his own overworked imagination. So successful was this misuse of the imagination, this creation of a monstrous fairy tale, that Swift proceeded to invent three more "journeys" for Gulliver.

The fictions of Swift I will not bother to defend, but that a Lemuel Gulliver traveled to Lilliput is certain. Gulliver's voyage there has been the subject of considerable inquiry among the Lilliputians, and the details of that great journey have been established by their historians beyond all doubt. I have, in fact, a copy of the authoritative version of these historical events written by Skkrrk Skkrrl. Unfortunately, this great classic I have not yet been able to translate. I hope to undertake that task at some future date and attach the translation as an appendix to these memoirs.

But to return to my own journey to Lilliput. I propose here to begin by setting out, with the skeptics especially in mind, how it is that I ascertained the exact location of Lilliput and managed to journey there. All this I accomplished despite being the subject of contempt and ridicule from the outset of my project. Alone I was in this wide, wide world. So complete was the disbelief in what I was attempting that after the first few rebuffs I spoke no more to any of my work. From then till now, I have lived in anonymity and obscurity. A lesser heart would have broken, but my faith in the importance of my work kept me going.

It is not my intention to settle scores here, but I must note that the Indian government, three universities here in India and elsewhere, and one important international society dedicated to exploration, all declined to participate in my project. All of them ignored my proposal for a team of explorers completely. The last attempt for help in my project I made personally and not through the mail. I cannot let pass without comment the behavior of this eminent explorer who had connections with a wealthy international society for exploration. He fidgeted, he looked at his watch, he strained to hide his disbelief. When I persisted in making my case, he got up abruptly from his chair and said, "Mr. Vishveswaran, we do not have money for crazy schemes with no substance in them."

Crazy schemes! Well, I wish to name no names here, but when finally relations are established between us and the great civilizations of Southern Lilliput (as indeed they will be when the Southern Lilliputians are good and ready) the world will know whom to credit for making the first overtures to the Southern Lilliputians. What about Gulliver? some of you may say. Well, what about him? He made no conscious attempt to establish relations with the Lilliputians of the South. Indeed, the few scraps of notes he has left of his trip to Lilliput are singularly critical of them. I dismiss him. He deserves no credit. It is I who first consciously, deliberately, made an advance to them. The significance of all this will not be, cannot be, forgotten.

But I must record how Gulliver's few notes on the Lilliputians fell into my hands. About five years ago, Mr. Norman Morrison, who comes of an old Anglo-Indian family, decided to emigrate to Australia to be with his daughter. I bought his house in Ooty from him. When I took possession of the house, I found in one room an old steel trunk with this note taped to it: "Mr. Vishveswaran, you tell me you are a historian associated with Madras University. Here are some things you may find interesting. These papers have been in my family for many, many decades. If you find them of no value, you may dispose of them as you wish. The scrap-paper man I'm sure will be glad to have them! Norman Morrison." And there in that trunk, between the pages of the diary of someone called Mrs. Valerie Morrison dating from the nineteenth century, I found four yellowing sheets of paper covered with very close handwriting. These were Lemuel Gulliver's notes on his accidental journey to Lilliput.

On reading these notes, I knew at once that I had made a discovery of immense importance. There was no doubt whatsoever in my mind that I was looking at a genuine manuscript—of someone who had really traveled to Lilliput. The quality and present condition of the paper, the nature of the script, the language of the narrative, all convinced me of the genuineness of what I was looking at. I should also mention here that I have considerable expertise with ancient manuscripts.

I remembered Swift's book too, of course, and went and consulted it. There were indeed similarities between the manuscript and the book. Swift's account of how Gulliver found himself tied down by the Lilliputians when he first regained consciousness in Lilliput is taken almost verbatim from Gulliver's manuscript. Some of Swift's description of the physical characteristics of the tiny Lilliputians and their civilization at the time is also real. But that is as far as the similarities go. Gulliver never befriended the Lilliputians, which is the term for all these tiny people rather than just those of one kingdom, as Swift would have us believe. The relationship between the Lilliputians and Gulliver was purely hostile. Both Gulliver's own notes and the Lilliputians' account of the incidents are very clear on this point. Gulliver remained for ten days (the chronology of the manuscript is confused, but Skkrrk Skkrrl's work is very detailed in its dates) in Lilliput, living off the meat and vegetable produce of the land and hiding from the Lilliputians whenever possible. Skkrrk Skkrrl writes of how Gulliver's wanton acts of depredation, inconsiderate behavior, and dietary needs left an entire agricultural district devastated and forced drastic measures to be taken. This area, the Karunar Punuk, is a desert even today. On the tenth day, Gulliver discovered a boat that had washed ashore, probably from his own ill-fated ship, and set out to sea. The matter of the similarities and differences between Swift and Gulliver is something that I plan to examine at greater length in a monograph that I shall prepare soon.

How Gulliver managed to return home to England can only be a matter of conjecture. Perhaps Lemuel Gulliver left more extensive notes on his great excursion into the lands of the Lilliputians some three hundred years ago. If so, I have not been able to find these notes. The manuscript that I do possess seems to indicate through allusions the existence of other material. The quest for the complete notes written by Lemuel Gulliver must surely be the greatest intellectual and scholarly challenge of our times. I hope someone who reads these lines will take up the quest.

Soon after having discovered Gulliver's manuscript in Mr. Norman Morrison's trunk I went to England on a grant for two months, ostensibly to study papers of the East India Company relating to the siege of Srirangapatnam, but really to see what I could find on Gulliver and his journey to Lilliput. I went to find anything I could that would help me make the journey to Lilliput that I had already decided to undertake.

I found, as I have already noted, nothing by Gulliver on his journey. I did find some little information on Lemuel Gulliver himself. I discovered that Lemuel Gulliver had indeed studied "physic" at Leyden (as Swift notes that he had). He had set out in 1699 on a journey to the South Sea Islands. This was the journey that led to his adventure in Lilliput. The next mention I found of him was in relation to three journeys made with Captain Charles Whacker to Surat and Fort St. George. The last journey, to Fort St. George (as Madras was then known), was made in 1707. I assume it was during this time that the manuscript relating to his journey to Lilliput was left behind in Madras and somehow, how I have never been able to learn, got into the Morrison family, who took it to Ooty. It is also of course possible that the manuscript was brought to Madras by the Morrison family at a much later date and the matter of Gulliver's last journey being to Madras is simply coincidence. At any rate, the only other mention that I found of Gulliver in all my research was that he had settled in Ireland for the last years of his life.

As you can very well imagine, all this took an immense amount of time and digging. When I returned to India I had of course very little to show on the siege of Srirangapatnam. So when I applied for another grant to go to England, it was refused. This did not deter me. Fortunately, I was independently wealthy and did not need grants to continue my important work. I sold the newly acquired house in Ooty and went to England and Ireland on my own. I spent many months looking at every single scrap of paper associated with Jonathan Swift that I could find. I came up with nothing relating to Gulliver. This was heartbreaking. I returned to India disappointed. I tried to get in touch with Mr. Norman Morrison in Australia, but could get no reply from the only address I had of him.

Where was Lilliput? Where exactly was it to be found? I had nothing to tell me except Swift's locating it in or near the Southern Indian Ocean in his book. How true was this? Could I believe it? I spent months agonizing over these questions.

And then I had the most wonderful good fortune! One day as I was idly looking at Mrs. Valerie Morrison's diary, I found a sheet of paper I had not looked at closely because it was clearly in Mrs. Morrison's handwriting and I therefore had little interest in it. It was mostly a description of an elephant ride that she had had with the Raja of Mysore through the jungles of his kingdom. But on the back, in what could only be Gulliver's cramped handwriting, were these figures and words—"55 degrees 7 South. 100 degrees 9 East." I had found what could only be the location of Lilliput! Forthwith I went to look up the most detailed atlas of the world I could find, and sure enough, all the atlas indicated for that area was the blank ocean. After months of fruitless and expensive search all over the world, I had found the answer to my questions in my own backyard (so to speak)! When all seemed lost, the answer was given to me.

Some may have found a few jotted-down figures insufficient

evidence to plan a long journey, but not I. I tried, as I have already described, to get various organizations interested, but lack of intelligence and imagination prevented them from seeing what I had seen—irrefutable evidence for the existence of Lilliput. In a way, I was glad that I was now alone in my project. I felt none could ever match my intense desire to reach Lilliput. What I did next was to sell everything, absolutely everything, that I had—my house in Madras, my stocks, my car—and invest most of the money in training myself as a pilot through the Madras Flying Club. I also learned how to parachute. I kept back only a little money in case I needed it later.

All these preparations were very expensive but easily done because I had enough money to do what I wished and no family to obstruct me. I had never married and both my parents had died some years before. I was an only child and my other relatives and I did not keep in close touch. After I had begun making my preparations to go to Lilliput, I kept myself at an even greater distance from them.

And so, a little before September 1991, when I knew summer would be approaching in the Southern Hemisphere, I left for Australia. There, in Albany, I acquired a plane (in not strictly legal ways, so I shall leave out the details) and set out toward the South Pole. On the third of September 1991, at two in the morning, I strapped on my parachute, made sure my bag of things was with me, and jumped out of my plane over 55 degrees 7 South, 100 degrees 9 East. The night air was chilly. My plane crashed into the sea many miles farther on, the Lilliputians told me later. As I rushed through the night air toward the darkness below, I wondered what I would find there.

Chapter 3

The next day I went to see Selvi with Carol. Carol had rented a room at the back of Chandran's house in Nungambakkam and I went to meet her there, since I had some errands to run in that part of the city anyway. Chandran's house is huge. There are two stories to it. The front room of the upper story is Chandran's study. One day I would like to have a study like it. It is large. There are three desks in it and four typewriters. In one corner sits a telephone that never rings because it has been unplugged. Chandran prefers that his son or daughter-in-law, who live with him, answer the phone below. Bookshelves of a reddish-brown wood stand against all the walls—some even stand in the middle of the floor, so that negotiating your way through the room is something like passing through a maze. Books are stacked on the floor all around. Many, I suspect, have not been disturbed in years, perhaps decades. There are only two chairs in the entire room. One is a hard wooden chair behind a desk, the other an armchair with a pile of cushions on it.

What I like about this room is its blissful disregard for order. I can imagine it taking shape and growing through the years that Chandran has used it. He throws a book on the floor. A few days later another book is placed on top of it, and a few days after that another still. Soon it is a stack. In a similar fashion, desks and typewriters and shelves sprout here and there over the years. Thus, as Chandran grows and changes in his exuberant and chaotic way, so does the room. At least, this is the way I like to think of the extraordinary room that is his study.

The study leads onto a large balcony that overlooks the front of the house. Here are placed potted plants and two or three chairs. This is where Chandran is usually to be found. One of the desks in the room is a small one with castors and Chandran usually wheels it out onto the balcony. Here he sits reading and writing and keeping watch like a sentinel on whoever enters or leaves the house, for the front gate is visible below.

Carol and Chandran were on the balcony when I arrived to take her to see Selvi. Chandran leaned over the railing when he saw me at the front gate and waved out from between the leaves of a potted plant. "Here!" he shouted to me in Tamil, his bald head bobbing between the green leaves of the plant like a brown nut. "Come up here! The front door must be open!" Above the leaves of the potted plant, behind him, Carol's face appeared like a white patch in the bright afternoon light.

The front door was indeed open and I made my way up to the second floor and through the study to the balcony. "Here is something I want you to give to Selvi," Chandran said in English as I appeared on the balcony, and handed me a yellow envelope. "If she gives you something for me, will you bring it to me tomorrow? That's a good boy. There's glory in being a messenger too. Remember Narada who carries the messages of Vishnu." He pretended to muse upon this for a moment. All of it, I think, was for Carol's benefit. "Of course, he also has the reputation of a troublemaker among the gods. . . . No matter! My messages are innocent. No one can make any trouble with them. Now go, or you will be late."

"You don't look like Vishnu," Carol interjected with a laugh. "At least not like the pictures I have seen."

Chandran leaned forward and patted her hand. "Alas, it is my lack of hair," he said with mock sorrow, "but I'm glad you think so, Carol. I'm glad you think so. Vishnu is such a degenerate god. Shiva's asceticism is much more to my liking." He smiled innocently.

Carol stood up and began to gather her things around her, slipping on her sandals, which she had taken off. "Well, I hope you have decided whether you are Vishnu or Shiva by the time I come back," she said.

"My God!" Chandran said in mock horror. "How you speak of the gods, Carol! I'm an old man. God will forgive me. But you, you who are so religious?"

I noticed the cross that hung around Carol's neck. "I'm sure God has a sense of humor," Carol said. "That's the one thing I'm certain of."

Carol and I took an auto-rickshaw to Madras Central, where we boarded a train to Krantinagar. At this time of day, the trains were not very crowded. From Krantinagar station we took another auto to Kuppancherry. Finding Selvi's house was not easy. The lanes ran in all directions without method and were not always named. When we arrived finally at what I thought was Selvi's house, it was only a little before four-thirty. The house was a low building with a thatched roof and two windows that were shuttered at the moment. I knocked on the door but there was no response. Under a tree, across the street from the house, was a cycle mechanic. He was sitting back on his haunches, watching us. "Is this Selvi's house?" I asked him. He nodded. Carol and I paid the auto-rickshaw and stood in the shade of the wall to wait for Selvi.

Across the street, the cycle mechanic was still watching us. He was a boy, about fourteen or fifteen years old, thin and shallow chested beneath the yellow shirt he was wearing. Around him were the instruments of his trade—a cycle-pump, a tray of dirty water in which to check for punctures, and a wooden box of rudimentary tools and other necessities, like glue. From one of the branches of the tree hung an old tire tube. The whole affair was not a grand operation. A cycle that he was working on lay on its side in front of him.

Selvi's house stands in a row of low houses with thatched roofs on them. The houses look old and the walls are uneven and dilapidated. Many of them are little more than huts. The street is a strip of hard-packed soil with stones in it. It had once been macadamized—patches of black macadamized surface show here and there. Thorny scrubs form fences around some of the houses. In the street, small, bare-bodied children played as we waited, shouting and chasing after one another. At one end of the street is a large well with a concrete wall around it. Women were drawing water from it. I looked to see if Selvi was among them, but she wasn't. At the other end of the street are three shops next to one another. One of them was a tea shop from which loud Tamil film music blared.

By the time Selvi appeared, hurrying down the street, it was well past four-thirty. "I'm late," she observed. "How late am I?" She was carrying a cloth bag under one arm.

She opened the door to her house and we went in. The room was bare except for some mats and bedding that had been piled neatly in a corner and four steel folding chairs that had been folded and leaned against a wall. A door led to a room within. Two windows with bars across them looked out onto the street outside. The paint on the wooden shutters of the windows was peeling off. When Selvi opened the windows, the sun shining through laid two striped patches of yellow on the cement floor of the room. In the middle of the wall opposite was a large dark patch. It had rained heavily a few days ago and the damp, I think, must have seeped into the walls.

Selvi took two of the folding chairs and set them out for us. She then disappeared farther inside the house and when she came back she had put away her bag and washed her face. She went across the street to say something to the boy under the tree. "I have asked him to bring three coffees," she said to me when she returned. "The lady will drink coffee, won't she?" She looked at Carol doubtfully.

"Of course, I will," Carol said, when I asked her.

"Let us begin," Selvi said, setting up a chair for herself. "We are already late."

And so we began the interview, if I may call it that. Carol had a cassette-recorder and we taped the whole session. My job, which was one of translating between Selvi and Carol, turned out not to be so easy. The appropriate words did not always come automatically. Fortunately, we have both Carol's and Selvi's original words on tape, and I am to spend some time in the following days transcribing the interview more fittingly. I have already begun this.

What will emerge in the transcription, I think, is an encapsulation of Selvi's life as she told it to us. This is what Carol wants. She began the session by saying (I have the notes right here in front of me), "I'm looking for personal testimonials, anecdotes, from workers. That is what I am collecting at this stage. Tell her that,

RK." And then she turned and addressed Selvi directly, "I guess I would really like you to begin by talking freely about your experiences as a worker, you know, what kinds of work you have done, stuff like that. And then maybe you can talk about how you got involved in the Domestic Workers Union. I'll ask more specific questions when I need to. Also, maybe if you could relate all this to your experience as a woman, as a female member of the work force, that would be good."

When I translated all this to Selvi, her response was "Why? What does she need this for?"

"There is this problem in India of large portions of the work force being unprotected," Carol said. "Especially in unregulated sectors of the economy, like domestic servants. I want to see what kind of movement there has been in the politicization of this work force, which is often female. This is a huge project, as you can tell. So I have decided to confine myself, to begin with, to an urban center in the south. But we will see what happens as the project develops."

With this, the interview began. My translations were really just rough approximations of what Carol or Selvi said. I discovered that there is a whole class of words in English for which I have no corresponding words in Tamil, and vice versa. Actually, and I am appropriately shameful of this, I found myself more comfortable in English than in Tamil.

I have found the process of interviewing Selvi and making a transcription of what she said quite interesting. How typical Selvi's life is I cannot tell. In its pattern of migration from the village to the city, it is predictable. Yet, it seems to me, she has also displayed an uncommon enterprise. For me personally, her story has been important because it has given depth and a material solidity to people who had earlier been simply names or faces. Figures in the street have taken on character.

For example. A few days after the interview with Selvi, I happened to be in Madras Central late one evening. A number of long-distance evening trains had come in and a crowd milled around on the platforms and outside the station, the peculiar smell of trains hanging over them. As I joined the crowd to make my way out of the station, a man passed me with a cloth bag very like Selvi's under his arm. He was a short man and I noticed his frayed shirt collar was brown with grime. Behind him, his wife followed, a child on her hip. The couple did not have the familiarity and sureness of people who had been living in Madras for a long time. They stopped outside the station and spoke to each other, seemingly uncertain of what to do. The porters in the red shirts and the taxi and auto-rickshaw drivers did not bother with them except to give them hard looks and shout at them when they got in the way.

When I saw the couple, I was immediately reminded quite involuntarily of Selvi. Had this couple too come to the city looking for a job like Selvi and her husband had so many years ago? Where I would once have passed without noticing the couple as people, a whole history seemed to jump into place for me.

All this has served to remind me of something I should never have forgotten—that a universe divides me and someone like Selvi in practice. What does it mean to say we are both Indians or we are both Tamils? This is not the first time I have asked myself such a question, especially since then.

During the interview (I'm copying from my notes), Selvi told us she had come to Madras some fifteen years ago from a village near Salem because her husband had come to Madras. She had not wanted to leave her village, she said, but what could she do? In those days, she did not think of her husband as different from herself. In Madras, work had not been easy to come by. First her husband had worked in Ambattur at a temporary job in a small factory making auto parts. The job had been lost because the foreman in the company had wanted it for someone he knew. One day, that foreman had called her husband aside and told him he need not come in the next day. Had there been a union in that factory? No, she did not think so. Her husband had not been officially appointed in the factory, so it would not have mattered anyway. Her husband had only been an errand boy. He was nearly thirty when he came to Madras, but he was only an errand boy. He carried files from one desk to another and, two or three times a day, went out to get coffee and tea from a stall on a corner. When the manager arrived in the morning, her husband had to carry his briefcase in from the car. She had always found this work more demeaning than her husband had. In the village they had been poor too, but at least they could call themselves farmers.

When her husband left the factory in Ambattur, he got a job as a laborer for a contractor. What kind of contractor was this? It was a building contractor. He built mainly houses. Her husband was paid a daily wage and worked when the contractor had some work going, which meant he did not work every day. He could not work for any other contractor at other times, for then his old contractor would not take him back. During the rainy season there was little construction work and then things were more difficult. However, they did not starve, for the contractor-sir would aid them a little. If things were very bad, they could go and stand before him with their hands pressed together in submission and he would throw them some money. As a loan. When work began again, this would be subtracted from the pay.

This was when she too had begun to work with her husband in the construction business. Her husband had not wanted her to, but she had insisted. They were both unskilled laborers, so they made very little money. They worked as a team carrying sand, cement, and bricks up to the masons. This was very hard work. One of them would fill sand or bricks or whatever into a tray and the other would carry it to where it was needed. Sometimes they would have to carry it up steps. She had seen pregnant women doing this work.

Skilled workers had it easier. A mason or a plumber or especially an electrician or a carpenter was paid much more and could order people around. They had boy apprentices who handed them nails and wires and ran their errands. Even the contractor-sir was more careful with these skilled laborers. Were there women electricians? Now when she thought about it she had never seen a woman carpenter or even mason. That was men's work. Only men could do such work.

There was no union here either. The contractor-sir would have thrown out anyone even talking about unions. Once, the son of someone for whom they were building a house, over in Adyar, had begun to talk about unions when the workers were around. The contractor had quickly led him away. Suddenly there was some detail about the shelves in the kitchen that needed clearing up and it was essential the son do it right then. At that time she knew nothing about unions but she could remember the electrician smiling knowingly. It was strange how these things came back. Little-little details. She had not thought about these things for a long time.

Selvi did not work too long as a construction worker. Her husband had persuaded her to give up the job and to work as a domestic servant for someone for whom he had done some little work on the side in Krantinagar. This had been about ten years ago. The people had been North Indians who had since gone back to Delhi or Bombay or wherever they had come from. She did not know it until later, but her husband had wanted her to leave the construction work because he had taken up with one of the women in the construction gang. Soon after, her husband had left her. Did she have any children by him? No, she had not had any children by him. Maybe that was why he had left her. Did she see him now? No, she did not keep in touch with him anymore. When something is over, it is over. She thought he still worked for the same contractor. She thought he was now a mason. Living alone had not been easy in the beginning, but she had become used to it very quickly. Now she was much gladder to be on her own.

At first she had not liked domestic work. She had thought it was a step down. In the construction work there had been other people to work with. You worked hard but you could talk and laugh and even flirt with the men as you worked. In domestic work you worked alone. Also, it was often demeaning work. She had even cleaned the toilet for the North Indian family. But she never did this anymore. It was also boring work. She still did not like this work. How could a human being like this? But she would not go back to construction work. There were some good things about domestic work. It was less hard on the body. And getting the women together and organizing them in construction she could never have done. She would have been beaten up or chased out. Or even killed. Many of these contractors were rogues.

After the North Indians had left, she had continued to work for the new people who moved in. These were Madras people and they had lived in Madras for a long time. They made her work hard. She even had to go shopping with them to carry the bags back. And they did not pay well. When someone came and offered to work for less, they dismissed her on some pretext. She had found this completely unjust. This was when she had begun organizing the domestic servants in the area, in Krantinagar. This had begun in a simple way. She had found that servants were constantly being dismissed when someone new came offering to work for cheaper rates. This new person often would not stay in the job but leave. What all this meant was very little job security for those who lived by doing domestic work in the area. Also, they had to take whatever they were paid and do all kinds of work. So she had got together those who had been working in the area for a long time in a group. When anyone in her group got dismissed unjustly, this group would not let anyone else be hired in the house that person had been working in.

How many of these longtime servants were in the group? About twenty at first, but soon others joined them. They would go talk to any new person who had moved into an old person's job and quietly advise her to leave. If she insisted on working there, they would make it difficult for her in all kinds of ways. If she agreed to leave, Selvi's group would try to get her a job where she would not be making someone else stand out in the street.

At first the employers tried to resist. One of them had even tried to put the police on them for intimidation but she and her people had not backed down. Most of the houses in Krantinagar had rich people in them. Many of them were Brahmin ladies. They did not like doing housework. Also, if they did not have servants, their neighbors spoke badly of them. Soon most of these ladies gave in.

Now many, many of the households in the area had her people in them. They got more pay, better hours, and they could not be spoken to this way and that way.

There had also been attempts at intimidation from the men of the women her people had chased away. Most of them were drunken fools who lived on their women's money anyway. Now new people mostly joined her group and it was better for everybody. It had not been easy getting things organized. It had not been easy at all, but now they had a good position in the area.

When had Shanthamma become involved? Shanthamma had come in two, no, three years before. Shanthamma had approached Selvi. She had been organizing women in other areas of Madras for much longer. Actually, Selvi had got the idea for organizing domestic workers in Krantinagar only when she had heard some news of domestic workers being organized in other areas nearby. She had not known of Shanthamma then. Later, Shanthamma had contacted her and they had talked numerous times. Shanthamma had told her that she should be official, she should register her union, collect money as subscription, and expand her activities, maybe even hold classes to educate the women. This again had not been easy. Domestic workers made so little money that many women did not want to have membership fees. And many of them were not interested in things like education. They could not think beyond the next hit film or the next shot of liquor in Velan's shop. But Shanthamma had provided money to get things started. She had also guided them in many different ways. She knew a lot about such things.

Now Selvi's group was part of Shanthamma's Domestic Workers Union and had a room for an office in the next street. Many women were actually coming for classes and things like that. What kinds of classes were these? Mostly reading and writing classes. A schoolteacher from Krantinagar Primary School who was sympathetic to them contributed her time. But sometimes they also had someone talk to them about unions and bringing up children and things like that. Many of these women were single mothers because their husbands had left them, or because they did not bother with things like marriage. As was well known, poor people often did not pay much attention to such things. Rich people liked to think this was because poor people were loose and immoral, but she did not think it had anything to do with immorality.

In this way, Selvi's group had grown a lot. Recently her branch of the Domestic Workers Union had even contributed money for a function at the Ganapathy temple in Ganapathy Kovil Street. So they had come a long way. But much, much remained to be done. Too many of the domestic workers were still not members. Even in Krantinagar and the area around. In other parts of Madras there was no such thing as a union. And even now those who were in unions were not paid well for the dog's work they did. When there were so many people without jobs living on the streets and things like that, a union could not do too much, could it?

This is a summary of Selvi's story as it emerged in the interview, perhaps not an uncommon life, except for her involvement in organizing the women of her area. I have put a summary of it down in my journal as a way of remembering it. Now I can look it up whenever I want to.

Chapter 4

I met land. And twenty Lilliputian officers of the Mildendo Peeg Immeegar. They were waiting for me as I floated down in my parachute. I did not know this until later, but two of their combat aircraft had been following my plane for quite a while. As my feet hit the ground, I was caught in a crisscross of powerful light beams that were blinding in their force. Two chochos came buzzing around me. They were the size of small birds. Below me, on the ground, the vehicles of the Mildendo Peeg Immeegar scurried around. I could not see them clearly because of the blinding lights, but their sound was quite distinctive. One was blown over as my parachute settled around me with what must have been for the Lilliputians a gale of air. I could see its dark shape toppling and turning once before coming to a rest.

"Bandur!" a loud voice electronically magnified hailed me (I did not know then the meaning of "bandur," but what followed was in perfect English). "Do not move! Keep perfectly still! I repeat, do not move! There are twenty of us here armed with many weapons that could destroy you easily. Do not move!" I obeyed the order to keep still without hesitation. I had come in peace. I was confident I had nothing to fear.

I waited, keeping carefully still, for a long time. I could sense activity out beyond the splash of light in which I was standing, but could not see anything clearly. Sometimes there was the sound of something, a vehicle, leaving or coming. How long exactly I waited I cannot tell. I was wearing a watch but did not dare to lift up my left hand to check the time.

Standing there in the night, waiting for the next orders, I had time to note with well-deserved satisfaction how right I had been about the existence of Lilliput. Understandably, I felt exultant. The great gamble had paid off! My calculations had been right! I considered once again how little are the things that make the difference in the great sweep of History. I could easily have bought some other house in Ooty. I could easily have disposed of Mr. Morrison's trunk without looking into it. I could have overlooked Gulliver's manuscript. I could even have lost heart and not followed the quest to this moment here in what was truly Lilliput. But I had not! That is the point, that is the crux. I had persevered and now here I was, a man standing at a crucial juncture in Earth's History. Such thoughts of satisfaction, which all will agree I surely deserved, passed through my mind as I waited.

When I had been waiting in the glaring light for some time and nothing had happened, I considered shouting out something to the Lilliputians I could vaguely make out beyond the circle of light in which I was standing. I had composed and practiced a little speech of greeting before leaving India. It ran as follows: "I come in peace. I am Valur Vishveswaran. Take me to your ruler." I had practiced these words in all the languages I knew—English, French, German, and even Tamil and Hindi. I had planned to speak these words to the accompaniment of various gestures, which I had also practiced. I would first spread out my arms and open my hands fully to indicate that I did not mean any violence. And then I would slowly lower myself to the ground and lie prostrate so that I would no longer be towering over the Lilliputians in an intimidating fashion.

Now I wondered whether I should enact this little ceremony. I finally decided against it because I was not certain if the loudness of my voice would frighten them in any way. I was also reassured that I had been addressed in English. Communication with them, even in an emergency, would not be a problem. As for being spoken to in English, I was only a little surprised by it. I had come prepared to experience wonderful things.

My legs were beginning to grow tired when the electronically magnified voice spoke again: "Bandur! On our instructions, step by step, lower your bag to the ground, take off your parachute, and then take off your clothes, one by one. Begin on the count of three. One, two, three . . ." And then I was slowly made to take off my things and place them on the ground. I thought they would not make me take off my underwear but they did. This bothered me a little but I did not have time to think about it, for when I hesitated for a moment, the voice rang out: "Do it! Now! At once!" So I did. When I was finished, I was instructed to step back for about ten paces, the beams of light following me, and left waiting again. Standing there in that bright patch of light completely naked was most uncomfortable. I kept wondering with some embarrassment if there were any female members in the Lilliputian reception party. Outside the circle of light, I could hear vehicles dragging away my belongings.

Fortunately, this time I did not have to wait long. Soon they returned my clothes to me, though not my other belongings or my watch. When I had dressed myself, the voice spoke again out of the darkness: "Do you see the three vehicles with red lights on them?" I noticed three flashing red lights ahead in the darkness and nodded, and then cautiously added "Yes," to test their response. They did not seem to find my voice too loud. "Follow the lights to where you will be kept," the electronic voice ordered.

The place I was taken to was an aircraft hangar which was quite large by their standards. Eight of their largest aircraft could be stored in it. For me it was too low to stand up in, but I could sit up in it and I could move around comfortably when I was lying down. The hangar was in the middle of the Karunar Punuk, the area that had been devastated and made desert on Gulliver's journey here centuries ago. I did not know of the Karunar Punuk at this point, but I had noticed on my way to the hangar how desolate the countryside was. There was virtually no vegetation except for tiny Lilliputian shrubs.

The journey to the hangar did not take long. The coordinates that Gulliver had jotted down in his manuscript and I had followed were in the Karunar Punuk. I had therefore landed quite close to the hangar. As we approached the hangar, the sky began to lighten in the east. Dawn was breaking. I could see a little more clearly. The vehicles I was following, I observed, were boxlike things that moved very fast so that they kept ahead of me very easily. They made a whirring sound. Some of these vehicles were behind me too. And some chochos, which are Lilliputian "combat aircraft" I learned later, swooped and danced in the air above me.

So it was with a sizable accompaniment that I moved into my new residence. I was given explicit instructions before I did so—I was to live in this hangar for an indeterminate time, food would be provided, arrangements would be made for my toilet, I could leave the hangar but only after I had given warning that I was going to come out, I could not leave the facility in which the hangar was situated, I was to await further instructions patiently and not attempt anything foolish because enough force to destroy me would be permanently stationed around the hangar. Once these instructions had been given, the vehicles that had brought me to the hangar moved away to a distance and made a circle around the hangar. Above me, the chochos continued to circle and weave in an agitated fashion. Of course I was not going to attempt anything foolish! I was only a little disappointed that I had not yet spoken to a Lilliputian face to face, but I was willing to be patient.

The first thing that I did was to crawl into the hangar and go to sleep. All the standing and waiting had made me tired. When I woke up it was bright light outside. After giving due warning, I crawled out of the hangar. The Lilliputian ground vehicles were still in their circular formation a little distance away. Standing next to them were a few Lilliputians. I observed them eagerly. They were, most of them, about the length of a man's middle finger. This I later found to be the average height of the Lilliputian males, the females being slightly shorter—about the length of an index finger. The Lilliputian men were dressed in dark green trousers and shirts and carried what looked like guns in their hands. They did not seem to be afraid of me.

"I come in peace," I said in English. "I am Valur Vishveswaran. Take me to your ruler." As I spoke I spread out my arms and opened my hands fully. And then I slowly lowered myself to the ground and lay prostrate. Looking along the ground at the Lilliputians, I could see them much more clearly. Their eyes and hair were bright blue and their skin color was a marvelous green. This I later found to be true of most Lilliputians of Mildendo that I met.

Two of the Lilliputians stepped forward and stood before my face. "We know who you are," one of them said. "We have gone through your belongings. I am the Alando Leed, the Chief Special Officer, of the Mildendo Peeg Immeegar. What is your purpose here?"

"I come in peace as a visitor," I replied.

"How do you know of us?" the other officer interjected.

I explained briefly the events leading up to my arrival in Lilliput and ended with a statement on how I thought I had much to learn from the Lilliputians and was looking forward to communicating with them. The officer accepted my comments with a gracious nod of his head.

"Consultations are being conducted," the Alando Leed said. "I will be back to talk to you later. Be prepared to meet me then. That is all we can say now." With these words, the two officers returned to the circle of vehicles the Lilliputians had made around my hangar, climbed into one of the vehicles, and drove away. I smiled at the remaining Lilliputians to show my friendliness and got up from my prostrate position to survey the area around me.

There were buildings other than the hangar in the facility that I was being kept in. It seemed to be some kind of an army camp. I walked around in the space available to me, being careful of what was underfoot. I thought it possible that there might be some misunderstanding if I inadvertently stomped on one of the Lilliputians. The army camp was quite large by Lilliputian standards. There were many buildings in it and many Lilliputians moved about around them. Some of them would stop to stare up at me as I stepped cautiously over them. I was careful to smile at them in a friendly way. Sometimes I waved to them with a slow, careful gesture, and then some of them would wave back to me. Throughout my tour around the camp, which really didn't take me more than fifteen minutes, two of the ground vehicles followed me. When I neared the boundary fence of the camp, perhaps half as high as one of our desks, a voice from one of the vehicles bellowed out a warning to me not to leave the camp. I nodded my head to show that I understood and sat down on the ground so that I could examine the countryside around at leisure.

As I was sitting there, however, an urgent need to pass water came upon me. I explained this to the Lilliputians and after consultations they led me out beyond the fence where I could relieve myself. The Lilliputian vehicles withdrew to one side and I turned away, so as not to expose my genitalia to their view; but as my water began to flow onto the ground, I heard a great cry of wonder rise up behind me. A desert land stretched away on all sides, marked only by what looked like roads. In the near distance were some low hills, which for the Lilliputians would have been nearly mountains. My water fell in a torrent on the ground but the arid soil sucked it up in a moment, sending up a pungent steam in return. Behind me, I heard what sounded like coughing from the Lilliputians. In embarrassment, I quickly finished my job and did up the fly of my trousers.

I then returned to the hangar which was my residence, disappointed that I had not seen anything more interesting. I had hoped to see towns, or at least villages, outside the perimeter fence of the facility that I was in. Waiting outside the hangar, when I got back, was a convoy of trucks and tankers. The trucks (or lana-trakas, as I learned later) contained bread (called ratha-ng) and various tiny vegetables boiled in saline water. The tankers, which looked like our oil tankers, contained milk and orange juice. One of the large Lilliputian drums (used probably to store gasoline—I seemed to detect a faint smell of gasoline when I first used the drum) served very well for a cup. For a plate I had a square sheet of steel. The food, I found, was excellent, the quality much superior to anything that we bandur produce here in our bandur lands.

Soon after I had finished my meal, the Alando Leed returned and demanded to speak to me, so we retired into the hangar. I lay flat on the ground on my belly so that I could more easily converse with him. Throughout the dialogue that followed, the Alando Leed walked to and fro in front of me, stopping often to turn and stare into my face if he found something that I said interesting or if he himself wanted to emphasize a point. I found his bearing to be proud and confident. He showed no fear of me. He was careful of what he said, but when he said it he said it with tremendous conviction. This was a trait that I found among most of the highborn of the Mildendans. It made them refreshingly easy people to communicate with, for they were hardly ever confused about themselves or what they wanted to say.

"I hope the meal was to your liking," he began.

I assured him that it was.

"Your entry into Mildendo is illegal," he said. "I hope you are aware of that? You do not have the requisite documents to enter my country."

I was a little taken aback at these words. I had expected a different kind of welcome. I hastened to repeat to him my reasons for coming to Lilliput in this fashion.

He listened to me impatiently, and then said, "Be that as it may. Your entry into this territory is not authorized. As the Alando Leed of the Mildendo Peeg Immeegar, it is my duty to inform you of this. You are not to take your status here for granted. Your presence here is, at the least, illegal. Given the enormity of your physical size, do not be surprised if we choose to treat your unauthorized entry into our territory as an act of invasion."

He paused to let his words sink in, and then continued, "I must tell you that we are not at all certain of the wisdom of a bandur visiting us at this time. We monitor you bandur very closely and we do not think you are as yet developed enough to appreciate the things we have achieved here. We find you to be much worse in your capabilities and attitudes than even the Northern Lilliputians." I did not at this time know anything about the Northern Lilliputians and therefore could not appreciate the true force of his comparison. Later, I would learn.

"I hear you, O Alando Leed," I said to him after he had finished speaking. He stepped back, grimacing as I opened my mouth and spoke. I am ashamed to admit this was because of my bad breath, which gusted out of my mouth and swirled around him where he was standing not far from my face, lifting the collars of his shirt and ruffling his blue hair. I have already admitted I am ashamed of this, but I would have you all remember that I had not had the opportunity to clean my mouth since I had set out from Australia. I doubt any other mouth would have fared better than mine. I turned my face in another direction and continued shamefacedly, "I hear everything that you say. I wish only to assure you that I mean no act of hostility against anyone in Lilliput. I cannot emphasize to you how important it is to me that I be allowed to remain here. I hope you will grant me this request and permit me to move around freely so that I may see the wonders of your land myself."

"That is to be decided yet," he responded from the distance to which he had retreated as I was speaking. "Consultations are yet going on. Your presence here is not totally unprecedented as you are well aware, but it is certainly unexpected. It is possible something will be worked out. Let us however"—he hastened to add as my face lit up—"wait and see how that turns out. I must leave soon, but I am ready in the meantime to answer whatever questions I can." He stopped and waited expectantly.

I had, of course, a million questions of every kind to ask him, but I was most immediately interested in getting practical information—where I was, in whose custody I was. I told the Alando Leed as much.

He hesitated for a few moments, apparently wondering whether he should respond to my request for information or not. At last he seemed to decide in the affirmative. "This is the Kingdom of Mildendo," he said. "The capital of this kingdom is the city of Mildendo. It is ruled by Queen Baataania. I am, as I have already told you, the Alando Leed of the Mildendo Peeg Immeegar, which is the Mildendan army and in whose immediate custody you are. My job is to monitor our borders against intrusions, of which there are many, especially from Northern Lilliput. You may consider me the chief of a kind of border security force. Any more questions?"

I sensed that he was in a hurry to be gone, and so I indicated that I had no further questions for him, though I did indeed have many things to ask him.

"Good, good," he said. "I shall leave now. Soon your belongings will be sent to you, including your cleaning articles, of which you seem to have great need. Arrangements are being made for your toilet. We have noted your special needs. Pits are being dug out in the desert. Water will be provided. Consult my subordinates outside at your convenience." And with that he was gone.

I lay back inside the hangar and considered all that I had been told. I had indeed been given important information, but many, many questions remained unanswered. The uncertainty regarding my legal status as a visitor to Mildendo also bothered me; there was nothing, however, to be done about that but wait. In the meantime, I decided, I would begin talking to any other Lilliputian who had the time for me.

As I was coming to these conclusions, there was the whirring sound of motorized vehicles outside the hangar and then the loud "thump" of some object being flung on the ground. When I crawled outside, I was delighted to note that my bag had been returned to me. I dragged it back into the hangar with me. My two pairs of trousers, two shirts, three pairs of underwear, card calendars for 1991, 1992, and 1993, wristwatch, two notebooks, many pencils, and the toilet items were all there. My camera and camera film, three magnifying glasses of varying degrees of power, and my documents (passport, checkbook, and birth certificate), to my dismay, had been taken away. The withholding of the documents I had expected after my conversation with the Alando Leed. The matter of the magnifying lenses and the camera confounded me. I was sure, however, that the Lilliputians had a good reason for withholding them, though I never ever found out what it was. Why, after all, would they withhold these items without reason?

As soon as I had finished going through my bag and its contents, I sat down with my notebook and wrote in it all that had happened to me since my arrival in Lilliput, including almost word for word the conversation that the Alando Leed and I had just had. This was a practice that I kept up throughout my stay in Lilliput. You may attribute this to the conscientiousness of a serious historian. After all, my purpose in coming to Lilliput had been precisely to explore that part of the world and record my experiences there.

By the time I was finished writing in my notebook, it was late in the evening, and I settled down for the night. Thus ended my first day in Lilliput.

The next morning began with the loud scream of a siren jerking me out of my sleep in a startling if also efficient manner. I opened my eyes to find that an electronic instrument of some kind, mounted on the back of a truck with a crane (known in Lilliput as a kon-traka), had been thrust into my right ear. A Lilliputian in a brown uniform was standing on the back of the traka. When he saw that I was fully awake, he turned and pressed a button to turn off the siren and gestured to me that I was to follow the traka out of the hangar.

The truck and three other ground vehicles led me out beyond the perimeter of the camp to where large pits (large for the Lilliputians) had been dug in the desert. They had been provided for my toilet. I was to do my business in them, using the pits as bowls to relieve or wash myself in. Two or three karunar (a kind of bush that grows in the desert and whose leaves are commonly used for bristles) had also been bound together to provide me with a brush. About two of our pails of water had been provided in six very large Lilliputian drums for my use. When I was finished, the pits would be covered over with earth, effectively burying my business out of sight. Three machines stood by ready to do this. They looked like large toy bulldozers. I could see inside their cabins, where the drivers were sitting in their brown uniforms. They had what looked like space helmets over their heads. I was later told that this was to protect them from the poisonous fumes the Lilliputians expected to be produced by my business.

As I went about my various toilet activities, the Lilliputians withdrew some distance. They did not, however, depart completely. The earth-moving machines and the four vehicles that had accompanied me out into the desert joined together to form a group in the distance. Some of the Lilliputians, drivers and soldiers, got out to watch me as I went about my toilet activities. My modesty was a little offended but there was nothing I could do about it. When I had washed myself and put on clean clothes, I washed my old, filthy garments as best I could so that I could lay them out to dry on the roof of the hangar, and I was ready to return to the camp. As we left, the machines began to fill in the pits I had used.

This was to be the routine almost every morning. After some days, I forced myself to ignore the Lilliputians watching me in the distance. The Lilliputians who were regularly assigned to this task of accompanying me out into the desert soon lost interest in my toilet activities. But there were usually some new Lilliputians with us every day and they would stand in front of the vehicles watching me with fascination. Lar Prent told me one day, much later, that the officer assigned to supervise this operation secretly smuggled in visitors and charged them high rates for the privilege of watching me going about my morning duties. Once, Prent averred, the officer had even smuggled journalists in and descriptions of me doing my business (with pictures) appeared in all the media. But I do not know if this information of Lar Prent's is any more reliable than his other lies.

Back at the camp, on the morning of my second day in Lilliput, I tried to talk to some of the Lilliputians, but none of them, I found, knew any of the languages that I knew. I did, however, manage to learn a few things from one of the soldiers who was on duty. If I were sitting outside the hangar, he would come up and walk around me in his proud Peeg Immeegar way, his little arms stiff by his side, and stare up into my face in wonder. If I said something to him, he would sometimes answer me very quickly in Lilliputian, but of course I could not understand any of that. If, however, I pointed to an object, he would tell me the name for it. Thus I learned a few Lilliputian words that day: the Lilliputian name for us is "bandur," which means "giant one"; an aircraft is a "cho-cho"; a ground vehicle of any kind is a "traka"; food is "ng"; sky is "parselan"; earth is "amarselan." And so on. . . . From the soldier on that second day, when I was left more or less to my own devices, I learned a few basic words of this kind.

The soldier's interest in me is not surprising. The average Lilliputian does not know very much about us bandur, except that our lands lie far, far to the north, even beyond the lands of the Northern Lilliputians, which are already considered very remote. In high school, Gulliver is discussed briefly, but the land from which he is identified as coming is described as being so remote as to be nonexistent for all practical purposes. Hence, the average Lilliputian knows of our existence but does not concern himself with us unduly.

My second day passed in the fashion I have described above, quite uneventfully. But on the third day, the Alando Leed reappeared. "It has been decided that since you are already here, you will be permitted to stay for now," he said. "You will live here in the hangar. An instructor will be assigned to teach you some basic facts about our ways, our language, and some of the other things you will have need to know. You may move around, but only after explicit permission has been obtained and you must be accompanied by three of our peeg trakas"—which is their name for the military ground vehicles—"at all times. I must warn you, in case you have not realized it already, that these peeg trakas are equipped with immensely powerful weaponry, the best our technology can provide. You would not be a match for even one of them. We also reserve the right to take any other necessary security precautions with regard to you. I will be your liaison in all matters. Clear?"

I nodded vigorously to show him that I understood. I was delighted at his words. I had been allowed to stay!

"I have kept one most important thing to the end," the Alando Leed continued. "We are keeping your documents with us for the moment. They will be returned to you when you leave us. We have, however, issued a temporary residence permit in your name. You must carry it with you at all times. Without it, you have no legal status in Mildendo. This is a most important matter."

With these words, the Alando Leed produced a card about a quarter of an inch in length. I took it on the tip of my finger and squinted at it, trying to make out what was on it. I could barely see, on one side of it, what seemed like a tiny photograph of me. Of course, the details of the face were not visible. I wondered when they had taken the photograph. I hoped I looked presentable in it. It would not do to appear threatening to an officer already intimidated by my size. I put the card in my shirt pocket, resolving to put it away in a safer place later.

The Alando Leed was preparing to leave.

"I have a request to make, O Alando Leed," I said to him.

"Yes?" he said, stopping in front of my face, his hands clasped behind his back.

"I wish tomorrow to see the city of Mildendo," I said to him, adding quickly, "but only if that is possible."

He considered my request for a long moment. "That is possible," he said at last. "I will see that preparations are made. Until tomorrow morning, then."

The next morning, after I had drunk a tanker-load of milk and eaten some thirty or forty of their apples, stems and all, I set out for Mildendo City, surrounded by numerous trakas of all kinds. Shackles were put on my wrists and ankles before we left. I had not expected this, but I did not complain. Given the difference in size between them and me, I felt that the shackles were perhaps justified. The shackles, I learned much later, had been secretly manufactured and kept ready many decades earlier for just such an eventuality. I marveled at the foresightedness of this. As soon as the Mildendans had knowledge of my presence within their jurisdiction, the shackles had been brought out of storage and transported to the army camp to be used on me in case of an emergency or if, as now, I was traveling away from the camp. Within the army camp itself, the Mildendans were far more confident of their ability to subdue me in any situation. The Mildendans, I think, had also decided that they might antagonize me unnecessarily if they kept the shackles on me twenty-four hours a day. Needless to say, they need not have feared any such thing of me.

The shackles were brought to the hangar on two trakas. When we were ready to leave, I was made to lie down with my wrists and ankles placed together. Cranes lifted the shackles out of the trakas and positioned them appropriately over my wrists and ankles. Workers in brown uniforms then secured them properly. The whole operation was carried out most efficiently and took no more than a few minutes. When I stood up (with some difficulty), I found that the shackles around my feet allowed me to walk without much discomfort but effectively prevented me from running or making any sudden movements with my legs. The shackles on my wrists similarly restricted the movements that I could make with my arms.

In this manner we set out for Mildendo City. The Alando Leed himself accompanied us, traveling in the lead traka of the Peeg Immeegar. We traveled as fast as my shackles would allow me to walk and within two hours we were climbing into the wooded hills that I had previously seen and leaving the lowland behind. We did not travel by the roads, of course, for they would have buckled and cracked under my weight, besides disrupting regular traffic. We traveled instead across the open countryside, the trakas handling all terrain quite easily. Their maneuverability was very great.

The countryside immediately surrounding the camp, as I noted earlier, is mainly a desert called the Karunar Punuk. Once it was a verdant and prosperous land, the Alando Leed told me later. It had been transformed to this sorry state after Gulliver's visit to Lilliput. Unable to handle Gulliver's depredations in any other way, the Mildendans had been forced to follow a policy of scorched earth. Devastating the land around Gulliver voluntarily, the Mildendans had gathered together massive forces on the hills to effectively isolate him in what was now the Karunar Punuk.

Such was the origin of the Karunar Punuk. The desert turned to grassland a little before the hills. Here, small collections of what looked like boxes became visible in the distance. These were Mildendan villages. Narrow ribbons of a gray material connected them to one another. Trakas of all kinds were traveling along them at great speed in both directions. Some of them pulled off the roads and stopped to watch us pass. My towering figure surrounded by numerous trakas, each of them two feet long and one foot high, must have made quite a spectacle.

Once we had reached the hills, it took us another half hour to get through them. Once through, we were almost upon Mildendo City, for it lay just beyond. The Alando Leed directed me to halt on a hill above the city. Two or three chochos came flying from the direction of the city and circled above us, the sunshine glinting on their bright metal wings.

I sat down on the side of the hill on which we were so that I could examine Mildendo City more closely. It made a strangely beautiful spectacle, for a black cloud, produced by a ring of mushroomlike structures on the outskirts of the city, lay all over it. I could not see below the cloud of smoke except when the wind shifted some portion of it now and then. And then what looked like red buildings and narrow streets showed briefly before the cloud swirled shut again.

Above the cloud, however, Mildendo City rose in tall towers and spires that stretched away into the distance. Long strips of silver flowed from one tower to the other, forming a web of connections among them. These were transportways along which vehicles moved at great speed. The whole city, I found, was built to a plan. The tallest buildings were in the center, some of them easily taller than I. These were surrounded by less tall buildings. And so on and on, until the structures were no longer visible because of the black cloud of smoke I have described.

Above the cloud was the glint and shine of steel and glass. The great buildings rose and fell in shimmering planes and rods, like some fantastic technological dream. A hundred different bright colors seemed to be flashing all over them. In the very center was the tallest of them all—a pyramidlike building that seemed to rise from a broad base to a single flashing point. From just below the tip of this building, silvery transportways reached out in all directions.

"The palace of Queen Baataania," the Alando Leed said to me, pointing with justifiable pride to the building in the very center. "And Mildendo City," he added, with an even prouder sweep of his arm over the great city below. "Isn't it beautiful?"

I agreed without hesitation. Mildendo City was easily the most wonderful sight I had seen until then. I wished the Lilliputians had returned my camera to me, so that I could have taken a picture of it.

As I was admiring the city from my perch on the hillside above it, an amazing thing happened. One of the transportways that extended out from Queen Baataania's palace contracted on itself and withdrew to the top of the building. A few moments later, it shot out in our direction, darting through the air like a white snake.

"Stand back," the Alando Leed cried, when he saw it traveling in our direction, and we all withdrew some distance.

The transportway came to rest against the side of the hill with a loud thump, and vehicles appeared on it and began to descend toward us. The Alando Leed went forward to meet them and there was some discussion between him and the Lilliputians who had just arrived.

"Queen Baataania wishes to observe you more closely," the Alando Leed said to me, when he came back. "She has been watching you from the windows of her palace and now she wishes to look at you more closely. This place, however, is not convenient. We will return therefore to the camp. After you have washed and cleaned yourself, you will be visited by her this evening."

Chapter 5

As Carol and I walked back through Kuppancherry after the interview with Selvi, I was reminded of my late night wanderings there of many years before. I did not recognize the places in Kuppancherry very well anymore. Where had Karuthan's shop been? Where exactly had the old beggar sat with his cardboard box? I could not tell. But a vivid remembrance of what Kuppancherry had meant to me all those years ago came back. "This has so many memories for me," I said to Carol. "I haven't been back here in so long." She nodded as if she understood. I felt very warm toward her. There was something tender and understanding in her manner. It was late in the evening by the time the interview with Selvi had ended and we were heading toward Krantinagar railway station. I confided to her about Kuppancherry as we walked through it.

Kuppancherry was the forbidden land of my childhood. It was a place of danger and disease. Unexplained things could happen to you there. It was the object of dire warnings from my mother—"Yes, you may go and play with Anand and Ramu and Meera, but don't cross the maidan to Kuppancherry," or "Go and buy some bread. But if Karimbhoy doesn't have any, don't go looking in some shop in Kuppancherry."

But interdictions have a way of becoming seductions. Kuppancherry proved a good locale for my mood during a certain stage of my adolescence. I often wandered in the lanes of Kuppancherry late at night with cigarette in hand. In my last year in high school, when smoking was an important rite of passage into adulthood for me, Kuppancherry was where I smoked that last cigarette of the day. Often I would stop at Karuthan's dimly lit shop for a glass of coffee under the kerosene lamp. I did not know it then, but looking back I realize Kuppancherry has proven my unlikely teacher in many intangible, unexplainable matters of life.

It was there one evening, I remember, that I began to discover the significance of bodies.

First it was the body of a beggar who habitually sat with his cardboard box of belongings in a corner formed by two walls, across from Karuthan's shop. Leprosy had denuded his hands of fingers, leaving little more than stumps. Wisps of hair hung wildly around his immensely wrinkled face. Gray rags were all the clothes that he had.

Standing in the dim light of Karuthan's kerosene lamp, I would watch this beggar night after night. He would mumble and talk to himself incoherently. Sometimes he would weep. Sometimes he would pull a dented old aluminum plate he had from the cardboard box and stare into it and bang it on the ground. Cupping the lit end of my cigarette in one hand, I would watch him as I smoked. Sometimes he would turn and stare in my direction almost as if he knew I was watching him, though I took care to hide my interest in him.

I wrote my first poem about this beggar. It was called "The Body of a Beggar" and it was a short description of the physical attributes of this beggar in the moonlight. I saved this poem for many years, but I can no longer find it. Before it disappeared, I would come across it every now and then within the pages of some book or the other. Once it occurred to me that it was a strange kind of love poem. It was sad and naive and sentimental and pretentious. And, of course, bad. But I wish I still had it.

This beggar made me inordinately sensitive to the physical appearance of the people of Kuppancherry. Human beings disappeared and bodies appeared in their stead. In Kuppancherry, I suddenly realized with a surprise embarrassing to me now, there were diseased bodies and dirty bodies and deformed bodies. Here were bodies of children, potbellied on stick legs, bodies of old women bent over the sticks or arms they were leaning on, bodies of young men and women walking home from work barefoot and tired. There must have been other bodies—not diseased, not deformed, not dirty—but I did not see them then.

Crossing into the lanes of Kuppancherry from Krantinagar at night, I had discovered a foreign country, an immense shadowland of huts and shacks and rude tenements unilluminated by the streetlamps that stood like sentries along the streets of Krantinagar—a strange, alien land inhabited by bodies that were not, I thought, like mine. In my soaped and combed body, I felt an interloper there, an unwelcome visitor. People hurrying through the dark streets would take in my clean shirt, my jeans, my Bata sandals, and look at me sharply, I felt, as if to ask what I was doing here. Who are you? I half-expected some figure with one arm and no fingers, taking form in a shadow, to cry to me. What are you doing here? What do you want? Why do you come here night after night?

No figure ever did. Night after night, I plunged deeper and deeper into Kuppancherry, exploring farther and farther. It was a place of sudden sounds and varied darknesses, a patchwork of grays and blacks, punctuated only now and then by a flash of yellow from a hut doorway or the bleak whiteness of a fluorescent lamp burning in a tailor's shop, his figure bending over the cloth for some school uniform or other. Muted sounds and darkness were everywhere. That snuffling sound was perhaps a dog or a pig or a child by the side of the road. That brief flash of light was perhaps a bicycle lamp.

Deep inside Kuppancherry, set back a little from the street, stands Velan's liquor shop. It's called Velan's liquor shop though it really belongs to Bhimanbhai Dwarkanath. Velan is just his front. Under the thatched roof of the shop are tables and hard wooden benches. A signboard with a number hangs over its entrance. Through this entrance a steady trickle of people flows in and out. If you happen to be in the vicinity of the shop late at night or early in the morning, you may find one or two bodies lying by the path that leads up to it. If you step closer and peer into their faces, you may discover that their eyes are red and sweat beads their faces. One of them, you may find if you are a youth named RK who should be in bed in Krantinagar, has two protuberances on the forehead. Another, who lies a little further down the path and whose veshti has ridden up to his waist, you may discover, with horror, has swollen testicles.

Everything in Kuppancherry was shadowy, dimly lit—except Velan's shop. As I approached it through one of the three lanes leading to it, there would suddenly be bright light, loud voices, and the hiss of food frying in the kitchen at the back. I would stand sometimes in the shadow of a shuttered shopfront some distance away and watch people going in and out, too afraid to go in myself.

My excursions into Kuppancherry lasted only a few guilty months. I entered college. A new world was there for me to explore. Perhaps the novelty of Kuppancherry began to wear out. Perhaps my need for a late night cigarette disappeared. As inexplicably as I had started, at any rate, I stopped. Fortunately, my mother, as far as I know, never learned of my excursions.

These are some of the memories that came into my mind when I was walking back to Krantinagar railway station with Carol a few nights ago. I resolved that night to write these thoughts down in my journal, but I have not had time till now, though I have made other entries in the journal. There has been the transcription of the interview to work on. Over the last few days I have met with Carol one or two times to work on the transcription. Long afternoons I have spent playing back the cassette of the interview, writing down Selvi's words in my awkward Tamil and translating that into English.

Carol has offered to pay me for the work but I have refused payment. I only want to be allowed to use the material for an article that I think I might want to write. I do have friends who work for newspapers, and Chandran has told me many times that if I write something worth publishing he will see what he can do. Freelancing seems an appropriate way to spend my time until Law College. A series of profiles of Madras's more unusual citizens would be worth writing. Selvi would fit in there admirably.

In the meantime, there is the announcement of the election to the state legislature from Krantinagar and Kuppancherry, that is, the West Madras constituency. The sitting member of the legislative assembly for West Madras died a few months ago and at last it looks as if there might be a by-election to fill the vacancy.

I was with Kulan when I learned of the election. I had run into him outside Krantinagar railway station. It was late in the evening. He was sitting on the backseat of the rickshaw with his feet up on the saddleseat in front. There were only two other rickshaws waiting with him in front of the station. The others must have already left for the day.

I had stopped for a moment outside the station because it had suddenly occurred to me that the short lane in front of Krantinagar railway station at night would be an excellent subject for a black-and-white photograph. In my dilettantish way, I have considered filling my time by taking photographs of Madras scenes. I probably won't, though, because photography is such an expensive hobby. It's so much cheaper to write a photograph than to shoot it.

The cycle-rickshaw stand where Kulan's rickshaw was waiting is opposite the entrance to the railway station. Through the entrance, Kulan can see railway tracks and platforms. If the photographer were positioned in roughly the same place, a tantalizing glimpse of the interior of the station would appear in the middle of the photograph, framed by the entrance. Tracks, two platforms, and perhaps one or two figures in postures of expectant waiting would be visible in that frame. The photographer would have to wait patiently to capture the figures in these postures. To one side of the entrance to the station is a flight of stairs, which leads to the overpass over the tracks. In this photograph of a night scene, the overpass would disappear mysteriously into the darkness of the night sky. The effect would be perfect if a man in a white shirt were climbing up the steps at that very moment.

Small shops and stalls stand against the outer wall of the station on the other side of the entrance. Most of them would appear closed in the photograph because of the lateness of the hour. Only two of them were still open the night I saw Kulan outside Krantinagar railway station. One was a lottery ticket stall. Beneath a hurricane lamp, different lottery tickets had been laid out in rows on a wooden board. The other shop had an electric light and was a stall similar to Joseph's. It sold cigarettes and soft drinks. From this stall a radio blared loud music into the almost empty street. The music, unfortunately, cannot be captured in the photograph, but the hurricane lamp and the electric light would appear as splashes of white. Also in the photograph would be the street itself, with scraps of paper, old shoes, and rotting vegetables lying in the dust. The refuse in an empty street would give the photograph an appropriate atmosphere of desolation. And in the foreground of the photograph, his slightly out-of-focus profile looking toward the entrance to the station, would be Kulan on his rickshaw, sitting on the backseat with his feet on the saddleseat in front.

Kulan noticed me as I paused to conjure up this photograph outside the station entrance and nodded to me. I stopped to talk to him. "How are you, Kulan?" I said to him in Tamil. He took his feet down from the seat in front. "So-so," he said. "How did the interview with Selvi go?" I told him it had gone well and described to him what she had said. He listened to me intently, his eyes fixed on me unwaveringly. A faint smell of stale sweat rose from him. He nodded when I had finished. "She is a good woman," he said. "She has worked hard for the Domestic Workers Union."

"Do you know her well?"

"Yes," Kulan said. "She and I have worked together sometimes. I came to know her through my union." When I looked blank, he pointed to a metal sign above him. *Krantinagar Cycle-Rickshaw Union,* the sign read. Below were listed many of the more common destinations in Krantinagar, like Kuberan A/C Theater and Krantinagar Shopping Complex. At one time fares had been given next to the destinations, but the numbers had since been scratched out. The paint was old and faded and rust showed through in places.

"I have never noticed this sign," I said to Kulan. "I didn't know there was a rickshaw union in Krantinagar."

"There isn't," he said. "I tried starting one some years ago. I didn't want much, only to get some common fares and some discipline in handling customers. It didn't work." He smiled bitterly. "You would think such a thing is up to the rickshaw-wallahs. But it isn't. I came to know Selvi in the early days of trying to set this thing up. Now I try to do whatever I can for the Domestic Workers Union. When they opened their office in Kuppancherry, I and some of my friends helped them fix the place up. It needed a lot of work. We helped paint the place and brought in the furniture in our rickshaws . . ."

Kulan broke off as the song that was playing on the radio in the stall outside the station ended and an announcer's voice came on. Time for the news, I realized. It was nine. Kulan was leaning forward, listening intently.

A woman's voice began reading the news in Tamil. By-elections had been announced in various constituencies around the country.

Kulan jumped out of the rickshaw and hurried over to the stall to listen more carefully. "Elections have been announced," the stall keeper repeated officiously to Kulan. He was a thin man in a white vest. His large eyes had a perpetually eager expression in them. He flicked his handcloth over the radio and fiddled importantly with the tuning knob. The newsreader's voice was interrupted by crackling and got worse instead of clearer.

"It's fine. Let me listen," Kulan said to the stall keeper in exasperation. The stall keeper turned away, offended. "I was only trying to make it better," he said.

The voice on the radio had already passed on to the next news item. There had been a big communal incident in Uttar Pradesh. Many men, women, and children of a "certain community" had been killed. The prime minister had denounced the killing. The state governor was on his way to visit the affected areas. Kulan returned to his rickshaw. The stall keeper pretended to be listening intently to the radio.

"Shanthamma may contest the election from here as an independent," Kulan said to me when he came back. "I wanted to hear if West Madras had also been included among the constituencies for which elections have been announced."

"I didn't know Shanthamma wanted to run for election," I said with some surprise. I have been trying to catch up on Tamil politics by reading some of the back issues of Chandran's Tamil weekly *Achamillai! Achamillai!* has carried stories of Shanthamma's organizing activities in Krantinagar, Kuppancherry, and adjoining areas, but it had not mentioned anything about her political ambitions.

"She is thinking of it," Kulan said. "She hasn't decided anything yet."

"Does she have popular support?"

"In Kuppancherry she does," Kulan said. "Many people there appreciate the help she has given in organizing the domestic servants. Shanthamma's Domestic Workers Union has a lot of support there. I don't know about Krantinagar." He paused for a moment and added with a smile, "Will you vote for Shanthamma?"

Would I vote for Shanthamma? I think I would, if I voted for anybody at all. But who can get excited about voting these days? The regular national parties, in years of holding power, have successfully communalized and corrupted politics.

The next day's newspaper confirmed that a by-election for West Madras had in fact been announced. Shanthamma, the story reported, had only said she was considering whether to contest the election. She had not yet decided. Sethuraman, the local politician of long standing, will be the candidate of the Congress (R) party. The member of the legislative assembly whose death had caused this by-election had also been a member of the Congress (R). Krantinagar and Kuppancherry have returned Congress (R) candidates for as long as I can remember.

While Shanthamma is still deciding whether to contest the election or not, the Congress (R) machinery has already gone into operation. They have the support of Bhimanbhai Dwarkanath, the very rich owner of local businesses, legal and illegal, who has been associated with the Congress (R) for a long, long time. The Congress (R) is well organized. Chandran is sure that the party knew of the election date well before it was announced. In the streets, evidence of its election machinery is already visible. Posters have begun to appear everywhere. At the corner of Ganapathy Kovil Street, the Congress (R) has put up a wooden shelter and a loudspeaker. All this is only possible because the Congress (R) must have had firm prior knowledge of the time of the elections. Since the Congress (R) is in power in the center and an ally of the ADRK here in the state, I would be surprised if the party did not manage to make sure it was properly prepared before announcing the election date.

Kulan and I, listening to the radio in front of Krantinagar railway station, knew nothing of all this. "Perhaps you will vote for Shanthamma if she stands for election," he had said to me. "Perhaps," I had replied, and turned to walk home.

Walking home that night from the Krantinagar railway station, a strange thing happened. I met Valur Vishveswaran, the one that the children of Ganapathy Kovil Street call White-Beard Grandfather (though, from up close, he does not look so old), walking swiftly toward the station. He appeared from around a corner and slammed into me before I could move out of his way. Even as I was reaching out to support him, he had fallen to the ground. I bent over him.

"Are you hurt?" I said to him.

He turned a face twisted by distaste toward me. When I reached out to help him up, he quickly scrambled away along the ground, an uncommon fear written across his face. "Don't touch me," he said. "Don't touch me." He got up on his own and backed away, as if he expected me to attack him. His eyes watched me unwaveringly to make sure I did not make any sudden movements. And then he turned swiftly on his heels and was gone. In a moment he had disappeared down the street.

Wondering at this strange incident, I stopped at Joseph's stall before going up to my apartment and mentioned it to him. Joseph was shutting up his stall for the night. "That's the way the White-Beard Grandfather is," he said, lifting up a wooden slat to put it in position over the counter of his stall. "He hates to be touched. Sometimes he comes out and buys a coffee or a tea from me but he will not take it from my hand. I must place it on the counter before he will pick it up. Once I asked him why he disliked to be touched. He looked at me straight and said, 'With hands as huge as those, don't you think you will crush my hands to pieces?' I think the children are right, RK-sir. I think the White-Beard Grandfather is crazy. He is so strange. He lives in that little room there. Even where I live is better."

Joseph finished placing the slats in position and locking up his stall. He stuck out his hands toward me. "You tell me, RK-sir," he said. "Are my hands so huge and ugly?"

I did not say this to him, but Joseph's hands, though not huge, are certainly big. His whole body is stocky and powerful, though you don't realize it at once. He has a certain presence. It is interesting to see how the loafers around his stall, like Mohan, defer to him. He is not a very talkative man. I have tried engaging him in a conversation once or twice, just to see what kind of life he has led. He has not told me much. The only subject he talks about at any length is his daughter, whom he wants to send to medical college. Or to engineering college. He is dreaming the middle-class dream.

Carol took me out to dinner tonight. We went to a restaurant in Adyar Gate Hotel, the kind of restaurant I myself could never go to. This expensive treat was a kind of payment for my help in various ways over the last few days, I think. It was not the best of days for such a treat. My father's death anniversary is coming up. My mother has been talking to the priest to make arrangements. She has been lecturing me on my attitude toward my part in the ceremony. My father was an atheist. I am an atheist. I find it hard to be cooperative in this matter. Finally, I will do what my mother wants, but it is hard to be gracious. We had a big argument just before I had to leave to meet Carol.

In the restaurant, Carol and I sat at a table by the wall, from which we could see the musicians who were performing that day. A jazz band was playing at the restaurant—mostly classics like Louis Armstrong's "Black and Blue" and "I'm Confessin' That I Love You," though once they played a jazz rendition of a popular Tamil film song. I resolutely put the argument with my mother out of my mind.

"Have you come here before?" Carol asked, looking at the menu. She had dressed up for the occasion. She was wearing earrings and lipstick. Her pink shirt had a silky sheen to it and daringly plunged toward her cleavage without quite making it. She had brushed her hair so that her face was framed in brown waves. Brushed in this fashion, her hair had surprising body. A faint smell of perfume rose from her. She seemed attractive in a quiet way. She had, I noticed, wonderful eyes, set wide apart in immense openness to the world. She had accented them with black eyeliner.

"You studied in the U.S., right?" she said, when we had ordered.

"Yes," I said. "For two years."

"Do you plan to go back to the U.S.? To study I mean."

"You know," I said, smiling. "When I was in the U.S., everyone would ask me if I was going back to India. Now that I am in India, everyone wants to know if I am going back to the U.S."

Carol's eyes widened and she looked at me directly. "I didn't mean anything by that," she said. "You should go back if you want to. You should stay here if you want to." She was concerned that she had offended me. I was touched.

We talked then about different things, but mostly about New York, which is the place in the U.S. I know best. Carol does not know New York well. She spent only a summer there long ago.

"Did you like it there?" she asked me.

I thought about New York. "Actually, I did," I said. "It was Manhattan, you know. The big city feel, I've always loved that." I remembered Terri Stead, who had produced a demo tape called "Big City Blues, White City Truths" and was trying to find a label for it when I left the U.S. months ago. She had very clear ideas about big cities. I had not written to her since my departure, although I had promised her I would. In my mind's eye, I could clearly see her blowing her saxophone with her band. She put so much passion into her music. When she leaned back and let it rip, her fashionably braided hair would fall away from her neck and her nipples would stand up and strain against her T-shirt.

"I have this friend," I said to Carol. "She has a real love-hate relationship with New York. She is black and grew up in the poorest part of the Bronx. She hated it, but she can't imagine living anywhere else."

Carol had grown up in Chicago.

"The U.S. was all right," I said. "But it wasn't home. Whatever that is."

And so we talked about whatever home was for a long time. The U.S. was home to Carol but she often felt more comfortable in Mexico or Guatemala. Most of her work had to do with Central America and she went there often, at least once or twice a year, sometimes more. Mexico wasn't too far from Austin, Texas, where she taught at the university. Now that she was beginning to do work in India, she thought she might go there less.

The food arrived, wheeled to our table by a serious-faced, elderly man. He had been composed by the management of the hotel in black trousers and a white jacket with gold bands around the collar, and flashed a smile every time he was spoken to. He arranged the dishes carefully on the table. I watched the sure movements of his hands and wondered in what part of Madras he lived, whether he was married, whether he had children and what they did. I wondered if he was religious.

When he had left, I said to Carol, "What do you mean you feel more comfortable in Mexico or Guatemala?"

She waited to finish chewing her mouthful of tandoori chicken and then said, "It's the strangest thing. The U.S. always seems unreal to me when I'm outside it. I mean, I know it's there and it's home. It's where most of my family is. It's where many of my friends are. It's where I grew up. It's where I live and work most of the time. I don't really forget that. But still it seems less real than, say, Mexico, many times." She paused. "I remember the first time I ever traveled outside the U.S. This was when I was an undergraduate, many years ago, when I traveled to Mexico with a friend. I had never been out of the U.S. before, not even to go to Canada. Coming back, we flew into Chicago's O'Hare Airport from Mexico. My father had come to pick me up and we drove home. As soon as we were back near my neighborhood, it suddenly hit me how sanitized the U.S. is. Everything was in order and in place—after Mexico, almost unbelievably in order and in place. Here was the place I had grown up in. I couldn't believe how ultraorganized everything suddenly looked. As if out of some fantasy land. You know?"

I nodded. "That is exactly the kind of feeling I have about the U.S.," I said. "Not about New York, of course, but other places. You know? U.S. in general. Something like that. I didn't think an American would have such a feeling."

Both of us were silent as we finished eating. When I was done, I pushed the plate away. The composition in black trousers and white jacket materialized at my side with a finger bowl.

The conversation took a more personal turn. Carol wanted to know if I had a girlfriend, whether I was hoping to get married. I was embarrassed by her questions. "You sound like my mother," I said to her. She laughed and told me about herself. She had been married, not to an American but to a Mexican who came from a very wealthy family. They had met in the U.S. as graduate students. She had gone back to Mexico with him but things had not worked out. He studied to be a lawyer because his family wanted him to and they had drifted apart. The divorce had not been easy since both were devout Catholics, though she was hardly orthodox.

It was then I set fire to the fuse that made the evening explode in our faces. For some inexplicable reason, I said to her in an accusing tone, "I'm an atheist."

I told her that I found the idea of a god too much. It was all so fantastic, that somebody somewhere was keeping watch over us all. Religion, I said, wagging my finger in her face, makes us resign ourselves to things. Carol was calm. She begged to differ and gave her reasons. "Jesus was a revolutionary, you know," she concluded.

We looked at each other without speaking. I wanted to say something more but did not know how to say it.

Carol had asked for the bill, and now the waiter appeared with it and waited quietly at the side of the table. I looked at him. "Are you religious?" I said to him. He looked back at me in surprise, not knowing how to respond.

"Look at people," I said in a voice I knew was too loud and angry. "I'm sure people just love being religious. That way they needn't do anything with their lives. I bet they go to temples instead of union meetings. I bet God makes it okay for them to be where they are." I was surprised at my own barely veiled rudeness to the waiter.

Carol said nothing. Her mouth was a tight line. She took out money and paid the waiter. Later, as we were leaving the restaurant, I caught a glimpse of the waiter through the doorway that led to the kitchen when one of the doors swung open. He was talking intently to one of the other compositions in black trousers and white jacket. He was bending over and rubbing the seat of his trousers, demonstrating something to his companion. His companion's face looked serious and concerned. And then the door swung back shut. I felt ashamed of myself.

After the air conditioning of the hotel, the air outside was warm and sticky.

"Well, that was rude," Carol said.

I was ashamed. "I know," I replied. "I'm sorry about that." I hastened to add something about how I still believed in what I said, but even to myself I sounded trite. I was saying all the right things in all the wrong words. I felt resentful and ashamed. I hadn't wanted to be rude, especially to a waiter who was simply doing his job. How did I know what he was really like?

Carol took an auto-rickshaw to her room. I volunteered to take her home. She refused. I felt a little sad and helpless. On my way home, I remembered that Terri Stead was an atheist too, but that made it only a little better. When I got in, my mother heard me and came out of her room. She did not look as if she had been asleep. I could not face her. I darted quickly into the bathroom. I could hear her get herself some water from the kitchen. I did not come out until she was back in her room. When I thought of the argument with Carol, I felt like crying.

Chapter 6

When evening came, I was ready for my interview with Queen Baataania. Another trip had been made to the pits out in the desert so that I could wash myself. The Lilliputians had provided a large quantity of their strongest industrial cleaning detergent. I poured this fluid over my body, pouring a little extra over my armpits and other such places, and scrubbed hard with two or three karunar bushes. From the karunar bush the Lilliputians make a brush that is used for scouring floors. I wished I had a mirror to help me comb my hair, but in its absence had to be content with running my comb through what I thought were the right places. I was intent on making a good impression.

The queen arrived in a long convoy of vehicles. There were many trakas in the convoy. Chochos kept watch overhead. "Be careful how you behave in front of the queen," the Alando Leed had warned me earlier. He had rushed into the hangar when the convoy had first been sighted on the horizon. I was in the process of pulling on a clean pair of trousers. It was not easy to do this lying on the ground. The Alando Leed had hurriedly averted his eyes and waited for me to finish, and then he had instructed me in the proper ritual for paying respect to the ruler.

The ritual that I went through was as follows. I was made to sit cross-legged in front of my hangar. As the queen got out of her vehicle and approached me, I bowed until my forehead touched the ground lightly (so as not to raise a huge cloud of dust). I did this three times. What this meant, the Alando Leed had told me earlier, was that I gave the queen command over my mind, soul, and body. The queen, standing at a distance, raised her hands thrice and waved them to signify her acceptance of my submission. This ritual is a very ancient practice. In the old days, when Mildendo was constantly at war with its neighbors, this was the manner in which defeated rulers had submitted to the ruler of Mildendo.

A large crowd of soldiers had gathered around to watch my

meeting with the queen. They stood just beyond the circle formed by the trakas in uniforms made of a special green substance called chulia that glinted and flashed in the lights of the convoy. As soon as the ritual had been completed, I was made to lie down on the ground and the shackles were put back on me. The top security officers of Mildendo had decided that this precaution was necessary.

The queen and the Alando Leed then advanced toward me, and the Alando Leed suggested that we retire to my hangar so that the meeting could take place in greater privacy. I entered my hangar first and lay down, as was my wont when talking to the Lilliputians, on my belly. A chair was brought in for the queen and placed in front of my face. She then entered accompanied by the Alando Leed. Behind them, ten soldiers appeared and stood just within the entrance to the hangar, their guns held at the ready.

When the queen was seated, I said, "O Queen, it gives me pleasure to meet you. I wish I could speak to you in your own language, but I have not yet had the time to learn it. You must forgive me for this."

"It is no matter," the queen replied with much dignity through the Alando Leed, who acted as translator. "We have not learned any of your languages either. So in this we are both mutually at fault."

"I intend to learn your language as swiftly as I can," I assured her.

"Your language, our scholars tell me," the queen replied through the Alando Leed, "is closer to Northern Lilliputian in its grammar than to High Lilliputian. It may therefore be better for you to begin with that dialect first."

The Alando Leed explained to me that Northern Lilliputian was a degraded form of Lilliputian. There were significant differences between Northern Lilliputian and High Lilliputian, but the speakers of the two dialects were mutually intelligible to one another for the most part.

"Thank you for your advice," I said to the queen.

"The Alando Leed has told me of your manner of entry into

Mildendo," the queen continued. "What you have done seems to us considerably brave. To jump out of an aircraft over an unknown place! How courageous!"

"My thoughts were all about Lilliput as I jumped," I said to the queen. "I knew I would find Lilliput below me. I only hoped that I would be able to make friendly contact with you Lilliputians. And now that you have granted me permission to stay in your country, my wishes have been fulfilled."

In this fashion, the queen and I kept up a pleasant conversation until it was almost time for her to leave. I found her, in everything she said, a modest and gracious person. The Mildendan monarch does not actually rule the kingdom, for there is a special class of administrators selected for this purpose. Despite this, I found Queen Baataania to be, in all my conversations with her, a well-informed person. The queen is something of a scientist and an economist, a very clear-headed pragmatist who is always interested in how to make her kingdom even more magnificent than it is. During our talks, the queen asked perceptive questions about my life as a bandur in my land and I answered her as best I could. Because of her intellect and her keen interest in her kingdom, the queen had earned great respect among her people and continued to exercise considerable influence over the affairs of her country.

Even at that first meeting with her, the queen gave evidence of her great intellectual curiosity. Before the meeting ended, the queen rose from her chair. "We are intrigued by your size," she said through the Alando Leed. "We wish to examine you closer up. Be prepared for our approach."

And the queen came up and stood near my face, staring up at me with interest. The length of my face was more than twice as much as her entire height. She leaned back on her heels, tilted her head far back, and examined my face carefully. Throughout her examination, she kept up a commentary in Lilliputian to the Alando Leed, who made notations in a book he had with him.

This examination took some time, but it gave me the opportunity to examine the queen carefully. She was only of average

Lilliputian height but her complexion was of an especially clear green. She wore a long robe, patterned in brown, black, and yellow, that extended to the ground. On her head, she wore a hat of the same colors over her thick blue hair, which had been done up in tight braids. Her hat was studded with many jewels. The queen's features were very delicate, her nose long and sharp, her mouth small above a pointed chin.

Queen Baataania appeared very beautiful to me, but I must say I did not appear in the same light to her. When I begged her to tell me what she had concluded in carrying out her examination of my face, she said, quite reluctantly, "You appear ugly and monstrous to us. The color of your skin is very strange, just like that of the Northern Lilliputians. How dirty and blotched your complexion is! And your nose—we have never seen a larger, more bulbous nose. Your lips, so thick and long! I believe your lips are nearly as long as my body at my full height . . ." Noticing the disappointment on my face, she stopped.

The queen's words saddened me greatly. It had been important to me that I make a good impression upon her, and now my ugliness seemed to have alienated her. She had found my skin dirty. The strongest industrial detergent in Lilliput had been of little help. "Do not be grieved by this, bandur," she said to me graciously. "Your ugliness is not your fault. If Yaaga, or God as I'm told you call him, in His wisdom has made you into such a monster, we are certain He has His reasons. We do not hold this against you."

At last the evening drew to an end. "Perhaps we will visit you again soon," the queen said, before she left. The soldiers who had been standing guard followed her out of the hangar, but the Alando Leed stayed back.

"It has been decided," he said to me, "that you be employed in some fashion during your stay in Mildendo. In this way you may earn your keep, which as you can very well imagine is considerable. It has also been decided that you will be most useful doing physical work because of your great size. From tomorrow, therefore, you will join the work team in Sector 420 of Mildendo City. Be prepared for this tomorrow morning."

I was pleased to hear this from the Alando Leed. I had myself been planning to offer my services to the Mildendans in any capacity that they wished, but the Alando Leed had preempted me. I let the Alando Leed know that I would do whatever work was assigned to me to the best of my ability.

The next morning, the Alando Leed arrived to lead me to the work I was to perform. We went back to Mildendo City but by a different route, so that we approached it from the plains and not from the hills. We stopped a little outside the city. The black cloud of smoke that habitually covered it lay at a height much greater than mine, and so I could see the portions of the city that were below the cloud much more clearly now than I had been able to do the previous day. The streets, I found, were long and narrow, and many of them ran straight, intersecting with other streets at right angles. They were lined with buildings, reddish-brown in color and often four or five stories high. I could look down two or three of these streets from where I was standing. In the distant center of the city, breaking through the black cloud above and disappearing from sight, were the towers and spires I had seen the day before.

The streets, in shadow because of the overhanging cloud of black smoke, bustled with activity. From some of the chimneys of the buildings, smoke rose into the air, mingling finally with the great cloud overhead. Many trakas of different kinds were moving along in all directions. Lilliputians thronged the streets in the gray light that lay in them, weaving their way around stationary trakas standing in front of the buildings. Some were climbing out of trakas, going into buildings, buying things from street vendors. Others were standing in groups, talking to one another, throwing a pandhu (a kind of wooden ball) among themselves.

Many of the Lilliputians in the street, I noticed, were not green-skinned like the Alando Leed or the queen, but had skin that was a kind of brown, something like mine, or black. Their hair too was not blue but black. Other Lilliputians were pink-skinned and yellow-haired. Intermingled with these brown-skinned, black-skinned, and pink-skinned Lilliputians were green-skinned Lilliputians much more like the ones I had seen so far. The varied hues of the people in the street suggested an ever-changing, mobile quilt of many colors.

"Your task," the Alando Leed said to me, climbing out of the traka in which he had been traveling, "will be to help clear certain areas in Sector 420 of the city. Sector 420 should be visible to you from up there, if you look carefully to the left of you. You will see a tall crescent-shaped building. Do you see it? Between that building and the river behind it is Sector 420."

Sector 420 appeared even more reddish-brown than the other parts of the city below the black cloud. Later, I would learn that the reddish color of these buildings was a result of rust. When we got closer to Sector 420, I could pick out the details better. Black, polluted water stood in stagnant pools in some of the lanes that led to the river. The houses here rose only to my waist. They were low and mean, and the streets little more than winding lanes. Doors and windows stood ajar. If I bent down, I could peer into some of the houses. The rooms were empty and the paint was peeling from the walls.

Sector 420 had been cordoned off from the rest of the city by the Mildendo Peeg Pleesa, which roughly translates as the Mildendo City Police. The streets leading into Sector 420 had been barricaded and the trakas of the pleesa stood at strategic points within the sector. Various work teams were making their way through the lanes to demolish the houses and clear the area. My job was to help these work teams in their task.

The Alando Leed took me to the freepar, or "foreman," in charge of the street in which I was to work, who had already been informed that I was to join his work team. He was waiting for the Alando Leed to bring me to him. He first knelt and bowed low to the Alando Leed and then turned to look up at me, his eyes full of wonder. He had never before in his life seen a bandur. The Alando Leed spoke to him for a few minutes and then explained to me what I was to do.

The task was fairly simple. Machines preceded me into the area to be cleared. The people living there had been warned to leave many days earlier. Now that the area was supposed to be clear, machines dismantled the buildings, bringing them down in a cloud of rubble. My job was to pick up large pieces and carry them out of Sector 420, which was one of the outermost sectors of the city, to the adjoining plain. Here, other machines waited to cut the pieces into smaller bits and carry them a little distance from the city, where a new town was being built for the people who had formerly lived in these buildings. The materials were to be used in the construction of this new town and the cleared area of the city made into parks and playgrounds. The whole project was part of the beautification of the city.

The task was simple but physically exhausting. When the Alando Leed had departed, I was left with the freepar and no way of communicating except through gestures, which meant that we took more time than required getting started. Most of the buildings had been constructed centuries earlier, and hence were made of heavy, primitive materials of a kind that would never be used in any modern Mildendan building of any quality. The items I was to carry out were often large pieces of iron or wood. Sometimes I also had to break these pieces into smaller ones for ease of conveyance. My shackles had been adjusted to increase my freedom of movement, but they were still enough to make some of the work unnecessarily laborious. I could understand the anxiety that drove the Mildendans to shackle me, but I resolved to talk to the Alando Leed the next time I saw him about leaving the shackles off, at least while I was working. I did not think the Mildendans had anything to worry about with so many of the trakas and the chochos of the Peeg Immeegar keeping watch over me.

The work was also complicated by the fact that I had to be careful not to let any piece fall, for there was always the danger that some Lilliputian would be crushed by what I had dropped. It was difficult to watch where I was putting my foot while carrying a large iron roof in my shackled hands. I had to be especially careful because many Lilliputians had refused to leave the designated parts of Sector 420. When the alarms warning them to leave the buildings and proceed to a relocation point were sounded, these

Lilliputians simply ignored them and hid within. They would wait in hiding, for as long as a week I was told, until the dismantling machines were almost upon them. And then they would appear to stand as living shields in front of the machines. For some inexplicable reason, they did not want the beautification of the city to go forward.

At this point, special officers of the Mildendo Peeg Pleesa, who had been deputed to do this work, would go into action and physically remove these miscreants. But some of them always escaped, and I had to be especially careful that I did not inadvertently stomp on them as they jumped up from the rubble to stop me from doing my work.

Once I was attacked directly by one of these crazy Lilliputians. This happened in the very first week I began my work in Sector 420. I had just picked up a heavy piece of rusted iron when a Lilliputian woman suddenly appeared on a large mound of rubble and addressed me in a loud voice. "Bandur!" she cried. "Bandur!" and followed this up with some Lilliputian words I could not understand then because I did not know the language. She waved both her hands at me and shouted the same words again and again. Her long black hair hung loose in a manner quite unlike the usual Lilliputian style. Her skin was black. She was dressed in a long gray robe that fell to the ground in loose folds and was so thin that she appeared to be little more than a skeleton.

I was so taken aback by the actions of this Lilliputian woman that I dropped the piece of iron I held in my hand. It fell to the ground, raising a great cloud of dust that surrounded the mound, the Lilliputian woman and me. Even I was convulsed by coughing and blinded by the dust. When the dust cleared, I found that the Lilliputian woman had been joined by a male Lilliputian, green-skinned and blue-haired. He turned and spoke to me in English. "I am Lar Prent," he said. "She meant you no harm. Let us leave in peace." Before I could respond, the two had climbed down from the mound of rubble and joined a group of accomplices who were blocking a machine's approach to a building by lying down in its path. Three traka of the Mildendo Peeg Pleesa were moving down what had formerly been a street to haul these Lilliputians away. I stayed to watch for a moment and then picked up the piece of iron that I had dropped and stepped over the rubble on my way to the collection depot outside the city.

Other than the infrequent distractions and interruptions caused by this handful of crazy Lilliputians, the work I did was hard but routine. It was also very productive work, as the freepar himself acknowledged to me once when I had learned enough Lilliputian to converse with him. I managed to carry out the remnants of many dismantled buildings in one day. These buildings were for me, after all, little more than large toy houses. At the end of a day's work I enjoyed the satisfaction of a job well done. I also enjoyed the exercise. The two-hour trudge back to my hangar in the afternoon, however, was difficult. I only wished my place of work were closer to where I lived.

I approached the Alando Leed about the removal of the shackles from my hands and legs. He listened to me patiently and twitched his nose (which is one of the Lilliputian ways of saying no). "Not possible," he said. "You will forgive me for saying this, but we have only your word regarding your feelings for us. We need to take all the precautions we can." The Alando Leed, however, did speak to some of the Peeg Immeegar officers who accompanied me out to Sector 420 every day and had them devise a new travel route that reduced the time to less than an hour and a half.

The evenings had been set aside for my study. A tutor named Edu Kator had been appointed to teach me the Lilliputian language. "Let us begin with Northern Lilliputian," he said on the first day. "You will find it easiest to learn and it will be sufficient for you to converse with speakers of High Lilliputian as well. Later, if necessary, you can learn some High Lilliputian." Over the following weeks, I made rapid progress in learning the Lilliputian language with my language teacher. My tutor's knowledge of English, though not very good, was adequate for our purposes. He was an officer of the Peeg Immeegar and had traveled into the bandur lands a few times on reconnaissance missions. The Mildendans and a few of the other Lilliputian nations regularly send secret missions into the lands of us bandur to monitor our progress. The average Lilliputian knows nothing of these missions—indeed, knows virtually nothing of us. I was curious about these missions, but my tutor would not discuss them with me and, in fact, seemed worried that he had even mentioned them.

Meanwhile, Queen Baataania often came to watch me at work in Sector 420. She would sit in her official traka and look on as I performed what must have seemed to the Lilliputians prodigious tasks of labor. Sometimes she came in a chocho and watched me from above. She seemed fascinated by the physical characteristics of my body and by my great strength. She often made the request that I take off my shirt when I worked so that she could watch my body muscles perform. This request was passed on to me by my freepar. I acceded to it quite willingly, although I was a little ashamed at the flabbiness of my body. After a few weeks of working in Sector 420, however, my muscles began to get some shape and firmness.

The queen frequently had a famous surgeon with her in her traka or chocho. It was the job of this surgeon to point out the various parts of my body and the muscles I was using to do what I was doing. The queen and the surgeon even had charts and diagrams with them. I would sometimes see them leaning out of the circling chocho, looking down at me, with pieces of paper in their hands. I would then raise my hand and wave to them, being very careful, however, in doing this, because the chocho often flew very close to me. Once or twice, the queen very graciously waved back to me.

I, for my part, worked even harder when the queen was present. I was flattered by the interest she was taking in my performance and tried to outdo myself. Where it would have been sufficient to carry one beam of wood, I would carry two. This proved very taxing upon me and on the days that the queen came to watch me there was a constant soreness in my body, but I was only too glad of the opportunity to erase the bad first impression I had made upon her. I told myself this was a way of showing the queen that there was indeed a reason why Yaaga had made me so huge and ugly; it was so that I could perform such prodigious feats of strength.

One particular day, when working in Sector 420, I managed to be of especial help. A group of the same Lilliputians who were doing their best to prevent the work from proceeding had barricaded themselves in a building so that the officers of the Mildendo Peeg Pleesa were unable to dislodge them. During the night, the Lilliputians had dug deep trenches all around the building and piled up rubble in such a manner that trakas were unable to approach it without exposing themselves to attack by stones from the building. This building was so situated that the area behind it could not be approached until it was cleared. The work had been brought to a full stop and all the freepars were in despair. There was talk of bringing in more reinforcements from the Pleesa or even calling in the Peeg Immeegar, but these were options that the Mildendans wished to avoid because of the publicity they would bring.

At this time, it struck me that I could quite easily do something that would have required tremendous effort for the Mildendans, even with all their technology. I conveyed to my freepar my idea and it was soon approved. Leaving the Mildendans standing at a distance, I quickly strode up to the building. From within, the crazy Lilliputians threw stones at me when they saw me coming, but these stones did not amount to more than pebbles to me. Standing close to the building, I began removing the roof bit by bit. This was strenuous work and took much longer than I expected because the building was very well constructed and there were many distractions. The barricaded Lilliputians stuck sharp sticks into my legs through the windows in the hope of stopping me. Once they rammed a long stick hard against my knee and I let out a loud yell that frightened them. The thick material of my trousers, however, protected me for the most part and the roof was soon off. After this it was relatively easy work for a chocho to drop officers of the Mildendo Peeg Pleesa into the building and clear it.

As the defeated Lilliputians began leaving the building in the custody of the officers, I returned to where most of the members of the work team were gathered. There were shouts of congratulations and applause all around me. The workers, some of whom were getting used to me and would wander over during the lunch break to watch with awe as I ate traka-loads of food, raised both their clenched fists above their heads in the traditional Mildendan gesture of approval. The queen, who was also present that day, showed her approval by making a similar gesture from her traka, and I was especially gratified by this.

In all this there was only one voice of disapproval. As I was making my way back to join my work team, a voice said to me, "Valur Vishveswaran, why are you so eager to do all this?" I turned to see the Lilliputian who had identified himself as Lar Prent standing alone on the roof of a half-dismantled building. Before I could say anything, he had ducked into the building and was gone.

When I rejoined my work team, however, the freepar came up to me and told me that he was so pleased with me, he was giving me the rest of the day off. I dismissed Lar Prent's words from my mind, quickly gathered my things together, and left for my hangar with my escort. I was not going to bother myself with the words of a strange Lilliputian who, for some inexplicable reason, had chosen to obstruct much-needed construction activity.

Chapter 7

Some days ago Carol, Chandran, and I watched the Tamil movie *Viduthalai*. The movie was something special that Carol was giving herself because she has been such a good girl and has managed to get so much work done in the last few days.

We watched the movie on Chandran's video recorder, which is in the living room on the ground floor of his house. I was supposed to translate the dialogue in the movie for Carol. I myself offered to do this as a way of atoning for my rudeness the other evening. I felt quite ashamed of my behavior at the restaurant. I wanted to make up with her. Carol accepted my offer without much ado. She was very sweet about it, dismissing my apologies with a quick gesture of her hands. Maybe one day we could have a more fruitful discussion about religion. I want to understand why she is religious.

Chandran joined us when the movie started. Carol had invited him to view the movie with us earlier, but he had refused, pretending that he was not interested. He was expecting Shanthamma to arrive any minute. As the titles began to roll across the screen, he appeared from the study, glanced at Carol guiltily, and sat down to watch the movie, saying, "I know the actor. I know him very well," as if that explained everything.

The actor that Chandran knows is Ravindran. He is the hero of the film. For twenty years and more he has been one of the biggest stars on the Tamil screen—he is now middle-aged, and still he plays the young hero of the movie. And still he draws the crowds. *Viduthalai* is the biggest Tamil film of the year. It ran in movie theaters for months. It is still running in Kuberan A/C Theater, here in Krantinagar. I pass the theater often. From a huge hoarding towering in front of the theater, the angry face of Ravindran watches over his devotees lining up at the ticket counters. Dressed in black trousers, black jacket, and red shirt, Ravindran is standing with his legs apart. A lock of hair falls over his forehead.

His left hand, which holds a gun, is pressed against his right cheek. The heroine is standing on his left shoulder and leaning on his left cheek. Dressed in a white saree, she is throwing a coy glance at the people gathered below.

Viduthalai is the story of a father and a son, both of whom are played by Ravindran. It belongs to that genre of Indian films, so common now, in which the hero is an upright police officer struggling against forces out to subvert India in any way possible.

The movie opens with Ravindran running through the dark streets of a large city at night. He is playing the role, at the moment, of a freedom fighter under the British Raj. Shots of wide, empty streets are shown. Ravindran's khadi kurta is torn and bloody. He pauses for a moment to catch his breath, leaning against a wall, and we see two pairs of headlights appear at the far end of the street. Two old-fashioned black cars with sirens and flashing lights are chasing him through the streets, but the hero is able to elude them by climbing over the wall. Blood is flowing from his chest and has soaked his kurta.

Frequently, the camera cuts to a close-up of Ravindran's face. Anger and pain chase each other across it. He stops to lean against another wall to catch his breath. On the wall is painted a tricolor flag and the words "Quit India." Ravindran coughs blood into his hand and wipes it on the wall over the word "India." "My wife . . . my son . . ." he says in a loud whisper. "My wife . . . my son . . ."

The two pursuing cars turn into the street, one from each end. There are shouts of "Catch him!" in Tamil with an English accent. Ravindran is trapped. The wall is too high for him to climb. He steps into the middle of the street, hangs for a moment in the bright headlights of the approaching cars, and falls to the ground. Boots approach the fallen hero. Rough white hands go through his clothes and come up with a photograph of a pretty woman and a child. The camera pauses for a moment over this photograph in a white hand.

The next scene shows the woman in the photograph, now much older. Her hair is touched with white here and there. She is wearing glasses. She is standing in the living room of a large house. Before the woman stands a young man in a police uniform. It is Ravindran again, but now as the son of the fallen hero. "You must be as brave as your father," the woman is telling the young man. "You must protect the India your father freed." Above them, on the wall, hangs a garlanded black-and-white photograph of the fallen hero.

From here the movie becomes the story of the hero's single-handed struggle against a gang of smugglers. There are long, violent sequences interspersed with romantic scenes between the hero and the heroine, who is the daughter of the chief villain (she doesn't know he is a smuggler). The chief villain is a former freedom fighter (like the hero's father) who has now succumbed to the forces of evil. The character of this villain is an interesting one. In a movie full of clichéd figures, this villain has some complexity. This unrepentant murderer and smuggler justifies his villainy by pointing to the violence of society in general. There is an element of the antihero in him. In the last scenes of the movie, when Ravindran takes the unconvinced heroine to confront her cornered father, the father freely admits his villainy and declares that he has done what he has done only for himself and for her. The heroine is aghast at what her father has said. Both Ravindran and the heroine excoriate him for his lack of repentance, and as Ravindran is about to take him into custody, he shoots himself. The movie ends with the hero and the heroine joined together in marriage in front of the hero's mother and the picture of the hero's father.

Carol watched the movie leaning forward, her elbows on her knees and her chin on her hands. She had tucked her hair behind her ears so that the intense expression in her eyes was visible as she watched the movie. Her eyes are really quite beautiful. Once she caught me staring at them and I had to look away hastily.

Carol thought the movie loud and gaudy in its colors, but found the story interesting. I found the story boring, and the colors and the sound interesting!

When the movie was about a quarter over, Shanthamma arrived to speak with Chandran. This was the first time that I have actually met Shanthamma. At this time, she had not yet announced that she was going to participate in the elections from the West Madras constituency. Chandran introduced her to Carol and me. Shanthamma is a tall woman with glasses and gray hair done up in a bun, very dark, with a wide mouth that is constantly smiling. Vasanthi, an attractive younger woman with long, thick hair, who is Shanthamma's longtime friend and companion, was with her. When Chandran told Shanthamma who I was, she turned and looked at me for a moment and said, "I knew your father. He was a good man."

Shanthamma is much younger than Chandran is or my father would have been if he were alive today. I know her association with Chandran goes back a long time. Shanthamma is Telugu. She is from southern Andhra Pradesh. She came from a poor family. Her father was a peasant who got involved in the Naxalite troubles in the years after Independence. He was killed in one of the encounters with the police and her mother moved with her to Madras when she was still a child.

Shanthamma's mother, who is now a very old woman, lives with her. In the couple of interviews of Shanthamma's that I have read (in Chandran's *Achamillai!*), she has always mentioned her mother. One gets the sense that her mother is an important figure in her life. In Madras, her mother had worked in all kinds of jobs to send Shanthamma to school and finally to college. She had sold vegetables from a cart, she had worked in a cycle stand in Guindy, she had been a domestic worker. Soon after she finished college, Shanthamma says in one of her interviews, she and her mother quarreled and separated. She had not seen her mother for years, but then, one day, all of a sudden she had realized she had been wrong to quarrel with her mother and had gone back to see her. Her mother was still living in the same place. Without a word, her mother had accepted her back.

In college, Shanthamma had become involved with a young Communist named V. Anand, who had later been elected to the parliament twice from a constituency in Andhra Pradesh. Shanthamma and Anand had been married for some years. But then there had been some kind of scandal surrounding Anand, some accusations that he had embezzled party money. There had been a bitter row over this and Anand had been expelled from the party. Soon after this Anand had died, of heartbreak at the party's betrayal Shanthamma has always held. All this had once caused a sensation in Communist party politics, but now few even remember Anand.

Shanthamma moved back to Madras from Andhra Pradesh after Anand's death and embarked on the career that has brought her to where she is now—a considerable figure in the trade union movement in Madras, someone who might stand for election from the West Madras constituency.

Before Chandran, Shanthamma, and Vasanthi retired into his study for the meeting, Shanthamma said to me, "Chandran has told me you have just returned from studying in the U.S. What did you study there?"

"History," I replied. "In New York."

"New York," Shanthamma said. "My daughter is in California. She is doing her Ph.D. in microbiology there. I wish she were instead doing history like you have."

The next day there was definite news that Shanthamma had decided to participate in the elections. I had gone to meet Lakshman at his house. He had invited me home for dinner. Lakshman and I have known each other for many years, since our days in college together. He is one of my oldest friends. He is now married and a subeditor at *The Hindu*. We have been trying to get together to do something ever since I have got back from the U.S. I had suggested that we go to one of the beaches near Mahabalipuram for a day. We could swim in the sea, lie in the sun, and maybe go into Mahabalipuram to look at the ruins of the temples. We were trying to figure out which weekend would be best. We have tentatively decided to go the weekend after next.

"There is news you may be interested in," Lakshman said to me as I was waiting at the bus stop. He had walked out to the bus stop with me after dinner. "Shanthamma has decided to stand for election as an independent from West Madras. You will see it in the papers tomorrow."

"I'm not surprised," I said to him. I explained my encounter with Kulan to him. "Isn't that great news?"

Lakshman nodded. "It will be an interesting fight," he said. He stopped to glower at a beggar who had placed himself before us. "Don't you have a job?" he said to the beggar. The beggar was a thin figure in a dirty white cloth, his face prematurely wizened.

"I have looked and looked," the beggar said. "Nobody will give me a job."

Lakshman looked at the beggar speculatively. "If I send you to someone who will give you a job, will you go?" he demanded.

"Of course. Definitely," the beggar replied.

"Here, I am going to write the address down for you," Lakshman said, and he began fishing out a piece of paper from his shirt pocket.

The beggar looked at him. "I don't know how to read," he said. "It would help me more if you gave me some money."

Lakshman looked at me. "What should I do?" he asked me. I shrugged my shoulders. He took out some change from his pocket and gave it to the beggar. "Go away," he said. "Don't bother us anymore. Try to do something useful with yourself." The beggar walked away down the street.

"He'll probably go and drink it away somewhere," Lakshman said cynically. "It's so hard deciding whether to give money to a beggar or not." He paused. "Remember the street plays that Kumar put on when we were in college?"

Kumar is a friend from college who had acted in numerous amateur theater productions. I remember him as a small, eager man with a great mop of long, curly hair and round glasses. His parents were divorced and he lived with his mother, who had a boutique in Adyar. He did not get along with his mother or father and did drugs with a dangerous, careless abandon. Every summer he would visit his father in Delhi and they would go trekking in the foothills of the Himalayas.

Kumar discovered politics with his usual eagerness in college. In the space of a few months he discovered that "the people" could be more than a phrase. And then he had a novel idea. He would put on improvised skits on topical issues in the street with his girlfriend. His girlfriend would play a woman standing at a bus stop or someone buying something at a shop, and Kumar would be a beggar or a hawker. Using improvised dialogues, they would develop a scenario that could get the crowd standing around involved in the skit, which would typically be about unemployment or women's rights or alcoholism or some such thing. Lakshman and I had often played bystanders in many of these skits. We would interject a couple of lines now and then to get the interaction with the crowd going. Sometimes the street plays worked and sometimes they didn't, but they were always interesting to do.

"What's Kumar doing these days?" I asked Lakshman. I had not thought of him in years.

"I'm not sure. Last I heard he was getting a degree in social work in Delhi."

Kumar and his street plays. I wonder if it would be possible to do some street plays again?

Today is Sunday. For the first time in days, I am not rushing around running errands for Chandran and the campaign to get Shanthamma elected. I am sitting at my desk in my room. I have been looking at two poems I wrote a few days ago. And then I started writing down all these things in my journal, things that I haven't had time to write down till now. Through the window I can see Joseph's stall, Ganapathy Kovil Street, and on the other side of it, the maidan between Krantinagar and Kuppancherry. Everything is bright and sunny outside, dripping with yellow. The maidan is empty except for two boys kicking a ball around. If I lean to the right or the left, sitting in my chair, more things come into view.

Leaning to the right, I can see the road that connects Ganapathy Kovil Street and Kuppancherry and runs along one side of the maidan. A truck, with *All-India Permit* painted along the side of it, is standing on one side of this road. A Sikh is sitting in the cab with his legs hanging out the open door. He is smoking a beedi. Across the road, in front of the shacks that line it, stands a naked black child watching something that I can't see down the road, in the direction of Kuppancherry.

Leaning to the left, I can see the small streetside Ganapathy temple opposite Anand Vilas and Mohan's cart under the tree by its side. Election posters already festoon the walls of the temple. Mohan's cart is bare and looks as if it has not been used in days. There are no piles of clothes on it. The coal-iron is not perched on its customary stand. Mohan has not been working at his cart for many days now. He has been busy doing election work for Sethuraman. I see him around with posters and things.

Also through the window, if I lean forward a little, I can see my mother standing and talking to a neighbor in front of the gate of Anand Vilas. She is on her way home from the vegetable market near Krantinagar railway station. She carries two bags. In one, I can see some purple eggplants peeping out.

This is the extent of my universe when I am sitting in this chair. If I lean to the right, I can see thus far to the left. If I lean to the left, I can see thus far to the right. The frame of the window will expand this much and no more.

Inside my room, a ceiling fan turns rapidly, making a wall calendar flap and flutter noisily. The sheets on my bed are rumpled and creased. I have had a snooze in the afternoon, despite my mother's disapproval. I have been sitting at the desk since I woke up. It will be time for coffee soon and Selvi will be here. If my mother has not come up by then, I will have to make the coffee myself. At the moment, this is not a prospect to be considered with pleasure. The effort of standing up and doing anything seems too much.

I should go back to the poems in front of me. I am dissatisfied with the last few lines of the second poem—it is really a single poem with two parts. I think I have something to say and I have tried various different ways of saying it. None of them seems to work. I want to convey something significant but quite simple and unoriginal—the duplicity of politicians. My latest attempt has been to use the metaphor of flowers and weeds. I have scored out the old lines and written the new ones above them. The whole sheet of paper looks a mess. I can't tell if the new lines are any good. I will have to write out the whole thing again even to begin making sense of it.

This bout of poetic creativity has been brought on by my involvement in Shanthamma's election campaign. Through Chandran, who in his capacity as Shanthamma's chief adviser is pretty much running the campaign, I too have become involved in it. Last time I was at Chandran's, the talk turned to Sethuraman and his political antecedents. There was the same tired, predictable record of political self-serving and the idea for this two-part poem took shape in my mind. Sethuraman had switched parties four times in his career. His connections with big business were solid. He was himself an industrialist. His brother had been accused of taking bribes on behalf of Sethuraman when Sethuraman had been given a powerful political appointment of some kind. And so on and on. Such lists always seem endless.

That's the sound of my mother letting herself in. Here is an opportunity to put away my poems and this diary in the drawers of my desk. I will have time for a shower before coffee. Selvi will arrive soon. She is supposed to come here to collect the posters that should have come back from the printers. I have told my mother that I want Selvi to stay for coffee. I am going to insist that she stay when she comes. Perhaps she won't, but I hope she does. How difficult it is to strike up a friendship sometimes. Especially between two people like Selvi and me.

Selvi is gone now. She did stay for coffee, though not without some hesitation. When I came out of the bathroom after my shower, my mother had let her in and she was sitting in the living room, perched a little uncertainly on the edge of the sofa. I had only taken a towel into the bathroom with me and had to dart out of the bathroom, through the living room and into my room with the towel around my waist. "One minute, one minute," I remember mumbling to her, hanging my head with embarrassment. I quickly threw my clothes on, pushed a comb through my hair, and went out into the living room.

"He has been sleeping," my mother said to Selvi. My mother was standing in the kitchen, in front of the stove.

"It's Sunday afternoon. I always sleep on Sunday afternoons," I said a little sharply. It is not true that I always sleep on Sunday afternoons, but I do not like my mother discussing me in this fashion.

"You are staying for coffee," I said to Selvi. I suspect there was a challenge in my voice.

"Okay," said Selvi after the slightest of hesitations. She had left her chappals with the other chappals at the door and was barefoot. I remembered that I had not taken off my shoes when I had gone to Selvi's house with Carol for the interview and felt a little ashamed. Selvi had a large cloth bag with her, which she had placed on the floor at her feet. She was sitting on the edge of the sofa, her large head leaning forward a little. Her hands were gripping the armrests lightly. The whole effect was of someone preparing to leap up from the sofa. It made me want to smile.

"Your father?" Selvi asked, pointing to the large framed black-and-white photograph that hung on the wall. I nodded. My father stared down from his habitual place above the door that led to my bedroom. The red mark that had been placed on his forehead shone in the light coming in through the window.

"You look just like him," Selvi said. She is the first person to think that I look like him. It is well known in my family that I do not look like anybody they can think of. "Chandran has told me about him. He did good work during the independence struggle."

"Yes, he was a lawyer," I said. "He defended many freedom fighters before Independence. To take up some cases, he sold his own property to get money. He gave up his practice after Independence to do social work." These days my father's reputation seems to precede me everywhere. Everyone seems to have heard of him. I was conscious of my mother listening from the kitchen. It was therefore important to repeat all these details.

My mother called me into the kitchen for the coffee. I brought back two tumblers of coffee and some muruk and kesari on two plates. Selvi stood up to take a plate and a tumbler from me before I spilled anything. I set my plate and tumbler of coffee down and switched on the ceiling fan to cool the steaming coffee.

"Sethuraman also claims he fought for India's independence," Selvi said. She took a careful sip from her tumbler. "After so many years, everybody claims to have fought for India's independence. Who knows what the truth is? People like Sethuraman are such an insult to people like your father and Chandran."

I nodded and a long silence followed. Selvi drank her coffee quietly and ate a little kesari from her plate.

"In Dr. Ranga's house, they make kesari often," she said.

She paused and then seemed to think some explanation was necessary. "I work there," she said. "I had never had kesari before."

Outside, a jeep went down Ganapathy Kovil Street blaring election rhetoric in support of Sethuraman. Both Selvi and I listened to it in silence. *Vote for Congress (R),* the loudspeaker screamed repeatedly, *Vote for Congress (R). Vote for Sethuraman! Vote for Sethuraman, Friend of the People, Man of Action! Vote for Sethuraman!*

"They have so much money," Selvi said. "We have so little."

I thought of the posters that Selvi had come for. "The posters are not ready yet," I said. "The printer could only give me a test copy to look at. Shall I get it?"

"Yes," Selvi said. "Let's look at it."

I went into my room and came back with the poster the printer had given me. I had designed the poster, which was in English. The printer had promised to have the posters ready by today. Selvi had come to take some of the posters so that they could be put up in Kuppancherry. Most of them will, of course, be put up in Krantinagar.

I spread the poster out on the center table. The poster has a picture of Shanthamma from the shoulders up. She is wearing glasses and looks very serious, very respectable. Above the picture is her name and below are these words: *Better for Everybody! Vote with Independence!* The poster is in black ink on white paper. Chandran and Shanthamma had okayed the poster before I had gone to the printer.

"I was thinking of the Krantinagar voter," I said to Selvi.

"Getting the Krantinagar vote will be difficult," Selvi said. "What does the poster say?"

I remembered that Selvi does not know English. I explained the poster to her. She looked at it critically for a moment, nodded her head and said, "It is a good poster. It is simple but good."

Selvi left without any posters. I promised to bring her an appropriate number the next day.

I have just returned from the printer's shop, where the printer is working late into the evening to complete the job. The printer's shop is by the railway tracks, just on the other side of Krantinagar railway station. I went there to make sure that the posters would in fact be ready by tomorrow as the printer had promised. The printer is a big man who towers over me. He was standing in the doorway of his shop, smoking a beedi when I came up, his fingers black with printer's ink. Inside the shop, an assistant was working at a machine in the light of a naked electric bulb. Behind us, a train approached Krantinagar railway station, swinging slowly from side to side as it slowed down. The yellow rectangles and squares of the doors and windows were largely empty at this late hour. Here and there a lone figure stood in an open doorway as the train swung past, legs wide apart, hand gripping the pole that divided the doorway for support.

"How is the work going?" I said to the printer.

He nodded his head without replying.

"Can I see one of the posters?" I said to him, trying to look past him into the shop.

The printer smiled at me, took his beedi from his mouth, and said, "Come back tomorrow evening. Posters will be ready. Can't you see how hard we are working?" The printer did not seem to be in any more obliging mood and there was nothing else for it.

Walking back this late in the evening, the silence of abandoned streets accompanied me at every step. A gray bundle on the steps of a shuttered shop outside Krantinagar railway station was somebody sleeping. The sleeping figure had pulled the sheet up over its head so that the face was not visible, only the two feet that stuck out from the other end, bony and gray with dust. Somewhere else someone coughed, and the dry racking sound went through the dark streets as if in search of something. It was past midnight and most of Krantinagar was sleeping. Only a faint sound of music punctuated by speechmaking could be heard in the distance, probably in Kuppancherry, as I walked down the street toward Anand Vilas. A dog was nosing around in a heap of rubbish that stood at the corner of the street leading to the stalls of the Krantinagar vegetable market.

A little further down, I encountered Kulan and Mohan putting up election posters. A watchman, sitting on his wooden stool outside the shuttered front of a large shop that sold stainless steel utensils, was watching them put up the posters on two blank walls on the other side of the street. The watchman seemed to be observing them with some annoyance. There was a woman sitting by him on another stool, a big woman with large breasts and long, wet hair that hung loose. The woman was flirting with him playfully.

Mohan was putting up a poster for Sethuraman. Three figures appear on the poster, Sethuraman with the prime minister and the chief minister. Sethuraman is capitalizing on his connections to power at the center and at the state level. In the poster the prime minister, the chief minister, and Sethuraman are shown striding forward with their hands outstretched as if to shake hands. Both the prime minister and the chief minister wear sunglasses and are a little larger than Sethuraman. All three have been given a rosy color. Below them, in Tamil, appear the words *Forward! Together!*

Mohan had a new bicycle with him on which he carried the things he needed. With a thick brush he applied glue on the wall and on the back of the poster and then slapped the poster onto the wall. He then slapped some more glue on the poster and smoothed it with the brush. A line of the posters extended along the wall to his left, dozens of Sethuramans, chief ministers, and prime ministers striding forward with outstretched hands.

Kulan was doing the same on another blank wall a little distance away. He had his cycle-rickshaw, in which he was carrying all the materials he needed, with him. The poster he was putting up shows Shanthamma with her fist raised. The fist seems almost as large as Shanthamma's face. The poster carries the words *Shanthamma! For the good of the common people!* in Tamil.

Kulan and Mohan did not look at each other as they went about their work. I stopped to speak to Kulan for a minute. He paused with his brush in his hand. His eyes were red and he looked tired. A row of Shanthamma posters stretched away to his right, not as many as the Congress (R) posters but enough.

"Tomorrow I will do Kuppancherry again," he said.

I nodded. "The English posters will be ready tomorrow," I said.

Election posters are beginning to appear everywhere. Even the compound wall of Anand Vilas is covered with them. Somebody has pasted Congress (R) posters right over the place where *Post No Bills* had been stencilled. Many years ago, during another election period, the residents of Anand Vilas tried unsuccessfully to take action against people who posted bills on their compound wall.

The compound wall of Anand Vilas is now covered from end to end with the same large posters of the Congress (R). Innumerable Sethuramans and prime ministers and chief ministers are striding out of the wall, threatening to take hold of passersby.

Chapter 8

With my help, Sector 420 was cleared in record time, despite the interference of dangerous rabble-rousing leaders like Lar Prent. In recognition of our record-breaking achievement, "Certificates of Good Labor" were given to the members of the work team of which I was a part. The ceremony was held in the cleared ground where the streets and houses of Sector 420 had stood only a few days earlier. Thraivarov Puur, the young and intense state official in charge of labor relations in Mildendo, himself gave us the certificates at the ceremony. Thraivarov Puur had been in the news lately because of his vigorous support for the program of beautification in Mildendo City. He had come out strongly in support of the program because he considered it an important provider of employment throughout the city.

For the ceremony, a wooden platform and podium had been constructed at the edge of Sector 420, with the level brown surface of the now cleared section stretching away as a backdrop. Members of all the different work teams that had helped clear Sector 420 were present at the ceremony, forming a crowd of green, brown, black, and pink in front of the podium. On the day of the ceremony, a few machines were already at work moving earth in the distance. Landscaping was to be done here in accordance with the plans that had been drawn up for the park that was to be laid out. Other machines were in the waters of the river that flowed by Sector 420. They were engaged in cleaning the river of its pollution.

In the speech that Thraivarov Puur made before the certificates were given away, he had a few kind words for me as well. I noted down the relevant portions of his speech, which were as follows. "The bandur," he said, "came to us from a foreign land, ignorant of our customs, of our language, of our method of work. He knew nothing of our work ethic. When my office was first approached by the Peeg Immeegar to find a place for him, I must confess I did not think it a good idea. I did not think a bandur could ever learn to work as a Mildendan. I am glad to say the last few weeks have proven me wrong. The bandur has shown that the enormity of his size and his physical strength have some use." These were the encouraging words that Thraivarov Puur spoke about me. When I knelt down and bent low before the podium to receive the "Certificate of Good Labor" (little more than a speck to my eyes) from Thraivarov Puur, I felt especially proud. I stored the certificate carefully with my residence permit when I got home to my hangar and I still have it with me.

As reward for our record-breaking performance, the work team of which I was a part was given a few days off before we were to report for our new assignment, which was to build a dam in the hills above Mildendo City. As the weather was turning perfect with the approach of summer in the southern hemisphere, I resolved to make use of these free days to see more of the countryside. The Alando Leed had finally relented a little and agreed that I could now leave my hangar without his express permission. I was still shackled and accompanied by traka every time I left the base in which my hangar was situated, but at least I was no longer restricted by having to refer to the Alando Leed every time I wished to go somewhere. By this time my command of Northern Lilliputian had also improved sufficiently for me to converse with most people I met. I had not had too much trouble in understanding the gist of even Thraivarov Puur's speech, which was in High Lilliputian.

Since my arrival some weeks earlier, there had been tremendous interest in me not only among the people of Mildendo but also in the adjoining countries of Blefuscu, Faaranaaser, Karamany, and even in the distant, savage lands of Northern Lilliput. The Mildendan administration had been careful until then to keep me insulated from all the attention that was focused upon me. No raiterovshit (the High Lilliputian word for "journalist") had been allowed to interview me. All the raiterovshits had been instructed to maintain a certain distance from me at all times. Despite all this, my presence in Lilliput was the subject of much discussion in the printed and electronic media of Lilliput. Stories about me appeared almost daily in the newspapers. The scinca (the closest translation would be "television") also covered me extensively. There were stories about me working in Sector 420, stories about my growing knowledge of Northern Lilliputian, analyses of my physical attributes. In the early southern summer of 1991, all of Lilliput was beginning to obsess about me.

In response to this obsession, the Mildendan administration decided to organize a public event for me, which took place four days after my work in Sector 420 came to an end. I like to think my good performance as part of the record-breaking work team helped the administration to this decision. Delegations from all the major allies of Mildendo—Blefuscu, Faaranaaser, Karamany, among others—were invited. There were even a few delegates from Northern Lilliput, thin brown-, black-, and pink-skinned men from different Northern Lilliputian nations who had traveled together in an old, primitive chocho that almost crashed into Queen Baataania's palace because of a malfunction. They barely managed to land at the chocho port and had to be rushed directly to the ceremony, where they made an incongruous contrast to the genial and well-dressed Blefuscudians and Karamanians.

The ceremony took place on a long beach that lies a little north of Mildendo City. Here, on this long bare strip by the sea, there was enough space for huge crowds to gather. This beach, because of its proximity to Mildendo City, was a regular place for public events of all kinds. In preparation for the function that had been organized around me, the Mildendan authorities had set up long rows of stalls that offered everything from things to eat to games of skill and fortune. The idea was to exhibit me not only to visiting dignitaries from other countries but also to ordinary Mildendans. The authorities wanted to turn the day into an occasion for fun and celebration for everyone.

When I arrived at the beach on the afternoon of the event, it was covered with Lilliputians as far as the eye could see. A crowd of Lilliputians was waiting in the great open space that had been prepared to receive me. Some of them were thronging the rows of stalls behind the open space. Others were in the water in their swimsuits. Tiny, inflatable balls of different colors bobbed on the waves. Two or three water vehicles of some kind, with laughing Lilliputians in them, were zipping back and forth in front of the beach at great speed. They looked like toy boats, but one of them suddenly lifted off the water, thrust out wings from its sides, and flew up into the air. In the bright sunshine, with the blue sea in the background, the whole scene wore a look of festivity and enjoyment. Many of the Lilliputians had been there since the morning. Chochos flew overhead, some of them of the Peeg Immeegar or the Peeg Pleesa and the others of various news media companies. The scenes of this festive event on the beach were being transmitted not only all over Mildendo but all over Lilliput.

As soon as the Lilliputians caught sight of me coming toward the beach surrounded by my usual contingent of trakas and chochos, they set up a great yell of welcome. Bands began playing as I came onto the beach and the people chanted "Mildendo vangamal kangara, bandur!" (which means "Welcome to Mildendo, giant one!") and threw their hats in the air. I for my part raised my hands, even though my wrists were shackled together more tightly than usual, and waved them in appreciation to the gathered crowd.

A kind of a chair had been constructed for me at one end of the beach and I was led up to this seat by my accompanying traka. When I had occupied the seat prepared for me, the crowd quieted down. I could tell that I was expected to speak, but I was so overwhelmed by the reception I was being given by the people of Lilliput that for the first few minutes no words would come out of my mouth. All I could do was sit in my chair and gaze at the huge gathering of small figures in front of me. Never would I have conceived a few months earlier that such a scene was possible! In front of me stood tiny, well-meaning men and women the length of my middle finger. Even after I had discovered the existence of Lilliput from Gulliver's manuscript and resolved to journey there, I had not imagined that I would find myself in a setting quite like this. I bowed again and again in speechless acknowledgment of the enthusiasm of the gathered Lilliputians.

At last I collected myself together and spoke to the crowd in my rudimentary Northern Lilliputian. I had composed a little speech with the help of my tutor, Edu Kator, and I now recited it. "I am glad to be here in Mildendo," I said, "in the greatest land in the world. Being here is the fulfillment of my greatest dreams. I love Mildendo! I love Mildendo!" At this little speech, the crowd broke out in loud cheers that lasted a long time. Afterward, the delegations from the various countries were led up one by one to where I was sitting. I bowed low to each one of them. Some of them asked simple questions and I answered them as best I could. The last delegations to be led up were those from Northern Lilliput, who just barely made it in time for the ceremony.

After these introductions of the delegations were over, I was asked to perform various tasks to satisfy the curiosity of the delegations and the gathered crowd. First a large transport traka, used to carry things, was brought onto the beach. I picked it up with ease and raised it high over my head. The traka was then filled with bricks and brought back. I picked it up again, but this time with a little difficulty. The traka was brought back a third time. It was now filled with pieces of lead. I again managed to pick it up, but only with great effort. For a moment, as it seemed that I would not be able to lift the traka, the crowd waited in suspenseful silence. When I managed to raise the traka with a quick jerk, there was a sigh of relief and the crowd burst into loud cheers.

After this, two combat chochos with their pilots sitting inside them were wheeled onto my hands and I was asked to raise them to the level of my shoulders. I did so carefully and slowly. I did not want the chochos falling off from my hands. When my hands were level with my shoulders, the chochos took off with a great roar, buzzed above my head two or three times and disappeared into the sky after flying low over the gathered crowd. Later, the pilots received commendations for their courage in putting themselves in my hands. I also earned much goodwill with the Mildendan authorities for my proper and safe performance of this particular trick. I had not had much previous notice for this daring trick. The two brave pilots had thought of it only two days before the event. We had had time to rehearse it only once. The pilots had been allowed to perform the trick on the condition that the Mildendan administration would not be held responsible for their safety.

The entire affair (meeting the delegations, the antics) lasted the whole afternoon. As evening approached, I was escorted back to my hangar. The afternoon had gone very well. I had clearly won the sympathy of the Lilliputians with my speech and my willing performance of the tricks. Hundreds of the Lilliputians in their private trakas accompanied us part of the way to my hangar, sometimes scooting ahead, sometimes following behind. Despite the broadcast of an announcement by the officials of the Peeg Immeegar warning all nonofficial traka to keep away from me for their own safety, one or two of the more daring Lilliputians even maneuvered their traka with immense speed and daring between my shackled feet as I walked. They were, however, promptly apprehended by officers of the Pleesa and taken away. After a certain point on the route to my hangar, the ordinary Lilliputians were not allowed to accompany us any longer. The area immediately around the Peeg Immeegar camp in which my hangar was situated was out of bounds to them. They stood where the barricades had been set up and waved again and again to me. My escort and I soon left them behind and arrived back at what I now considered my home—the hangar.

Later that evening, the delegation from Blefuscu came to visit me in my hangar. I was delighted to find the Alando Leed with them. I had not seen him in many weeks.

"Bandural vangamal kangara," I said to him and the delegation, proudly displaying my newly acquired knowledge by giving the traditional greeting—"The giant one welcomes you"—which is the same in both Lilliputian languages.

The Alando Leed smiled and gave the traditional reply, "Vangamal bandural vangamal!"

"I am glad to see you, O Alando Leed," I said, continuing to speak in Northern Lilliputian. "It has been many days since you last visited me. It seems you no longer have any time for your giant friend. Are you well?"

The Alando Leed laughed appreciatively. "Your command of Northern Lilliputian has increased greatly since I last saw you. I am indeed well, bandur. Well, but busy. As you should know, policing the borders of Mildendo against infiltrators is a full-time job."

I could not help laughing at the Alando Leed's little joke at my expense, but I also knew that the unauthorized entrance of the Northern Lilliputians into Mildendo was a real and serious problem for the Peeg Immeegar.

"I have brought some visitors with me," the Alando Leed said, pointing to the Lilliputians who were with him. I recognized them as the Blefuscudian delegation I had met earlier that day. There were three of them, all dressed in gorgeous gold-embroidered robes befitting the representatives of the most powerful country in all of Lilliput.

Blefuscu lies to the east of Mildendo, across a large channel of water the Lilliputians call the Tritrade Sea. The Tritrade Sea is named for the island of Tritrade, which is reputed to have disappeared in a great cataclysm centuries earlier. The entire Tritradean civilization was destroyed in this great catastrophe. Not a single Tritradean was reputed to have survived.

It was my tutor who told me this story. Now that I had made substantial progress in my study of Northern Lilliputian, my tutor had been instructed by the Alando Leed to conduct lessons in the history, geography, and culture of Lilliput. Speaking of the disaster that had overtaken Tritrade, my tutor said, "The Tritradeans were a terrible and vicious race. They held slaves. Their brutality was famous throughout Lilliput. But they were also a great civilization."

My tutor had also spoken to me about Blefuscu a number of times. Blefuscu is the greatest of the Lilliputian nations, greater even than Mildendo, whose glory is in the past rather than in the present. The Mildendans and the Blefuscudians have fought various wars with each other, but now for many decades they have been at peace. It was Queen Baataania's grandfather who had reconciled the two nations by magnanimously ceding disputed territory to Blefuscu. Since then Blefuscu and Mildendo had cooperated closely in all matters.

Blefuscu, unlike Mildendo, is not a monarchy. It is best described as a republic. Its ruler, called the sycodent, is elected by the people of Blefuscu every four years and two months. At the time that I was in Lilliput, the term of Vico Karunar as sycodent of Blefuscu was coming to an end and the process of selecting the sycodent for the new term was under way. Vico Karunar was standing for sycodent again. The delegation that came to visit me from Blefuscu bore an invitation from him.

The Alando Leed introduced the Blefuscudians to me one by one and I nodded to each one in welcome. The name of the leader of the delegation was Nat Vathesims. He was an old man, his green skin wrinkled with age. His long robe was covered with the many ribbons of honor he had earned in serving the Blefuscudian government. His blue hair had touches of gray in it, and his features had the cast of one who, over a long life, had wielded much authority. My tutor, who had turned into my source of information in general, told me later that the choice of Nat Vathesims to head the Blefuscudian delegation indicated the importance the Blefuscudians attached to my arrival in Lilliput. The respect in which Nat Vathesims was held was clear from the way in which the Alando Leed deferred to him.

Nat Vathesims stepped forward once the introductions were over and stood looking up into my face. Accompanied by his two colleagues, he then slowly and carefully walked around my stretched-out body.

"One hundred and twenty-six paces," he said, when he had returned to the spot in front of my face from which he had begun. "You have an enormous body, bandur!" Nat Vathesims had a low voice. I had to strain my ears to catch his words.

"How tall does he stand?" Vathesims asked the Alando Leed.

"Six kais," the Alando Leed replied. One kai is approximately one of our feet.

"As high as a four- or five-story building," Nat Vathesims noted.

The Alando Leed agreed.

"I have an invitation for you from the sycodent of Blefuscu," Nat Vathesims said to me. "Sycodent Vico Karunar would like you to visit Blefuscu as his guest." He spoke slowly and carefully, to make sure, I think, that I understood him.

"Such an invitation is an honor," I replied. "I have heard much about Blefuscu. Nothing would give me greater pleasure than to visit your country. The only thing that keeps me from visiting Blefuscu is my responsibility to my work team. As soon as I have sufficient time, Blefuscu will be the first place that I will visit."

I did visit Blefuscu before I left Lilliput but I will narrate the incidents that occurred during my visit, both happy and tragic, in their proper places. It will not do to get ahead of my story.

Only a few days remained, after the day of the public event and the visit of the Blefuscudian delegation, before I was to recommence work with my work team. I spent the days walking around the countryside of Mildendo accompanied by my traka and chocho. I spent one day trekking in the hills above Mildendo City. The hills were filled with small mountain villages, which looked very pretty perched on the cliffs overlooking the valley in which Mildendo City stood. The villages made a great contrast to the city below, which was visible from some of them. At this distance, because of the great black cloud that lay over its lower portions, the city looked like some fantastic construction floating in midair.

The villages in the hills consisted of small stone houses. They looked very quaint and ancient from the outside but I was told that inside they were filled with all the latest amenities that technology could provide. These villages had traditionally been peasant and goatherding communities, but for many years now, prosperous Mildendans who worked in the city had been moving in and buying out these villages. These Mildendans from the city preferred the clean atmosphere of the mountains to the dense and muggy air of the city. The commuting time to the city from the villages in the hills was not very great, especially in a fier-traka, a kind of vehicle which was capable of both flying at low speeds and running along the ground very fast. These fier-traka were useful for flying down from the hills to the valley floor, where they would join the other traka on the transportways leading into the city. Early in the morning, you could invariably see scores of these fier-traka floating in the air above the valley like little insects.

Another day, I traveled through the desert land of the Karunar Punuk in the opposite direction from Mildendo City. A little distance from the Peeg Immeegar camp in which my hangar was situated the Karunar Punuk came to an end and a countryside full of small towns began. At the center of each town was a factory, from the chimneys of which smoke often rose into the air. This was a heavily populated, industrial area of Mildendo and the towns were numerous and close to one another. They all gave an impression of a quiet and efficient existence.

Everywhere I went, Lilliputians came out of their homes, and sometimes even offices, to observe me. Some of them would speak to me. They had all seen my figure on scinca in innumerable news stories, but the size of the real thing always seemed to amaze them. A few of the Lilliputians were bold enough to ask to be lifted up in my hands, but the officers of the Peeg Immeegar, who accompanied me everywhere I went, refused to permit it. This, nevertheless, did not prevent some of them from climbing into their fier-traka and flying close to me.

Another day I went to the beach to swim and lie on the sands a little. It was a beautiful day with bright sunshine. The beach was a private one set aside for the exclusive use of Queen Baataania. She had permitted me to use this beach since it was not considered safe for me to be swimming in the sea in close proximity to Lilliputians. The Mildendans were worried about this for both physical and biological reasons. The best Mildendan doctors could not be confident that even minute traces of the body fluids that I might emit while in the sea would not have some kind of effect on

Lilliputians. Mildendan scientists had in fact decided to use this opportunity to conduct various experiments connected with my emission of body fluids. These experiments were to be conducted in the sea after I was done there. Similar experiments were already being conducted in the soil near the area of the Karunar Punuk where I habitually went to do my toilet.

Because of these semiquarantine regulations, I had the beach all to myself. Since I was alone on the beach, it was considered sufficient to keep a watch on me from a distance. My shackles were removed to permit me to move freely and my accompaniment of trakas and chochos withdrew a little way. This was the first time that I had been given so much freedom outside the camp in which my hangar was situated.

Since I did not have swimming trunks of any kind with me, I swam in my underwear. The seawater was slightly chilly when I first went in, but as the day wore on it became warmer. The water here was calm because the beach was in a kind of inlet. Fronting the beach was the beach house of Queen Baataania, a large, ornate structure with wide windows to let in the sun and the sea breeze. Behind it was an extensive garden with tiny trees and shrubs. With the permission of the chief Peeg Immeegar officer present, I put my eye to one of the second-floor windows of the beach house to see what the interior was like.

The room I looked into was a large hall with plush carpets and wall hangings. One entire side of the hall was taken up by a tarunol, which is a kind of piano, with the keys arranged on four different levels. I had never seen a tarunol before, but my tutor had once described it to me and I recognized it from his description. The Lilliputians play the tarunol by dancing over it, by stepping from key to key. Teams of seven or eight are required to play the tarunol. Much practice is required to play it. Every performance is not only a musical one but also one of acrobatic skill. As the tempo of the composition increases, the movements of the players become faster and faster, until the jumping and leaping musicians are whirling at great speed over the keys. In Blefuscu, as I will narrate at the appropriate time, the tarunol is not only a musical instrument but also a political one of some consequence.

I found this glimpse of the interior of the beach house very interesting. When I had finished observing this room, I was going to put my eye to another of the windows, but a servant walking into the hall as I was about to withdraw gave such a screech of fright on seeing my eyeball pressed against the window that I hurriedly decided otherwise.

In the afternoon, I slept in the warm sun after lunch, which I had brought with me in my bag. There were seventy-five apples in a Lilliputian sack, fifteen large loaves of bread, and a large gasoline drum full of milk. It was a lighter lunch than I usually had but it was sufficient. I had my notebook with me and I spent time going over my notes, making additions and corrections, until I dozed off.

I was awakened from my light sleep by a hissing sound. When I opened my eyes, two figures were standing on the sand by the side of my head, hissing into my ear. One I recognized to be Lar Prent. The other was the woman who had confronted me one day in Sector 420. She looked much more respectable this time, her long hair braided and tied up in the conventional Lilliputian fashion.

"Do you remember me?" Lar Prent asked. "We have met twice before." He spoke in Northern Lilliputian.

"I remember you," I said to him. "You are Lar Prent. But I'm not sure I should be talking to you. Did the Peeg Immeegar let you in?" I looked over to where the chochos and three trakas of the Peeg Immeegar had been stationed in the shade made by the beach house. The figures of the officers were at such distance that they were only faintly visible, leaning against their vehicles.

"What are you afraid of?" Lar Prent said to me. "Surely you are too large for us to harm you."

When I did not reply, Prent pointed to his companion and said, "I don't know if you remember, but you have met her too. This is Fargo Withrun." His companion stepped forward and bowed to me gravely. "Lilliput vangamal kangara, bandur," she said, welcoming me with a great expansiveness to all of Lilliput.

"I know you both are troublemakers," I said to the two of them. "I think you both should tell me what you want, before I call the Peeg Immeegar."

"All we want is to talk to you," Fargo Withrun said. "Surely that is harmless?"

"All right," I said. "What do you want to talk to me about?"

"Nothing very serious," Fargo Withrun said with a smile. "Do you like it here? Are you happy? Do you like your life here?"

"Yes, I do," I replied. "But what does that have to do with you?"

"Why?" Fargo Withrun asked. "Why do you like it here?"

I showed my amazement at her question. "Why not?" I said to her. "Would you not be interested in going to a completely alien place where no one that you knew had ever gone before? A place that was completely different from any place you had ever known? Would this not interest you?"

"Yes, that would be interesting," she admitted. "My grandparents came here from Akalan in Northern Lilliput many years ago. They often speak of how they felt when they arrived here."

"It's not the same," I said to her. "I'm a bandur. It's very different when you are bandur."

"Maybe," she said. "Maybe."

"But, bandur, you are a prisoner here," Lar Prent said. "Does this not bother you?"

"I'm not a prisoner," I said indignantly. "What makes you think I am a prisoner?"

"You may not go wherever you wish. You are escorted everywhere you go. You are forced to wear shackles. Does all this not make you a prisoner?" Lar Prent wanted to know.

"I am indeed allowed to go wherever I wish," I replied. "Only a few days ago the Alando Leed gave me complete freedom in this respect. As for the rest of it, you know perfectly well they are precautions meant for the protection of you Lilliputians. I can understand why they are necessary."

"Have you visited Puur in western Mildendo?" Fargo Withrun asked suddenly and, it seemed to me, quite irrelevantly. "My parents live there. I'm sure they would like to meet you. Perhaps you should go there." She added with a smile, "If the Alando Leed permits it, I would gladly take you there."

There was the sound of a traka approaching at great speed across the sand of the beach. The Peeg Immeegar officers had noticed the presence of Lar Prent and Fargo Withrun. Lar Prent turned to look at the approaching traka.

"It seems our conversation is at an end," he observed. "Your friends have noticed us."

"It looks as if we must go," Fargo Withrun said. "You tell us you are happy here, bandur. You say you have been treated well. This may be so. Who am I to say whether you have been treated well or not? That is for you to decide. But I'll tell you our reason for coming here to see you. We want you to consider only one thing—will you consider whether you have seen everything that there is to see here? Is this all there is to see in Mildendo and Lilliput? Or is there more? Is what you see how things are? Or are they different? Will you at least consider these questions?" Fargo Withrun was speaking hurriedly to complete what she was saying before the traka arrived.

"Of course there is more to see in Lilliput," I said to her. I was a little surprised that she thought I would think otherwise. "I have not been to Blefuscu yet. Of course there are things that I do not know about. That goes without saying. I have just arrived here." I was annoyed that she considered me so simple.

But Fargo Withrun did not have the time to respond to me. The traka arrived in a shower of sand and four officers jumped out. "Your presence here is not authorized," one of the officers cried to the interlopers. "This is royal property. You are trespassing."

"Ask yourself who your real friends are in Lilliput! Ask yourself that, bandur!" Fargo Withrun shouted, as she and Lar Prent were bundled into the traka and taken away.

Later I mentioned the incident to the Alando Leed, when he came to see me in my hangar that day.

"Don't bother yourself with those two," he said. "They are not of importance. There are always people who are never happy themselves and cannot tolerate other people being happy. Lar Prent and Fargo Withrun are two such people. Their driving force is an irrational hate of all things everybody else values. They are failures themselves and cannot live with that. Therefore they have to direct their anger and hatred at anything and everything out there. They cannot tolerate anybody else trying to achieve anything. You yourself have seen their behavior when you were working in Sector 420. Did you not find them unreasonable? They want to deceive you into thinking they are your friends. You should be warned of this, but we need not concern ourselves too much with them. They are insignificant. Forget them."

Chapter 9

It is clear that Vaduvel, the printer I had engaged to make the English posters, is a rogue. We still don't have the posters and they were supposed to be ready three days ago. I have gone back and checked the printer's shop numerous times but it's always closed. The metal shutters are pulled down over the doorway. There is only silence within. I have shaken the shutters loudly, but there is no reply. When I ask the men at the grocery store next door if they know when the printer will be back, they shake their heads and spread out their hands to show ignorance.

Chandran has made emergency arrangements to have the posters ready by tomorrow through a printer that he knows in Mylapore. He is certain that the printer in Krantinagar has been bought off by Sethuraman's men. I think he may be right. When I went to check up on the printer again this morning (one last time), Mohan appeared from an alley that led behind the shop. When he saw me in front of the printer's shop, he came up to me, clucking sympathetically. I thought I saw a look of sly amusement in his eyes.

"Oh, you want to see Vaduvel?" he said. "But he is gone out of town! He won't be back for many days." His voice dripped mock concern. "Have you given him something to do?" he asked.

I did not reply but stepped into the alley from which Mohan had emerged. It led to a door at the back of the shop. When I knocked on it, a woman came to the door.

"I want to talk to Vaduvel," I said to her.

The woman shook her head. "He is not here. He has gone to his village," she said.

"Why don't you check inside?" I asked her and tried to look past her through the doorway.

The woman paused to glare at me. "I have told you he is not here," she said, and shut the door in my face.

When I reemerged from the alley, Mohan was leaning on the

counter of the grocery store, laughing at something with the men. They interrupted their laughter to watch me pass down the street. Chandran and Shanthamma have decided to file a complaint at the Krantinagar police station against the printer. Aside from the fact that an advance has been given to the printer (which he will no doubt give back as soon as he "returns" from wherever he is supposed to have gone), it is surely important to let Sethuraman and company know they can't do anything they like.

In the meantime, Sethuraman has stepped up his campaigning activity. He and his people have been ceaseless in their efforts around Krantinagar and Kuppancherry. It is important both for the prime minister and for the chief minister that the Congress (R) win this by-election in West Madras. The ruling coalition in Madras needs all the seats it can get in the legislature and New Delhi needs its alliance with Madras. Voter resentment is rumored to be running high. A strong showing in this by-election would be important in establishing the credibility of the governments at the center as well as at the state level. Hence, the floodgates of money have been opened. Sethuraman and his people are in the process of pouring money on everything in sight. If they could pump currency notes through the water pipes to get elected, they would do it. Jeeps have been going up and down the streets blaring their campaign rhetoric in support of Sethuraman. In Kuppancherry, there is afoot a not very subtle strategy of buying up lower-class votes. Cotton veshtis and sarees are being handed out to prospective voters.

Last evening, the chief minister himself appeared here in Krantinagar to address a gathering in support of Sethuraman. Preparations for this meeting started two days ago. A platform of bamboo poles and wooden planks was set up at one end of the maidan in front of Anand Vilas. I could see this makeshift stage from the window of my room. A few hours later, huge, larger-than-life cutouts of the chief minister and the prime minister sprouted on either side of the stage. The cutouts were very realistic and looked as if they would stride forward at any minute to greet the little men and women below them. Enormous garlands hung around the necks of the cutouts.

The crowd for the meeting had already started gathering late yesterday morning. By evening, a big crowd was milling around in front of the stage and large speakers, which had been placed at various points in the field, were blaring out Tamil film songs. Not everyone in the crowd was from Krantinagar or Kuppancherry. Trucks standing along the edge of the maidan had brought some of the crowd from other parts of the city. Joseph's stall was doing great business. It was festooned with Congress (R) posters. Joseph keeps his politics to himself but I think he has his connections to the Congress (R).

Early in the evening, I placed myself at my desk in my room to watch the proceedings. I had binoculars with me to observe things more clearly. I could see the stage quite well through the window. If I leaned to one side, I could see most of the crowd as well. With the binoculars, the stage appeared to be right outside the frame of the window. On the stage, a few chairs had been placed behind a mike. Banners of the Congress (R) festooned the back and formed a colorful backdrop.

Soon after I had placed myself at my desk, a man appeared on the stage and began to lead the crowd in shouting slogans. It was almost as if everything had been waiting for my arrival. I watched the man's face through the binoculars. Beads of sweat ringed his lips, which twisted and curved as he mouthed the words. Once in a while, a drop of sweat would shake loose, drop past his crooked teeth (one of which was missing), and disappear down the deep, dark cavern of his mouth. Volunteers began to bring the crowd to order. Sethuraman was about to arrive with the chief minister.

Sethuraman and the chief minister arrived in two jeeps and were accompanied by numerous police vehicles. Bhimanbhai Dwarkanath, the owner of Kuberan A/C, was with them. I recognized his corpulent shape in the jeep with Sethuraman. He is a prominent figure in West Madras. He owns all kinds of property here in Krantinagar and Kuppancherry, the most important of which is the opulent Kuberan A/C Theater. Because he is always giving money to various organizations and individuals in this area, he has attained the status of a local demigod. This is a role that he avidly cultivates. He would like to convert West Madras into his personal fiefdom.

The three men were led onto the stage. Introductions were made by Bhimanbhai Dwarkanath, who spoke in a high-pitched voice. For someone who is originally from the north, he speaks Tamil very well. And then Sethuraman took the stage. Sethuraman is a lean, elderly man, with sharp, pencil-thin features. He began in a quiet way, all dignified and statesmanlike. He had his hands calmly clasped behind his back. He would often pause and purse his lips together before starting each new sentence. Even in the binoculars his eyes looked hooded and expressionless.

Sethuraman began by saying he was honored that the chief minister, whose services to the country were legion, could be with them this day. He said he was glad that so many people had remembered the many achievements of the chief minister's government and turned out in such a large crowd to show their support for him. He knew many of them had also remembered his, Sethuraman's, services to the people of Krantinagar and Kuppancherry. That is what his volunteers told him and he believed them. He, for his part, vowed to keep working for the people of Krantinagar and Kuppancherry and, hand in hand with the chief minister, make life better for everybody.

Sethuraman spoke all this in a quiet, pleasant tone, as if he were speaking to friends about well-understood things. And then Sethuraman's manner began to change. His eyes remained hooded and expressionless, but an edge crept into his voice. He lifted his head and glared at the crowd. He swept his eyes over the crowd, as if to challenge them. There were ruffians and criminal elements, he continued in his new harsh tone, who had no loyalty to the nation and were now trying to win the elections by any means. He hoped the people would not be misled by them. The fact that these criminals and ruffians were led by a woman should not confuse the people, Sethuraman said. Only that very day he had learned a bit of information about this woman, Shanthamma, that saddened him greatly. He had learned that over the last few years Shanthamma and her people, who called themselves a union, had begun to terrorize the innocent working people. He had been told they were extorting money from people. They were forcing people to give them money or else remain unemployed. Sethuraman paused to glower at the crowd. He brought his hands from behind his back and shook them sternly. Now these same people wanted the people of Kuppancherry and Krantinagar to elect this terrible woman as their representative. Were they going to elect her? No! screamed the crowd on cue. No, of course not, Sethuraman agreed. The voters of Krantinagar and Kuppancherry would not be fooled by the fact that the leader of these people was a woman, would they? No! yelled the crowd, again on cue.

And then Sethuraman began to wind down. He became calm again and hid his hands behind his back. That was not the way he had learned to do politics, he said. When he had been in the independence struggle, morality had been an important issue. Now everything had changed. Ruffians and criminals had taken to politics. This is what they all had to fight. This is what he and his good friend Bhimanbhai Dwarkanath and the chief minister were all fighting against. This is why he wanted this gathering to vote for him. This is why he wanted them to listen carefully to what the chief minister, who had given up valuable time to come here, had to say.

When Sethuraman sat down, there was a great round of applause and much shouting of slogans, and then the chief minister rose to speak and the crowd quieted down again. The chief minister is well known for his oratory. He has the reputation of being a great Tamil scholar and he writes his own speeches. I would have liked to hear him speak, but I had promised Chandran that I would run an errand for him and so I had to leave. As I was walking down the street toward Krantinagar railway station, the chief minister was repeating what Sethuraman had said, only in his own, more ornate style.

Sethuraman's attack on Shanthamma shows he is worried about

her challenge. There are four other candidates who oppose him in West Madras, but it is only Shanthamma that he focused on in his speech. The others are not serious candidates.

When I returned home, it was late and the rally was long since over. Only a few stragglers were still in the maidan, which was littered with scraps of paper and other refuse. Workmen were dismantling the stage at one end. The cutouts of the prime minister and the chief minister still stood on each side of the stage. In front of one of them stood Valur Vishveswaran, staring up at it. He reached out and touched it once, and then again.

"Ay!" one of the men working on the stage shouted. "Ay! White-Beard Grandfather! What do you think you are doing? Leave that thing alone!" It was Mohan.

Valur Vishveswaran did not seem to have heard him. He reached out his hand to touch the cutout again, running his fingers over its rough surface and tilting his head back to regard the head. Mohan dropped his tools and walked over to him. He gave Valur Vishveswaran a push. "Leave it alone, Grandfather," he said. "Go on home."

Jolted out of whatever he had been thinking, Valur Vishveswaran backed away a few steps, his face contorted by horror and fear. Mohan followed him, his fists held by his sides in a threatening manner. The men working on the stage stopped to watch this little drama. Valur Vishveswaran kept backing away, saying something in some strange language I could not understand. And then he turned and was gone, disappearing swiftly into the compound in which his room stood. Valur Vishveswaran's sudden departure took Mohan by surprise. He stood looking after Valur Vishveswaran for a moment. "How strange he is," he said, turning toward me, forgetting for a moment that I was the enemy. I turned into Anand Vilas and did not reply.

So my life these days is filled with the election and Shanthamma's campaign to get elected. I feel as if I have involved myself in the campaign totally. I constantly run errands for Chandran, who sits magisterially in his house and helps direct the campaign. I see him almost daily. Sometimes he will want me to take something to Shanthamma or carry a message to someone or the other, and I will take his grandson's moped (which is now virtually at my disposal) and set off to do it. Sometimes he will have me go through newspapers and magazines for news items to do with the elections, especially Shanthamma's campaign.

It is now November and there are only two weeks left before election day. The work can only get more hectic. But I have told Chandran that I will not be available this weekend. This is the weekend that Lakshman, Sameera, his wife, and I have already set for going to Mahabalipuram. I have invited Carol to come with us and she has taken up the invitation enthusiastically. When I asked her, she was just entering Chandran's house. Her backpack was on her back, and her thumbs were hooked in the straps. There was a black smudge on her nose that I wanted to reach out and rub away. Or at least tell her about. She took off her sunglasses and nodded her head vigorously in response to my words. "Of course, of course," she said in that eager way of hers.

I'm glad she's coming. It will be fun to have her along.

Carol has been working quite hard on her research. Now that I am busy with campaign work, I am not able to help her as much as before. She has found a sociology student from Stella Maris College to be her interpreter and help. Since Carol is quite interested in Shanthamma's campaign, she is around a lot and I have been seeing a great deal of her. We talk together a lot. I find it quite easy to talk to her, but we have both been a little wary of each other too.

Chandran was understanding when I told him I was abandoning him for Mahabalipuram for some time.

"I am glad you are emancipating yourself from me, RK," he said. "But you won't forget to return to your slavery when you get back, will you? You have worked hard. We need hard workers like you."

Instead of going for a day, we are now going to spend the night in one of the beach resorts near Mahabalipuram. This would have been unaffordable for Lakshman, Sameera, and me, except that Chandran has given us a contact. When I told him I was planning to go to Mahabalipuram, he suggested that we spend the night there and pulled out a white address book from under a pile of handbills for Shanthamma's campaign. He gave me the number of one Mr. Elango, who owns the Palm Trees Beach Resort outside Mahabalipuram. "Call him before you leave and tell him you know me," Chandran said. "He will give you discounted rates." Mr. Elango has indeed agreed to give us heavily discounted rates for a one-room cottage all four of us will share. We plan to leave early Saturday morning and return on Sunday evening.

I am looking forward to this trip to Mahabalipuram. All this electioneering is getting to me. I need some distance from it. I'm tired of seeing posters of Sethuraman on every second wall. I'm even apprehensive about turning and finding Shanthamma's face staring down at me from some tree or other. I hope in Mahabalipuram I never have to think of Sethuraman or Shanthamma, even for a moment.

We left for Mahabalipuram at about seven on Saturday morning. Lakshman and Sameera were on their motorcycle. Carol and I were on the moped I had borrowed from Chandran's grandson. Usually the trip can be made in an hour and a half, but because of the moped it took nearly two and a half.

As soon as we had left Adyar and Injambakkam behind, the road began to open up and the sea appeared to our left, beyond the strip of beach sand. There was not much traffic on this road at this time of day. Every once in a while a car or a motorcycle would pass us, moving in the direction of Mahabalipuram. Sometimes a bus or a truck would appear. If it was traveling in the opposite direction, toward Madras, the wind from its passing would buffet us especially hard, and I would have to grip the handlebars firmly to steady the moped.

Lakshman on his powerful motorcycle found it difficult to keep back with us and ended up traveling far ahead. He would stop at intervals to wait for us to catch up. Every half an hour or forty-five minutes we would come up to Sameera and Lakshman sitting on a wooden bench in front of one of the numerous shops that appeared on the way to Mahabalipuram, eating nuts or drinking Thums-Up. Sameera, sitting cross-legged on the bench in her jeans, would wave to us as we went past, and a few moments later they would pass us on the motorcycle.

As we left the city farther and farther behind, everything began to appear less seedy. The villages through which the two-lane highway ran were small and poor, but they did not seem to have the grimy, unappetizing meanness of the city slums. In the morning freshness, with a light wind blowing across the road and gray waves breaking rhythmically on the beach to our left, the villages actually seemed peaceful and happy—despite the painted billboards by the side of the road that sold various commodities priced well beyond the capacity of the villagers and the squatting, barefoot women waiting for a bus who watched us pass with God knows what thoughts in their minds. I had to keep reminding myself that the billboards and the women were signs of a deeper reality I was missing as we went past on my moped. The sea, the palm trees, the frequent red- and white-painted temples, the women spreading out hay on the road, the young boys swimming in a creek who stood up to wave to us, the young man sitting by a mound of tender coconuts selling coconut milk—all these pastoral images were seductive beyond measure.

"Quite pretty!" Carol said, shouting into my ear to make herself heard above the wind. I nodded my head in reply.

"I think I could easily live here, in one of these houses," she said. We were passing a large house, set back from the road and mostly hidden behind tall hedges. An empty expanse of beach spread out behind it. "At least for some days," she added.

Carol shouted something else into my ear but a sudden gust of wind from a passing truck blew it away. I shook my head to indicate that I had not heard what she had said.

She leaned closer and spoke into my ear, "I said I was reminded of my grandfather's house in San Diego. I used to visit there in the summers. I would swim naked in the sea at night. One day he found out and gave me hell. I was reminded of that."

We stopped once on the way to Mahabalipuram. The dust from

the road was making my throat dry and I needed a drink. Carol too needed some respite. The moped had a single bar at the back for the passenger to hold on to. Carol was holding on to the bag in her lap with one hand. With the other, she tried to hold on to the bar.

"Maybe this moped wasn't such a great idea," she said, climbing off and pushing her sunglasses up into her hair. Her face was dusty from the road. Two small boys, one of them naked, appeared from the shade of a tree to watch her. The penis of the naked boy was a tiny thing.

Carol bought two Campa Oranges from the little shop in front of which I had stopped and handed one to me. I took a big gulp from the bottle, the sweet coolness forcing its way past the dry constriction of my throat. I considered the moped for a moment.

"Maybe you should keep the bag in your lap and hold me round my waist with both your arms," I said to Carol. "That way the bag won't fall off and it will be easier for you too."

"You don't mind?" Carol asked.

"Of course not," I said, shaking my head.

And that is what she did when we set off again. She tried to keep from leaning against me too much and I tried to pay no attention to her, but the pressure of her breasts on my shoulders was a constant reminder of her body pressing on me. The young men we passed looked at us with knowing smiles on their lips.

The cottage at the Palm Trees Beach Resort was small but sufficient for our purposes. There was a kind of kitchen-cum-bar opposite the doorway, with a minirefrigerator in it. There was no stove, but there was a notice informing us that the use of a hot plate was allowed. Since we had brought no hot plate with us, the information was a little irrelevant to our situation. Most of the room was taken up by a double bed with a mosquito net over it. On the other side of the bed was a doorway which led to a bathroom with a shower.

It was decided that Lakshman and Sameera would share the bed, while Carol and I would sleep on the floor, on bedding we had brought with us.

"One of the few benefits of being married," Sameera said, lifting up the mosquito net and climbing into the bed, where she stretched out luxuriously. "Husband!" she said in a mock-imperious voice to Lakshman. "Get in here!"

There is something tomboyish about Sameera. She has short thick hair parted on one side. The few times I have met her, she has always been dressed in jeans and shirt or jeans and kurta. I don't know Sameera well. Lakshman became involved with her when I was in the U.S. She too works for *The Hindu*. That is how they met.

Since Sameera is Muslim, things were not without problems in their little romance. Lakshman comes from a very orthodox Tamil brahmin family. His father, who was a civil servant in the Tamil Nadu state government before he retired, is also a renowned Sanskrit scholar. I know Lakshman's family well. Lakshman has not given me all the details, but I cannot imagine that his family did not have a lot of trouble with this marriage.

Lakshman declined to follow Sameera's instructions. "I'm going to check out the beach," Lakshman said. "Anybody coming with me?"

"I need a shower first," I said. I was feeling dusty from the road trip.

Lakshman, Sameera, and Carol went down to the beach, which lay about a hundred yards away behind a row of bushes and trees. After my shower, I waited for them at the cottage for some time, and then I changed into my swimming trunks and followed them. Carol and Sameera were coming up the path that led from the cottages to the beach. "Where were you? We are going to get our swimming things," Carol said to me. "Lakshman is still on the beach." I gave her the key to the cottage.

Lakshman had taken off his shirt and was lying on his stomach in the sand. "Hello," I said, settling down next to him.

He rolled over on his back and looked up at me, shading his eyes against the sun with one hand. "Carol is nice," he said to me. "Did you know her in the U.S.?"

I shook my head.

"She told us this funny story about falling asleep on the beach once in Mexico and not waking up until well past dusk. She had the hardest time finding her way back to her friend's house."

"You should go and get your swimming trunks from the cottage," I said to Lakshman. I felt strange talking to him about Carol.

I went for a walk along the beach while I was waiting. There were many people on the beach, since it was a beautiful day with bright sunshine. The long, unbroken strip of sand curved all the way round to Mahabalipuram two or three miles away. The stone spire of the Shore Temple at Mahabalipuram was clearly visible in the distance, where the strip of sand curved out into the sea before seeming to come to an abrupt end. Two or three catamarans belonging to the fishermen in the area were out. At this distance, they seemed little more than black lines drawn on the greenish-gray water.

A little way down the beach was an open-air beachside restaurant attached to the Palm Trees Beach Resort. People had pulled plastic chairs from the restaurant out on the beach, and were sitting watching their friends and relatives playing in the sea. On the other side of the restaurant, a few bamboo sheds had been constructed for the convenience of people who wanted to change into bathing suits.

When I returned to the path from the cottages, Lakshman, Sameera, and Carol were already in the sea. "Here!" Lakshman shouted out to me, waving both his hands. I ran into the sea to join him. The water was cold and very salty. The sea was quite rough with large waves breaking at regular intervals close to shore. Carol and Sameera, who apparently were both strong swimmers, had swum out beyond the breaking waves. Lakshman and I stayed in the shallows, where the seabed was always within reach of our feet. Neither of us was a good swimmer, and we felt belittled and envious of Carol and Sameera.

Lakshman watched them. "How arrogant," he said, "swimming out all the way out there to show off. That's just like Sameera."

As we watched, a tall, muscular man with a handlebar mustache and long hair that flowed down his neck ran with great splashing strides into the sea and swam with sure ease beyond the waves to where Carol and Sameera were. He threw a big smile at us as he ran past. Lakshman was certain the smile was scornful.

Carol swam back when she saw I had returned.

"Hi!" Carol said as she came up to where we were. She had taken off the cross she usually wore around her neck.

"I suppose Sameera has no intention of coming back yet?" Lakshman asked her.

"She's a great swimmer," Carol said.

"That's the Shore Temple," I said to Carol, pointing to the stone structure which stood facing out to sea where the crescent made by this stretch of beach ended.

"Is that the Shore Temple of Mahabalipuram?" Carol said, turning to look. "I have read a lot about it."

"We'll go into Mahabalipuram tomorrow," Lakshman said, "before returning to Madras."

And then Sameera came back and started to make mischief, splashing water at Lakshman. Lakshman ran up onto the sand and refused to come back in until Sameera promised that she would not splash water on him. Sameera turned to find new targets.

"Not me!" Carol cried. "The men! Let's turn on the cowardly men!"

"Oh no, you don't! If I get splashed, you get splashed," I said, and grabbed hold of Carol. Sameera pounced on me to free Carol and Lakshman rushed back into the sea to protect me from Sameera. A huge wave came up and toppled all four of us into the swirling water and sand. When we came up, spluttering and laughing, with water running from our eyes, I was still holding Carol's hand.

"Well, you didn't manage to get free," I said, gasping for breath and coughing up seawater.

"I could have, if I had really wanted to," Carol said, and jerked her hand away. She ran up out of the sea laughing. I must admit she has a nice figure—thin bony shoulders and a slim neck, with a proper fullness to her hips. The water had plastered her hair to her skull, so that you saw how small her head really was. It made her look a little like a bird. Sameera, Lakshman, and I followed her out of the water through the crowd of small urchins that had gathered to watch our childish antics in the sea. Three matrons, who were sitting nearby in plastic chairs brought from the restaurant, turned their scandalized eyes away as we went past them. Sameera stuck out her tongue when she was behind them. Lakshman, Carol, and I burst out laughing. "We are behaving like four naughty children," Lakshman noted, as a concession to our adulthood.

That day and the next morning we spent pretty much on the beach. When we were not in the sea, we spread out towels on the sand and lay on them and talked. Lakshman and I reminisced about our college days, while Carol and Sameera listened. Carol was very knowledgeable about Navajo religion and told us some interesting things about it. I was interrogated about Shanthamma's election campaign, which suddenly seems to be posing a real challenge to Sethuraman. Sameera described to Carol her feelings about the recent massacre of Muslims in U.P., in which scores had been murdered and thrown into canals while the Provincial Armed Constabulary had stood by and watched and sometimes itself participated in the massacre. Carol and Sameera fell to talking about religion. I made sure I kept quiet. In the evening, after dinner at the beachside restaurant, we pulled out chairs and sat out on the sand until late at night, talking about what our favorite movies were, about how nothing would happen to the murderers in U.P.

The next day we went into Mahabalipuram late in the morning. Lakshman, Sameera, and I had been there many times before, but this was the first time for Carol. We went first to the Shore Temple and the rock temples. And then we had lunch at a restaurant in the town and went to see the Arjun's Penance rock carving. The state government was in the process of cleaning the rock mural, so that one half of it looked bright and clean and the other half looked dark and encrusted.

Lakshman and Sameera did not seem to notice anything different or strange between Carol and me.

Carol engaged a guide. She listened intently to him, her eyebrows drawn together in concentration as the guide described to her how there had been a Pallava harbor here in Mahabalipuram centuries ago and how the Pallava kings were responsible for most of the temples and rock carvings. He explained the Arjun's Penance mural to her in his peculiar English, picking out from the crowded drama of the mural the penitent figure of Arjun sitting cross-legged. In another part of the mural, he pointed out a monkey also in a posture of penance. Carol was completely absorbed in what he was saying. The guide was so flattered by this that he took us around the complex of caves and sculptures that surround Arjun's Penance with more than usual care, before he took us up the hill to where the ruins of the ancient lighthouse stand.

"Imagine," Sameera said, standing on one of the broken walls of the lighthouse when we were up there. "Here, two thousand years ago, lamps were lit to guide ships into a harbor that has now disappeared." From the prominence of this hill, a sweeping vista was visible all around—the beach and blue sea forming a perfect picture in the yellow sunshine to one side, the trees and buildings of the town crowding together on the other.

Inspired by the scene, Sameera recounted the story of Bali the Asura to Carol—how Bali the demon-king had been vanquished by Vishnu, who had taken the incarnation of a pigmy priest to accomplish this. "Bali had conquered all existence, you see," Sameera said to Carol, "and needed to be put in his place. So Vishnu gave up his divinity temporarily and came as a pocket-sized priest and demanded alms of Bali, who was renowned as a religious and generous king, even though a demon. Right here in Mahabalipuram, in this very place, it happened." Sameera's tone compelled us all to look out speculatively over the scene that lay below us. "When Bali asked him what he wanted, Vishnu asked for only as much land as he could cover in three strides. After all, how much could a dwarf cover in three steps? As soon as Bali had agreed to this, the little priest, who was so much smaller than the great demon Bali, grew to such huge stature that he covered all earth with one step, all the rest of existence with the other step, and had nowhere left for his third step. So when Vishnu turned and demanded from Bali a place for his foot, you know, for his third step, Bali had nothing left to offer but his own head and Vishnu crushed it to bits with his foot. And thus the demon was destroyed." Sameera paused to let the dramatic climax of her story be savored. "Bali agreed to the priest's demand even though he knew who the priest really was. Because he couldn't refuse anyone who asked him for anything." She turned and gestured to the land around us. "Isn't that a great story? Mahabalipuram is where this is supposed to have happened. According to one of the legends, that is how it got its name. This is Maha-bali-puram—the place of Great Bali. Or the place of the great sacrifice—the word *bali* itself means sacrifice also."

The guide, who had been listening to this recitation with some concern, said, "Only Asura is not only demon, madam. Means much more. Asura not always evil. And name of brahmin was Vamana. Vishnu come as Vamana." He wanted to make sure that we understood he knew the legend too. And then it seemed to occur to him that he might have offended Sameera by his attempt to demonstrate his knowledge. "Madam knows Hindu stories very well," he said to Sameera on our way down the hill, to make sure he had not offended her. "Madam very religious, yes?" He had no way of knowing Sameera was Muslim.

When we had come back down the hill, Carol paid the guide and discharged him. He wanted to take her to the Shore temple and the rock temples but since we had already been to them we declined. We returned to where we had left Lakshman's motorcycle and the moped, by the shops selling stone sculptures and handicrafts. Carol bought an exquisite small sculpture of Radha and Krishna in romantic play from one of the shops after Sameera had beaten the price down with some consummate haggling. I did not go into the shop with them, but sat in a restaurant nearby and had a cold lassi. By the time we left for Madras, it was late afternoon. We stopped only for a short while in Cholamandalam Artists' Village on the way back.

Chapter 10

The construction project in which my work team was now involved—the building of a dam—was located in an extension of the hills that lay between the Karunar Punuk and Mildendo City. Here, a large river flows toward the plain on which Mildendo City is situated. This is the same river that flows through the city. I call it a large river because that is what it is considered by Lilliputian standards.

At a point where the river flows through an especially narrow ravine, the Lilliputians had decided to put up a dam that would form a lake behind it. In this manner, they planned to control the flow of water into Mildendo City and create a reservoir of water for irrigation purposes up in the hills. This was a massive, multifaceted project. When I say the project was to build a dam, I am only capturing part of the whole story. A whole series of canals was also to be constructed. A number of hydroelectric plants were to be set up in the vicinity. A pleasuredome was to be created in the middle of the artificial lake, to which the Mildendans could retire to engage in all kinds of exciting water sports. Such were some of the programs that were part of the project as a whole.

This project up in the hills had been planned in conjunction with the redesigning of the city below. Some of the inhabitants of the city displaced by the redesigning were to be moved to townships that were to be begun along the margins of the artificial lake. Here, the displaced inhabitants would be sold land cheap by the explos (roughly translatable as "corporation") that was involved in the project. Queen Baataania's government would build the dam, the explos would develop the area, and the displaced citizens of Mildendo City would form vibrant new farming communities in the clean, modern townships. In this fashion, all of society would benefit from the project.

Similar projects had been completed all over Mildendo, indeed in most parts of Lilliput except the North. Northern Lilliput, I was told by my tutor as we were discussing the details of the project one day, had neither citizens nor governments with the necessary foresight to carry out such projects. It was, he thought, the great tragedy of the North, as Northern Lilliput was commonly referred to.

Since my new work site lay much closer to my home than Mildendo City, I had a lot more free time. I left home for work much later and arrived back much sooner. This was a welcome change, though I did miss Mildendo City itself, for I had always found it an exciting place. Often during lunch break in Sector 420, I would position myself in such a way that I could watch the comings and goings in one of the streets. I found this an endlessly entertaining thing to do. And then there was that first sight of the beautiful spires of the city rising out of the black cloud as we came down the hills every morning. I missed all this in my new work site.

In comparison, in the hills, there was the quietness of the wilderness. The hills were covered with a thick layer of greenness since it was summer in the southern hemisphere by now. Here, the stunted trees of the Lilliputian forest were often not much taller than I am. They spread thickly in all directions, appearing very much like a tall field of strange bushes. Every day I traveled from the desert of the Karunar Punuk into this thick forest. Were it not for the path made by the trakas, some of which were huge and stood as high as my knees, I would have had difficulty making my way through the forest to the work site.

Because of my excessive height, I frequently found myself looking into the nest of some Lilliputian bird or the other in the forest. Some of these birds were quite large by Lilliputian standards, one or two of them as big as my clenched fist. They were perhaps eagles or hawks, but I am no ornithologist. The birds themselves did not seem to know what to make of me. If I stood still for a long period of time, they would alight on my head. They seemed to mistake my hair, which had grown long, for the branches and leaves of some strange tree. For this, I was made much fun of by my colleagues on the work team. More dangerously, however, some of the birds would fly very close to my head. My eyes were constantly in danger from their sharp claws and beaks.

Once, one of the larger birds gashed me terribly on the cheek, just below my left eye, and copious amounts of blood began to flow. I tried to stanch it with my handkerchief but a chaeen (surgeon) had to be called to attend to me. Standing on a traka, he made me lie down, took one look at my cheek, and called for an entire cart of fresh sackcloth to be brought to him. This he had workers dip in a drumload of white liquid medicine and apply to my cheek. Under his supervision, two workers standing on a traka dipped each piece of sackcloth in the drum and flung it onto my left cheek. A third worker, standing on my other cheek, leaned over the mound of my nose and smoothed each piece into place with a pole.

This treatment was extremely painful. The white medicine had a stinging effect on my cheek and acted as an adhesive between the sackcloth and my skin. When, the next day, it was time to remove them, the pieces of sackcloth would not come off until plenty of water had been poured on them. As each piece of sackcloth was removed, there was a stabbing pain in my cheek. The treatment, however, was effective. The flow of blood stopped almost immediately. And by the time the pieces of sackcloth were removed the next day, the wound was well on its way to being healed. I was grateful to the chaeen for his prompt and efficient treatment of the gash.

This incident with the bird frightened me, for it made me realize how vulnerable my abnormal size made me. A minor cut had proven something of an emergency; if I had a major accident, would the Lilliputians have the necessary capability to treat me? I was confident that they had the necessary knowledge. I was worried about instruments and facilities. Clearly, my enormous size would make any treatment of a wound or sickness quite special.

When I spoke to the chaeen about my concern for my medical safety, he was frank with me. He thought that most of my medical needs could be met by a chaeen with present facilities, but there were of course no guarantees. There was always an element of risk, he said, nodding his head. Also, how would I pay for the extra-special medical attention that I would need? What I earned on the work team was barely enough to pay for my maintenance. The government could not be expected to invest huge amounts of money to produce the special facilities that I, a single individual who had arrived in Mildendo without invitation, would need. I would simply have to face this risk, the chaeen advised me, or go back to my country as soon as possible.

Later, I learned that the chaeen had written a scholarly paper about the gash in my cheek and the special conditions involved in treating it. He concluded his paper by discussing some of the questions regarding my medical needs that I had raised with him. This paper made a big splash in medical circles in Lilliput and the chaeen quickly acquired quite a reputation because of it. I was glad that I had in an indirect way been of benefit to him.

As for the birds that had caused this injury to me and daily plagued me by their dangerous fluttering over my head, I finally managed to be rid of them. My job as part of the work team was to help in clearing the forest. A kind of spade, appropriate to my size, had been provided to me as a tool. With this tool I dug up the trees. If they were of a manageable size, I carried them as they were to a clearing where trakas waited to haul them away to sawmills. If the tree was too big, a sawing machine would cut it in half, before I carried the pieces away. As the forest began to thin, the birds also began to lessen in number. Over time, as the work progressed, most of the birds probably flew away. But every once in a while one of them would turn up dead underfoot or in one of the branches of a tree. This was, as you can well imagine, sweet vengeance.

A few days following my recommencing work, Queen Baataania graciously visited me again to see what kind of progress I was making in my education. This was the first time that she came without the Alando Leed. I was able to converse with the queen in Northern Lilliputian quite fluently by now and this pleased her greatly. She was much concerned about the gash in my cheek, of which she had heard from the Alando Leed. I assured her that the wound was well on its way to healing. She also tested me in my knowledge of Mildendan history by asking me a few elementary questions. When I was able to answer all her questions correctly, she was delighted.

To show her how much I had learned, I deliberately turned the talk to Mildendan religion and philosophy and repeated to her what I had been told by my tutor. The Mildendans see the world as having been created for them by Yaaga. They believe Yaaga (the Mildendan word for God) is the Original Being whose immediate children are the ancestors of all Lilliputians. The children of Yaaga were created one day, before anything had come into existence, when Yaaga was asleep and dreaming of perfection. Suddenly the children stepped out of Yaaga's dream and began pouring out of his nose, ears, mouth, and eyes. When Yaaga awoke he was delighted to see the huge crowd of his children standing about him, in the nothingness of nonexistence.

Yaaga then created the universe because his children were bored and had nowhere to play in all the nothingness that was about them. Daily they were growing more and more listless and would not even eat. And so he created the whole universe as a playground for them. For many millions of years the ancestors of the Lilliputians played together happily in their playground, but one day some of the children of Yaaga began to make mischief and do evil things and Yaaga had to punish them. Those who had not done anything bad, he took and put aside, and gave to them the gift of success in everything they did. Those who had been evil he left alone and disowned and decreed that they would forget who they really were. This is why many Lilliputians, especially in Northern Lilliput, have forgotten that they are descendants of Yaaga and do not believe in Yaaga anymore.

The Mildendans believe they are descended directly from the good children of Yaaga. They believe that they and other descendants of the good children of Yaaga (like the Blefuscudians and the Karamanians) have the mission of bringing the world to greater and greater perfection in consonance with "the Dream of Yaaga" as set out in the Southern Lilliputian holy book called *The Dream*

That Yaaga Dreamt. I have already begun translating this most sacred of books and hope to finish it (with complete annotations) in a few months.

This is the central idea of Mildendan religion and philosophy that I summarized for Queen Baataania. The queen listened to me patiently, asking pertinent questions now and then to make certain that I really knew what I was talking about. At the end of my summary, she knelt down and offered up a prayer of gratitude to Yaaga that His dream was becoming the dream of more and more creatures in the world, that even bandur were now being touched by the dream. She invited me to join her in her prayer, which I gladly did. This was the first time that I prayed to Yaaga and I have never been the same since then.

When this serious talk of religion and philosophy was over, we were silent for a few minutes, the queen preoccupied by something on her mind. She sat in her chair in front of me as I lay on my side, her blue hair done up in a very simple style. Unlike any other time that I had seen her, she was dressed in a most functional attire. She was wearing a uniform similar to the kind that the soldiers of the camp wore. The reason for this I was to discover in a few moments, when she stood up and made a request that surprised me because I was not expecting anything of the kind.

"We wish," she said, "to inspect your body more closely. We must ask you to ready yourself so that we may climb onto you. As you can see, we have come appropriately attired for this."

I was, of course, taken aback at her words. Nothing had prepared me for this request. I did not know how to respond. The queen noted my confusion and came and stood in front of my face.

"Do not be alarmed," she said, in a kind tone. "The prospect of our climbing onto your monstrous body is disconcerting to us too, but the demands of science must be met. We wish only to take some measurements and inspect your anatomy more closely. If you will lie flat on your back and stretch out your arm so that we may use it as a ramp, this will be over soon."

Queen Baataania's explanation reassured me. I lay back on the floor of the hangar and stretched my arm out as she had requested so that she could use it as a ramp to climb up on my body. Queen Baataania had come well prepared for this expedition. The uniform in which she was dressed allowed her great freedom of movement. She also had a sturdy cane with her, with which to steady herself, and a notepad.

The queen carefully picked her way up my right arm. The cane was needed when she came to the depression at my elbow, for she almost slipped and fell there. When she was on my chest, she let out a sigh of relief and said, "Your skin is much more slippery than I expected." She made an appropriate note of this on her pad.

On my chest, she had the rougher material of my shirt for traction and this seemed to help her. "We will examine your face," she now informed me and carefully made her way down the incline of my chest toward my chin, climbing over the collar of my shirt when she got to it. She balanced herself precariously on the bony surface of my neck and leaned against my chin to look into my face. I was careful to keep as still as I could, regulating my breaths so as to give her as firm a surface to stand on as possible.

The queen placed both her hands on the tip of my chin and raised her head over it to look into my face. When she saw the deep dark cavern of my nostrils looming over her, with tentacles of hair reaching out, she let out such a scream that the soldiers standing just inside the hangar knelt down on the floor and aimed their guns at me. I believe if the queen had not stopped them, the soldiers would have fired. The queen hurriedly scrambled back to my chest and lay there for a time recovering from her shock. I lay still, not daring to move.

When she had recovered a little, she climbed down from my body and turned to me and said, "That will be all for today. But we will return soon to continue this expedition. You must be prepared then to allow us onto your body again." She looked exhausted and unwell, but determined.

I had some misgivings about the queen climbing onto my body after what had happened, but she assured me that when she came back she would be mentally prepared for all the surprises my body might hold for her. And indeed there were no mishaps again, until of course the last time, and then it was not her fault at all.

Only two days later, the queen was back. The queen began again with my head, in which she seemed especially interested. She had a traka driven into the hangar and parked close to my head. The back of the traka had a seat attached to an arm that could be extended or retracted. The queen climbed into this seat and had it extended over my face. From here, hanging over my head in a basket of steel rods, she began taking measurements. She had a small instrument with her to do this. She would look through this instrument and be able to ascertain the length of my nose or of the convex surface of my eyeball.

Using this instrument, the queen measured all the dimensions of my head and face, including my skull, and calculated the volume of my head. "One hundred and three kukais," she informed me. "Fifty Lilliputians could stand inside your skull."

The queen also had other instruments with the help of which she made a note of other information, such as the temperature of my body or the thickness of my skin. These measurements were taken over the course of many expeditions over my body, for the queen became a regular visitor to my hangar. The immensity of my body and the detail in which the queen was noting the information required that she make numerous visits. She was interested in noting all kinds of information—the average length of a strand of hair on my arm, the precise shade of brown of my skin (she did this by comparing my skin color to that of some Northern Lilliputians), the speed at which my fingernails grew.

Twice she made her way carefully from my collarbone to my shinbone, stopping when necessary. As always, she had her notepad with her, in which she made marks now and then. She cautiously picked her way across the folds of my shirt, skirting the cave of my shirt pocket, stepped across the belt of my trousers, and made her way down my leg, crawling on all fours once she was past my knee. When she had reached my foot, she let herself down to the ground and spent a long time writing up her discoveries in her notepad before she forgot. The next day she repeated this exercise over my back, beginning at my shoulder and making her way again to my feet.

The purpose of these expeditions was scientific. The queen was interested, as she herself told me a number of times, in discovering among other things the exact lay of my body and what potential the enormous size of my body had. When I wanted to know what she meant by potential, she said to me, "Each of your muscles is approximately twenty-five times as long as ours. Your skin is something like twenty-five times as thick. Surely the potential of all this must be of interest to anyone?"

To help her in the study of my body, the queen sometimes brought experts with her—a surgeon or a professor of anatomy or a physicist. These experts would sometimes accompany the queen onto my body, but most of the time they stood on the back of a traka with charts and books and powerful computers ready for consultation and advised the queen on the possible meaning of the measurements and observations she made. In this fashion, the queen amassed an enormous amount of data about my body over the course of a number of expeditions.

Not surprisingly, the queen's interest in my body led me to consider my physical appearance with greater interest. My body I thought was in good shape because of my daily physical activity at work and I always took considerable trouble with my toilet, making certain that I shaved every day even though I had no mirror and only a limited supply of blades. It was my hair that caused me shame. I had last had a haircut long before, in India, and my hair had now grown long and unkempt, hanging well below my shoulders.

My tutor, Edu Kator, also noticed the unkemptness of my hair. "Your hair is getting long and unruly," he said to me one day.

"Exactly my thoughts," I said to him, pushing my hair back from my forehead. "But how am I to have a haircut? Who in Lilliput will cut this forest on my head?"

When my tutor realized my embarrassment over the length of my hair, he spoke to the Alando Leed, who kindly made arrangements to have the matter taken care of. The tutor came back to me and said, "Do not worry. Everything has been arranged. Just keep yourself free tomorrow morning. Someone has been engaged to cut your hair. For payment, he is to receive the hair that he cuts. He will surely sell your hair for a lot of money to a furniture factory or a fence-making company."

The next morning one of the machines the Southern Lilliputians use to harvest their crops arrived outside my hangar with a great clattering noise. Gray steam rose into the cool morning air from two pipes that stuck out from it. These machines are not large even by Lilliputian standards, measuring only half as big as my head, but there is something mean and dangerous about them. Running on eight wheels, four on each side, they look like squat animals. Long rotating scythes extend like teeth along one side of the machine. The sharpness of these blades is proverbial in Lilliput.

I had seen these machines in operation in the fields many times before. The machines travel at great speed through the field. The driver of the machine sits in a cab high above the rotating teeth. As the blades slice through the stalks, they travel through a chute and appear gathered and tied together in neat little bundles on the other side of the machine. In a very short time, a field of waving plants is turned into an expanse of harvested bundles. Even though Lilliputian plants are expectedly small, the farms can be large affairs, some of them consisting of hundreds of acres. So great is the efficiency of these machines, however, that I have seen a few of them run through an entire farm in a matter of hours.

The driver of the machine that appeared in front of my hangar that morning was a little man (even for a Lilliputian) with a bald head and, as I soon discovered, a strange sense of humor. He had friends among the soldiers on the base in which my hangar was situated. He had told them what he had been asked to do and word had spread through most of the base. A large crowd arrived with him to witness the harvesting of my hair. The crowd of spectators stood in a large crescent in front of the entrance to the hangar. There was a rumor later that the driver of the machine had charged many in the crowd a fee for the privilege of watching the hair of the bandur being cut from as close up as possible.

On the driver's instructions, I lay down on the ground outside the hangar. The driver and an assistant spread my hair out behind me with a rake. When everything had been arranged to the driver's satisfaction, he climbed into his machine, which had been parked a little to the side where I could see it. Seated in the cabin, the driver bowed to the left, bowed to the right, and set his machine going. It lurched forward and disappeared from my range of vision. I heard it snorting and gnashing as it moved behind my head over my hair.

On its third and final pass, the machine rolled toward my head with a loud hiss of steam and a great clanking of metal. The experience of this vicious-looking machine rushing toward my head was quite terrifying, but the driver, before climbing into his machine, had warned me very carefully to keep perfectly still. "Do not move if you do not want me to tear all your hair off your head and leave you bald," he had said to me, running his hand over his own bald head in a comic way as he did so. The crowd standing behind him had laughed uproariously at his little joke.

And so I lay terrified but perfectly still as the machine approached closer and closer. It seemed to be making its way directly for my ear when, with a sudden jerk of the steering rod, the driver swung the machine to the side. I could hear the singing blades of the machine pass within inches of my ear. Fearing any moment to have the skin scraped off my skull, I lay there with the immobility of a block of wood. In a moment, the machine had crossed once again over the carpet of my hair and the singing of the blades was at my other ear. My head had been subjected to tremendous, painful jerks in the process, but it seemed otherwise unharmed.

I lay without moving for many minutes, recovering from the experience of having my hair cut by a Lilliputian harvesting machine. When I finally sat up and looked around, my erstwhile hair lay tied together by the machine in neat bundles that stood like an arc of pillars on the ground. A little distance away, the driver was standing up in his machine, which was emitting little spurts of steam, and bowing to the applause of the crowd. My hair had been cut in a neat straight line across the back of my head, just above where the collar of my shirt began. I did not, however, have the inclination to admire the precision of the haircut. My scalp was still stinging from the tremendous jerks of the machine. Such an ordeal was far from anything I had expected. I was only glad that the affair was over.

The driver of the machine, however, had other ideas in the matter. He felt that he should have taken off at least another inch. He walked around me, looking up at my hair and shaking his head critically. He motioned for me to lie down again on the ground, but I was not ready to subject my head once more to the attentions of his machine.

The driver, however, was unprepared to take my refusal for an answer. He insisted on cutting my hair one more time. He loudly proclaimed that his professional reputation was involved in the matter. His name would be mud in all the farm country beyond the Karunar Punuk, he declared, if it was thought that he was not capable of getting the job done exactly as he had been instructed. He had been instructed to cut the bandur's hair as short as possible. He would do it. Also, his payment for this service he was rendering to the bandur, as he was sure the bandur well knew, was the hair that was now his to sell. He felt he was entitled to at least another mikai of the bandur's hair. All this the driver proclaimed to me and the crowd in a loud voice.

The crowd backed him in the dispute and despite all my arguments I could not prevail over him and the crowd. The Alando Leed had to be called in to mediate, for no one knew who else could be said to have authority in this matter. Fortunately, the Alando Leed happened to be on the base at the moment. He arrived on the scene with a scowl on his face. He was not happy at being disturbed for such a trivial thing.

When he saw that more hair could indeed be cut, the Alando Leed was at first inclined to side with the driver. He tried to persuade me to submit to the machine again, saying, "He is being paid for his services only by your hair. Your wages are hardly enough to pay for an entire harvesting machine."

I agreed that I could not pay for the machine with my wages, but I did not think the driver was coming off badly in the bargain. The hair he had already harvested was considerable. My hair was so short now that the machine would have to pass very close to my head. I was frightened of this and submitting to the machine was simply not something I could countenance. Explaining all this, I begged the Alando Leed to intervene on my behalf.

When the Alando Leed saw how set I was against it, he finally agreed that I need not consent to the machine again. The driver of the machine felt cheated. He would have argued with the Alando Leed except that he was in awe of him.

Before the driver left with the bundles of my hair that were his, he drove his machine directly up to where I was sitting cross-legged on the ground and stood up in his machine, his green face greener with indignation. "You bandur are savages," he said, "and you deserve to look like savages." And then he drove off with a great clatter and the crowd trailed away behind him, some of them muttering and throwing hostile glances at me.

This trivial incident caused a greater uproar than it deserved. All the media, electronic and printed, covered it in great detail. The driver of the machine soon became something of a folk hero as the brave Mildendan who had stood up to the dishonest bandur. I did not receive good press in this matter. Even more unfairly, the Alando Leed came in for some mudslinging too.

The reason for this was as follows. A factory owned by the Alando Leed's family was the largest producer of papodee, a kind of Lilliputian toothpaste, in all of Lilliput. A few days earlier, when I had mentioned to the Alando Leed that I was running out of the toothpaste I had brought with me, he had come up with a scheme by which his family's factory would donate papodee to me. In return, I would be used by the company that produced the papodee to advertise its product.

Just the day before the incident of my haircut, I had received the papodee from the company in a public ceremony. An especially large drum, appropriate to my size, had been manufactured for the purpose, with the famous shining-teeth-in-a-face logo of the company painted on it. This drum, which stood thrice as tall as an average Lilliputian, was presented to me at the ceremony with much fanfare. All the media had covered it. Soon pictures of the drum of papodee being handed to me were being put out by the company all over Mildendo.

Now, after the controversy surrounding my haircut, rumors had it that the Alando Leed had sided with me because of the connection I had with the papodee factory owned by his family. The fact that sales of the papodee had picked up tremendously after the publicity I had brought to it only added fuel to the rumors. Both the Alando Leed and I knew that there was no substance to them, but this did nothing to stop the speculation.

The rumors were especially unpleasant to the Alando Leed because he prided himself greatly on his honesty and his loyal performance of his job. I believe it is from this time that he began to feel some resentment toward me. His later hostility toward me should properly be seen in this context.

Chapter 11

I suppose I should set it down in writing. I know I have been avoiding even thinking about it. If I can't write about it here in my private journal, where can I?

Carol and I made love, once, in Mahabalipuram.

There, it is written, and the page hasn't gone up in flames.

It happened on Saturday evening. After dinner, Carol, Lakshman, Sameera, and I sat out on the beach until late at night, talking. A full moon was out and had painted a white splash on the waves. The indistinct outline of a catamaran that had been drawn up on the beach lay some distance away like some mysterious sea beast. Any moment, I expected it to rise up on its four legs and lurch toward us. Carol and Lakshman had been discussing the massacre of Muslims in U.P. again.

"This night reminds me of a scene from some movie," I said, when both of them had fallen silent. "I've been trying, but I can't remember the name of it. It's a romantic movie. Boy and girl fall in love. Boy and girl not allowed to marry by families. Boy and girl commit suicide by walking hand in hand into sea. That was the movie, but I can't remember the title of it."

"How sad!" Carol said.

"Anyway, it has all these great romantic shots of the seashore," I said.

"It is a romantic night, isn't it?" Sameera agreed. And we fell to talking of various romantic movies that we had seen. Soon after, Lakshman and Sameera decided to turn in for the night and went off toward the cottage. Sameera took Lakshman's hand in hers and they disappeared, walking hand in hand, into the trees that lay between the cottages and the beach.

Carol and I sat silently for some time. Everybody else who had been sitting out on the beach had also turned in. Only two of the men who worked in the beachside restaurant were still sitting there, playing cards and smoking cigarettes under the lone light.

Neither Carol nor I seemed to feel like turning in for the night. We sat facing the sea and the white round of the moon, which gazed down on us like the face of some strange god. It was as if Carol and I, its devotees, had been summoned here for an audience, and any minute now a voice would ring out of the dark sky and speak to us.

"Do you want to go for a walk along the beach?" Carol asked.

We set off barefoot along the margin of the sea, where the waves pushed out farthermost, straining forward desperately with hissing and foaming fingers before falling back with a sudden rush. Our sandals were in the cottage. We left our footprints behind us, abandoning them in the half-light of the moon god to the jealous fingers of the sea, which would strain forward in a moment and rub them out. Carol was wearing a loose sleeveless dress that reached down below her knees. Underneath it, she was wearing a white T-shirt. The dress had large pockets in the front and she had thrust her hands deep into them. The breeze was lifting her brown hair from her face and neck. She looked as if she were walking forward with single-minded concentration, as if she urgently needed to find something when she reached the end of the beach. I could not see her eyes but I knew they had her typical faraway look in them. The expression on her face seemed so exquisite in spirit, I suddenly felt this urge to take her in my arms.

We stopped at the catamaran when we came up to it. It was no longer a sea beast but a flimsy, flat thing made of pieces of wood bound together. Carol and I ran our toes along the edge of it. The wood was still damp from the sea.

On an impulse, I took Carol's hand in mine. She turned her face toward me with an uncertain look on her face, but did not take her hand away. "I want to kiss you," I said, and found her mouth with mine. I could feel her hand creep up and press against my back.

One of the bamboo changing sheds was nearby. I pulled Carol into the shed and shut the door. And we made love for what seemed a long time on the sandy floor of the shed. When it was over, I said, "I thought it happened this way only in stories teenaged boys tell in dormitories."

Carol was silent in the darkness. I reached out and touched the palm of her hand with my finger. She raised herself on her elbow and lay looking down on me, her breasts soft white swellings in the darkness. Her cross was resting against her right nipple. I had not noticed it in our lovemaking. Suddenly there was the sound of someone rattling the door of the shed. Carol and I lay perfectly still. Someone rattled the door again and went away.

"We should leave," Carol said.

"Maybe someone else needs the shed," I said, laughing. I felt happy.

We threw our clothes on and stepped out of the shed. One of the men who had been sitting in the restaurant was standing by the catamaran. He was a short man in a white uniform. "Go," he said to me in Tamil as we passed him. "Go back to your room and go to sleep." I did not translate this for Carol.

We made our way back to the cottage quietly, walking so close that we brushed against each other at every step. Carol walked with her head bent, as if she were thinking of something. When we reached the cottage, Carol took my hand in hers, gave me a quick kiss on the cheek and said, "I'm going to have a shower."

Lakshman and Sameera were asleep, lying separately on the bed in a very demure fashion. The bedding that we had brought with us had already been spread out for Carol and me on each side of the bed. I lay down and shut my eyes. Carol came in after her shower and switched off the light. I lay awake for a long time, but I could not tell if Carol too was awake.

I did not sleep much that night. I woke up before any of the others did, had a quick shower, and went out to where some hammocks had been strung up between trees that stood around the cottages. A gray dawn was just beginning to break. It was so peaceful in the hammock that I dozed off again. When I came awake, it was much brighter and Carol was making her way through the trees toward the hammock. She was still in the dress and T-shirt she had been wearing the night before. She looked as if she had just woken up.

"I need to talk to you," she said. "About last night." She paused. "There is something I must tell you. Last night was not okay. I think you should know that. I made it happen too, I know that, but it was not okay." She stopped and looked at me. She had her fists thrust into the pockets of her dress. In the morning light, her face appeared gray and fretful. Her eyes looked puffy. "I don't do things like that usually," she added. She turned abruptly and headed back to the cottage, walking laboriously through the sand.

I wish I could discuss all this with someone. I have been trying to understand what happened—both why we did what we did that night and why it ended the way it did. I know I have been feeling attracted to her. I'm not stupid. I know how I felt. But nothing like that was supposed to happen. Now I can't even understand why I found her attractive at all. I mean, she is nice, I suppose. But why did I find her attractive in a sexual way?

"I don't do things like that usually!" Such self-righteousness. How could she talk to me like that?

I wish I could talk to somebody about all this.

Maybe it's better that there is nobody to talk to. Maybe it's best to get this whole stupid thing out of my mind once and for all. I should resolve not to write about this in my journal anymore. I should behave normally to her whenever I see her and never bring this up. And that will be that. I should also remember this is Madras. My mother would be devastated if she ever knew. I don't think Sameera and Lakshman guessed anything. We were strange the next day, but I doubt they realized why.

I wonder why she went along that night. I hope she wasn't fucking my ethnicity. I wouldn't be surprised if she was.

Today Shanthamma was campaigning in Krantinagar. I accompanied her as she went round to all the apartments and shops and businesses located in this area. I know many of the people here in Krantinagar. After all, I have only lived here all my life. It is for this reason that I volunteered to accompany her. I have not been able to get enthusiastic about the election campaign for some days now, ever since I returned from Mahabalipuram. But I have begun to feel guilty—I know I can be useful, even if only in a small way, to Shanthamma's election effort in Krantinagar. I'm sure my impeccable bourgeois credentials have some value here.

Shanthamma's campaign vehicle is Kulan's rickshaw, appropriately done up for the purpose. It has been transformed into a chariot for the woman warrior's use. The seat at the back has been removed, and a low platform constructed in its place. Bars have been placed along the sides and in front of this platform. When the chariot is on the battlefield, Shanthamma is usually standing up on the platform and holding on to the bar in front of her. Every now and then, she takes her hands from the bar and places them together in greeting to the people in the street, some of whom stop to watch the procession pass. Standing up in the chariot is, however, a precarious affair and she is always forced to return her hands hastily to the bar in front for support.

Kulan is in charge of operating the chariot. He usually pedals slowly up the street, in the middle of a small group that surrounds his rickshaw. A group in front, led by Selvi, marches along, holding a banner and shouting slogans. The small procession is usually orderly but a few khaki-clad policemen always accompany the procession. Sometimes a police jeep goes ahead. The political atmosphere in Krantinagar and Kuppancherry has not been good for the last few days, ever since it has begun to be clear that Shanthamma has genuine support here, not just among domestic workers but among all kinds of people. People are tired of politics as usual. They seem to be responding to Shanthamma's obvious sincerity. She may actually be a challenge to Sethuraman and his money machine. Tension has been building up. Newspapers have reported "a minor clash between Sethuraman's supporters and Shanthamma's supporters." What actually happened was that a few of Sethuraman's no-good goondas harassed some members of the Domestic Workers Union and the women took off their slippers and went at the goondas.

Shanthamma, Selvi, and I formed the core of the campaigning

team today. It is we who entered the shops and houses to solicit support while our unlikely army waited for us in the street. We made an incongruous trio. Shanthamma is tall and dignified. It is perfectly conceivable that she should be one of "us" in Krantinagar. After all, she recently moved to a house right here in Krantinagar, all the way on the other side from Anand Vilas. Yet there is something about her that lets you know that she wasn't always a Krantinagar person. There is still something of her mother in her.

Selvi is dignified too, but in a different way. No one would mistake her for one of the tenants of Anand Vilas. She is very neat and precise in her ways, there is a certain personal delicacy about her, but her hands are rough and hard with washing clothes and sweeping floors. She does not have the wide knowledge of the world that Shanthamma does. She is, however, learning. Even over the last few weeks that I have known her, there have been changes in her. Selvi has begun to operate as Shanthamma's unofficial chief aide. I think she would like to make a career for herself in politics as Shanthamma has. In order to take part fully in the campaign to get Shanthamma elected, she has temporarily stopped working. She operates out of the Domestic Workers Union office in Kuppancherry, which has been converted into a kind of campaign headquarters. She and Chandran and Vasanthi, Shanthamma's longtime friend and companion, have taken on the role of campaign advisers to Shanthamma.

I felt strange today making campaign visits with Shanthamma to Anand Vilas, where I have lived since childhood. Shanthamma, Selvi, and I began at Apartment A-1. I have known Dr. Kannan and his wife, who live there, for years. Their son Venu is my age. We went to high school together. Whereas I went on to do history at Loyola College, Venu went to IIT and is now an engineer making a lot of money. My mother does not say anything to me, but I know she silently compares Venu and me to my disadvantage sometimes.

The thought that I know most of the people who live in Anand Vilas was in my mind as I accompanied Shanthamma in her campaigning. Most of the people in Anand Vilas, I know, are amused by my association with Shanthamma. Some are scandalized. Only a few think charitably of me. I had already warned my mother that I would be going through Krantinagar with Shanthamma this day and that it was possible we would come to Anand Vilas. She took my warning quite well, though she must have been thinking of what her friends in the building would say. It is not my association with Shanthamma that she disapproves of but rather my refusal, as she sees it, to settle down.

When we reemerged from Anand Vilas into the bright sunshine outside, Shanthamma decided to take a short break from campaigning and Selvi went off to Joseph's stall to get her a drink. Since Joseph is a Congress (R) man, he is an enemy. But there is no other cold drink stall close by. Shanthamma's war chariot was standing under the tree that grows by the temple across the street. Shanthamma climbed into the chariot to rest. She sat on the floor and put her feet on the wooden step that had been attached to help her climb into the rickshaw. She looked uncomfortable and tired, an unlikely candidate for political office.

Looking at Shanthamma's little campaign team, all gathered together in front of me, I could not help thinking how different it looked from Sethuraman's well-funded machine, which had put on the rally in the maidan a few days ago. The little group accompanying Shanthamma had gathered around the small Ganapathy temple to wait for us. One or two of the group had entered the temple, the gates of which stood open, and were sitting on the cool cement floor in the shade. Ganapathy, his elephant head looking straight ahead, watched them with godly indifference from his niche at the back of the temple. Two policemen had wandered over to Joseph's stall and were sitting on the benches with cold drinks in their hands. Their sticks leaned against the side of the stall. The stall is covered all over with posters of Sethuraman. The reach of Bhimanbhai Dwarkanath, the owner of Kuberan A/C Theater, is long and deep in West Madras. Many of the small businesses in the area are personally beholden to him for money advanced. Joseph seems to be one such businessman.

It was interesting to listen to the talk of the group around the temple. I joined them. Kulan was also among them, leaning against the wall of the temple under the shade of the tree and listening to the men and women around him. They were talking excitedly. The mood seemed upbeat. Support for Shanthamma has been growing in the past few days. It is possible, just possible, that Shanthamma will win.

One man was loudly considering precedents for such a happening. It is not uncommon for trade union leaders to be elected. But an independent who was virtually unknown five years earlier? Who is also a woman? There were not too many such cases. No, sir, there were not. No, sir. But maybe Shanthamma could make it happen!

I turned to see if Shanthamma was listening. She smiled back at me. Suddenly the tiredness seemed to have vanished from her face and I could see a glow in her eyes, behind the glasses.

The man who was speaking began speculating about the things that could be done for Kuppancherry if Shanthamma was elected. School . . . that was one thing Shanthamma could get for them. And water. Street taps could be installed. At the end of the dry season in May and June, water was always a great problem. Sometimes they had to go to Krantinagar and beg for water from the big houses with wells and large water tanks. Street taps would save them from such humiliation. . . .

Someone brought ice from Joseph's stall. The man who was speaking paused to put a piece of ice in his mouth. I too took a piece. I pressed it against the roof of my mouth so that it would last and I would not be tempted to chew it. The sun beat down on Ganapathy Kovil Street. It was fierce, too fierce for November.

Before moving on, Shanthamma decided that we should visit the rooms in the compound next to Anand Vilas, which we had missed. I had never been inside this compound before. Formerly, it was simply a vacant lot. It is now a row of drab, functional, single rooms built recently by a real-estate shark to capitalize on lonely lower-middle-class men who can't afford anything better.

This is the compound in which that strange man, White-Beard Grandfather, lives.

The first door we came to was his. I knocked on the door. The door opened after a moment and White-Beard Grandfather thrust his head out, his gray beard appearing dirty and unkempt this close up. Behind the tangled jungle of his hair, I could see into the room a little. I noticed a huge, ugly green overcoat hanging against the wall. It was a bizarre-looking thing.

"Hello," I said, instinctively speaking in English and holding out one of the English pamphlets for him, "this is Shanthamma, who is running for election from this area." Shanthamma brought her hands together in greeting and smiled. "We would like to ask you . . ." Valur Vishveswaran quietly shut the door in our faces. I looked at Shanthamma. She shrugged. I left a pamphlet outside the door and proceeded to the other rooms. Only one of the men who lived in the rooms was home. He was a tired-looking man with sad eyes who listened to everything we said and took everything that we offered him. We left pamphlets outside the doors of the other rooms.

When we came out again into Ganapathy Kovil Street, our group had re-formed and was ready for us. Shanthamma climbed into the rickshaw and we set off down the street, carrying banner and shouting slogans. The policemen trailed behind us. We turned into one of the streets leading to Krantinagar Shopping Complex. Covering the shopping complex took the rest of the afternoon. By the time I came home, I was very tired.

I have done some more work on my poem in two parts. I feel it is now ready to grace the pages of my private journal.

Two Portraits

1. The Leader
O magnificent mind! O Leader sublime!
O maker of laws, I praise you in rhyme!

Your achievements to date are legion:
You've supported the cause of every region
From the north to the south, the east to the west,
According to the present site of your backside's rest;
You've shed tears for the poor and given to the rich
Only rules and laws and budgets and such;
Political diplomacy you've mastered,
Courses through oceans of intrigue you've charted
(And if, most times, you go round in a circle,
That's only because this world is spherical).
You believe in peace, but are all for war.
You are pro–free press but love the censor.
In joining parties you show no delay,
Seemingly embracing the contrary way—
Yet only is all this, Soul of the Nation,
Sign of universal imagination,
Which making its home in your spacious brain
Heroically weds opposites with no great strain.
So accept this offering, O Friend of the People,
Made humbly in verse by a loyal disciple;
And if you should rise one day to reign,
I know you'll embrace me if only in your brain!

2. *The Citizen*

Every few years comes an invitation:
"Commit suicide with the rest of the nation.
Between morning and evening may you be seen,
Selling your soul for the sake of Mr. Clean.
Come one, come all, and mark with your cross,
The next five years as a miserable loss."
O Face in the Street, what will you do?
They give you ten rupees and promises too.
They take you in trucks to sit on the beach
And listen to the Leader making a speech
For Mr. Straight and Mr. Straighter

(Each for the Leader till yesterday a traitor).
Haven't you heard, O Face in the Street?
The Leader's achieved yet another feat
By leaving his old cronies to join a new party,
Not from ambition, but from charity!
He was moved with grief at the new party's plight,
And that was the sole cause of his latest flight.
But where will *you* fly to, O Face in the Crowd?
Who will *you* accuse when the squabbles grow loud?
These are the gods you have voted to power,
These the weeds you have elected your flower.
But maybe I'm wrong and you've suffered enough,
Maybe it's time for you to call their bluff!

Chapter 12

Soon after I began working on the dam in the hills, I had another encounter with Lar Prent and Fargo Withrun, those two rebellious troublemakers.

The day of the encounter, during lunch break, I had found myself a secluded spot in the shadow cast by a low hill. In front of me was a slope dotted by the stumps of trees. At the bottom of the slope, the river was visible, with the skeletal outline of the dam beginning to take shape where the river was most narrow. In a few weeks, the steel rods would take on concrete form and a wall would emerge to dam the river and control the forces of nature for the benefit of civilization. It made me pleased to think that I was a part of this process.

I had retired to this secluded spot to eat my lunch because I was giving myself a treat that day and I wanted to enjoy it in some privacy. In addition to my ten sacks of apples, thirty loaves of bread, and drum of milk, I had allowed myself twenty-five pieces of pulpai, a most exquisite Lilliputian sweet. It was not often that I was able to buy such delicacies. My wages were hardly enough to meet a thirteenth of my needs, in fact, and I was being subsidized by the government of Mildendo, a situation of which I was quite ashamed. I had therefore been looking forward to this rare special lunch I had allowed myself with much excitement.

When Lar Prent and Fargo Withrun appeared, walking hand in hand up the slope through the stumps of the trees, I was about to start on the pulpai. I had spread the twenty-five pieces of pulpai on the palm of my left hand and was about to put the first piece, half the size of a fingernail, in my mouth. I stopped in surprise when I saw Lar Prent and Fargo Withrun approaching me. The last time I had seen them, they had been apprehended on the premises of Queen Baataania's beach house and bundled away by the Mildendo Peeg Immeegar. Now, here they were, not just free but wearing the distinctive overalls of my own work team!

The two of them came up to me and placed themselves between my feet. Lar Prent threw back his head and looked up at me. "How are you, bandur?" he said. The two of them stood close together. I looked down at them from between my knees.

"Nice haircut," Fargo Withrun said with a smile. She too had cut her hair short. In her short hair and overalls, she looked almost like a man. She stood a quarter of an inch taller than Lar Prent and this only heightened the effect.

"You are quite a celebrity, bandur," Fargo Withrun said. "The world can't get enough of you. Everything you do is news." She laughed.

I didn't like the tone of her voice, which was snide, and ignored her.

"You, Prent," I pointedly said to her companion. "How is it that you are here?"

"We have joined your work team, bandur," Lar Prent said to me. "We are here to help build the dam."

"But how did that happen? When I last saw you, you were being taken away by the Peeg Immeegar. What happened after that?"

"And the Peeg Immeegar was indeed glad to have us," Lar Prent admitted. "They handed us over to the Peeg Pleesa, who were going to put us away where we could do no more mischief. There are old laws which declare royal property sacred. On this count, they were going to put us in prison for many, many years, something they have been wanting to do for a long time. They were tired of releasing us from custody only to have to arrest us again." He paused. "After a few days in prison, we decided that that was not an interesting future."

"You don't know about Mildendan prisons, bandur," Fargo Withrun said.

"But you are here, in my work team," I said, still not understanding.

"There is a plan under which prisoners like us can be released if we promise to be good citizens in the future," Lar Prent said. "We went before the judge and signed a statement renouncing our past activities—you know, stopping the work in Sector 420 and things like that. And here we are."

"Sounds like a good plan to me," I said to them.

Lar Prent and Fargo Withrun looked at each other in embarrassment.

"We also had to give them some information that they wanted," Fargo Withrun said, turning her face away.

"What kind of information?"

"Let's not talk about it," Lar Prent said. "This is not a thing we are proud of."

Fargo Withrun had an expression of shame on her face. "It was a terrible thing to do," she said, as if she were thinking aloud. "We have no more friends in the world."

"I see," I said, beginning to understand. The two of them were telling me they had betrayed their friends. I thought about that for a moment. Lar Prent and Fargo Withrun had given out information about people who made it their business to disrupt the daily activity of state and citizens. I could not think of it as betrayal. "Do you regret your decision?" I asked them.

Fargo Withrun answered for both of them. "No, we don't," she said emphatically. She was holding Lar Prent's hand, and she now raised it to her lips and kissed it. There was something sweet and intimate about the two of them standing hand in hand in the afternoon sunshine in the overalls of my work team. I suddenly began to feel kindly toward them.

"The old life was not easy," Prent explained. "Always rushing off to stop something there or to start something here. Never, never living quietly in one place. The time we were trying to stop the demolition of Sector 420, we never slept in the same place for more than two days. For one whole month, I never ate a hot meal. After some time, you begin to grow tired. Deep within your mind there is a fatigue. You run around doing things. And what comes of it? Nothing. Nobody changes. The people in power remain the same."

There was a long silence as the three of us thought about what Lar Prent had just said. I was moved. There seemed to be something sad about the painful way in which this Lilliputian was finding out some of the commonest truths.

"What is that in your hand, bandur?" Fargo Withrun asked, breaking the silence and pointing to the hand that held the pulpai. The hand was resting on my knee, high above her, where she could not see what was in it.

"Just some pulpai," I said.

"Pulpai!" Withrun exclaimed. "That is something they don't give you in prison. I haven't had any pulpai in so long."

"Do you two want some?" I asked, lowering my hand reluctantly.

Lar Prent declined, but Fargo Withrun quite shamelessly took four pieces and put them in her bag.

I regarded Lar Prent and Fargo Withrun as they stood between my feet, close together and still holding hands. "Are you two married?" I asked them.

"That is one word to describe us," Fargo Withrun said with a laugh.

"We are not married but we have an understanding," Lar Prent said.

I was interested in this Lilliputian romance. It was not often that I got to learn personal details from Lilliputians. I met most Lilliputians in an official capacity. Here was an opportunity to learn something more. "Have you been together long?" I asked them.

"Actually, it was you who brought us together, bandur," Lar Prent said. "Remember the incident in Sector 420?"

"You mean the time Fargo Withrun confronted me after I had helped clear that barricaded house?" I asked.

Lar Prent nodded his head. He described to me how he and Fargo Withrun had begun to see more and more of each other, until, finally, they had taken the vow of departal, which is not formal marriage but a vow not to have sexual union with any other person.

"And now here we are," Fargo Withrun added. "In the hills

above Mildendo City. Helping clear the forest to build a dam. Maybe we *will* get married. Maybe we will have our children in one of the townships that are to be set up." Her voice was ironic.

"We made our decision, Fargo," Lar Prent said to her. "We decided it was time to think of ourselves. It was time to think of where our lives were going." He turned and explained to me, "We are not entirely happy about working here, on this dam, even though we asked to be sent here."

"Why?" I asked, surprised. "What's wrong with building a dam here?"

Fargo Withrun gave me an impatient look. "We are destroying an entire forest here, can't you see that?" she said. "Look," she turned and pointed behind her to the stumps of trees stretching away down the slope, "does this not bother you? Here, just a few weeks ago, there was a thick forest. It was one of the oldest forests in all of Lilliput. Now that monstrosity of a dam is going to rise up in its place."

"But think of all the benefits of building the dam. There will be towns. There will be more production of food. People will be able to live here in comfort and prosperity. Does this not count for more than a forest?"

"Will they really?" Withrun asked, with a skeptical tilt of her head. "Believe me, bandur, I have seen many such projects. They promise much, deliver nothing. If you are here three years from now, you will see how the townships look—run-down, poor, just like Sector 420."

"I don't believe you," I said to her. "Other people have told me about these townships too and I have seen similar townships myself. They are nothing like what you describe." I added triumphantly, "Also, your ideas are full of contradictions. Since Sector 420, as you yourself admit, was poor and run-down, why did you stand in the way of its demolition? Your ideas about this project make no more sense than that." My voice, I will admit, had a little exultant loudness in it. There was something a little annoying about the self-righteousness of Fargo Withrun and Lar Prent.

"As you wish, bandur," Withrun responded, with what seemed

indifference. "I will no longer argue with you. I have no more interest in the larger picture anyway. The world is as it is. I mean to do my job, look after myself, and let the world go on its way."

"If you dislike building a dam here so much, why did you choose to work here?" I asked. I wanted to see what answer they would give to that.

Lar Prent, who had been silent during this exchange between Withrun and me, replied, "After the project is completed, all the people who worked on it are to have first preference on houses in the townships. Fargo and I would like to buy a house and live here in the hills."

"Even though you mourn the death of your beloved forest?"

"Even though we mourn the death of our beloved forest," agreed Fargo Withrun. "And how much there is to be mourned. This forest used to be filled with birds, the most beautiful birds in Mildendo. Now they are all dead or gone." She turned to look at Lar Prent for a moment, as if an idea had just come to her. "Maybe we will build some kind of an aviary, or something, when we buy the house."

Lar Prent was taken with the idea. "Yes," he said excitedly. "We will try to bring back some of the birds that have been driven away from here. The aviary will be an oasis in this desert. We'll have all kinds of plants and birds in it. It will be our way of saving something for future generations."

"It will be expensive," Fargo Withrun reminded him. "Where will we get the money for it?"

"Maybe I'll go ahead and apply for a job with a takalat," Lar Prent said. Takalat is the High Lilliputian word for "institution of higher learning." When I was in Blefuscu, later in my stay in Lilliput, I would learn much more about takalats.

Lar Prent and Fargo Withrun were looking at each other excitedly. They seemed to have forgotten my presence there. I wanted to cut in and ask what made Prent appropriate for a position in a takalat. I had not thought that Lar Prent had academic credentials. But the siren for us to return to work sounded right then and we had to go back to our respective work sites.

Lar Prent and Fargo Withrun said hurried goodbyes and rushed away. They did not want to be late. They had to get across the makeshift bridge to the other side of the river, where they had each been assigned to operate an earthmoving traka. Apparently, they both had experience in that kind of work.

I reluctantly put away my pulpai and prepared to return to my own work site. I had not been able to enjoy even a single piece. In addition, I had lost four to Fargo Withrun. I was annoyed about this. In the days following, I saw Lar Prent and Fargo Withrun around the dam site often. Sometimes, if they had a few moments, they would stop and talk to me. But this was not something that I encouraged them to do.

Later on the day of my first meeting with Lar Prent and Fargo Withrun at the dam site, the Alando Leed visited me in my hangar. This was his first visit in many days. Having reviewed some complicated verb conjugations in Northern Lilliputian that Edu Kator had taught me the day before, I was writing up the day's happenings in my journal. As always, I was trying to recapture in idiomatic English the flavor of Lilliputian words. This was not an easy thing to do and took time. I often spent hours writing up my experiences of the day, but the result is that I have extremely detailed descriptions of my stay in Lilliput. This is what I have reproduced here in this account of my journey to Lilliput, trying to be faithful to how I saw things right then, as events unfolded. In the interest of immediacy of effect, I have tried not to write with the retrospective knowledge I now possess.

When the Alando Leed stepped into the hangar, I put away my journal. I had been lying on my stomach. Now I turned on my side so that I could face the Alando Leed. The low roof of the hangar did not allow me to stand up or even sit up fully. For this reason I had taken to spending most of my time outside the hangar. But when it came to studying or writing in my journal, or receiving visitors, I preferred to do it in the privacy of my hangar.

"Well," the Alando Leed said. "I was here on some other work and thought I would look in on you." The base in which my hangar was situated is one of the three main bases of the Mildendo

Peeg Immeegar. This fact brought the Alando Leed to the base quite often. "The Blefuscudian ambassador came to me with a message from Nat Vathesims. The Blefuscudians are still interested in having you visit them. You should consider this a great honor and be pleased about it."

"I am," I said to him.

The Alando Leed nodded. "How was your day?" he asked politely.

"As usual," I said to him. "The proximity of this new work site gives me more free time. I am grateful for this."

"As long as you use your time constructively," he replied.

"I study," I hastened to explain to him. "Don't you think I have made tremendous progress in my knowledge of Northern Lilliputian?" I did not want him to think I was lazy.

"Yes, I do," he agreed. He smiled. "I heard you bought yourself some pulpai today during lunch. Did you enjoy it?"

"It was," I said, trying to capture my exact feeling, "karul." Karul is not a word that translates easily. The closest word to it in English is "exquisite."

"But I did not eat the pulpai until this evening," I added. "I was interrupted in my lunch by Lar Prent and Fargo Withrun."

"Ah, yes," the Alando Leed said. "I was told that too. And how are those two? Endless worries they have given the Peeg Pleesa and the Peeg Immeegar over the years. What did you three speak of?"

I summarized for the Alando Leed all that had been said between us. The Alando Leed listened to me carefully, sometimes asking questions to clarify details.

"I am very concerned about them," he explained to me when I had finished. "They are such a talented couple. I hate to see them wasting their lives." He turned reflective for a moment. "I too had my wild days when I was young. But at a certain time you have to realize what is truly important in life and settle down. If this is what they are beginning to do, I am glad for them. Are they happy working on the dam?"

"They seem to have a lot of doubts about it, but they do want to settle down. They seem to be reconciled to the idea that they will have to compromise if they want to lead normal lives. I think they are tired of the old life that they used to lead."

His face had a doubtful expression on it. "Why do they want to work on the dam?" he asked.

"They want a house of their own. They kept talking about how they would like to buy a house in one of the townships in the hills after the project is over. And Lar Prent said something about looking for a job in a takalat. He would like that, I think. If he can find it."

"Maybe, at last, they are beginning to grow up," the Alando Leed said. "As long as they realize they have to grow up and stop being children, they will be fine. This is a land of opportunities for those who know how to use them."

After the Alando Leed had gone, I went back to my journal, reflecting on my life in Mildendo. I thought I was beginning to settle down too. I was happy and never thought of India. I had a steady job and a daily routine. I did not make a lot of money by Mildendan standards and, in fact, because of my extra needs, the pay was especially inadequate and the government had to support me. But I took great pride in the immense amount of work I was able to do because of my size. I was also proud of my progress as a student. I was most proud, however, of the great estimation in which people like the Alando Leed seemed to hold me. I was gratified that the Alando Leed thought highly enough of me to stop and look in on me from time to time, and this despite the bad publicity he had gotten over the case of my haircut and the papodee. I was above all gratified that I had been given this opportunity to observe the wonderful achievements of Mildendo.

But this general feeling of well-being that I had was to change very soon. In fact, within a couple of weeks. What follows is an account of the incident that proved to be my downfall in Mildendo. It is with considerable shame and disgust that I am going to record the details of this incident. I want to make it clear right from the outset that Queen Baataania was not to blame for anything that happened. The tongues that spoke ill of her after the incident (and had begun to speak badly even before, as I learned later) should all have been cut out and thrown into a fire as the Alando Leed suggested. This ancient punishment custom of the Mildendans would have been an appropriate response to such calumny. I would even have offered my own tongue to show that I took responsibility for the incident, were it not that I had something even more appropriate to offer (as I will describe in the right place).

This is how the incident came to pass. One day Queen Baataania visited me. Only two Lilliputian attendants accompanied her, the soldiers who usually came with her remaining outside. I was to learn the reason for this soon.

Under Queen Baataania's instructions, the two attendants began to set up charts and diagrams on wooden stands along the walls of the hangar. These were large diagrams by Lilliputian standards, some of them as large as my hand. On examining them closely with Queen Baataania's permission, I realized they were detailed projections of my body from every important perspective. They had been produced under Queen Baataania's supervision. The lettering on most of the diagrams was too small for me to make out, but one of the diagrams had a caption that read "Bandur—Frontal Projection."

Queen Baataania was pleased when she saw that my knowledge of written Lilliputian was also beginning to be quite good. I was grateful that all the long hours my tutor and I had spent going over the magnifications of the Lilliputian alphabet (the same in the South and the North) and of many Lilliputian texts were beginning to pay off.

When her attendants had finished setting up the diagrams, Queen Baataania dismissed them from the hangar and, turning to me, said, "As you can see, we have brought with us various anatomical diagrams of your body. We have made some predictions regarding the details of your body structure based on our earlier examinations of you. We intend today to examine you more closely to confirm these predictions and gather fresh data. For this purpose, it is necessary that you undress yourself fully. We shall leave the hangar now and return in a little while. When we return, you must be fully undressed. Understood?" And without waiting for my reply, Queen Baataania left the hangar.

This request, I realized now, was the reason for the absence of the soldiers and the attendants from the hangar. Her request put me in something of a quandary. I had never before undressed completely for Queen Baataania. She had climbed onto my body numerous times. She had often asked me to remove my shirt when I was engaged in labor. But this was the first time that she had asked that I remove all my clothes. Yet Queen Baataania did not seem to think she had asked me to do anything terribly unusual.

My moral sensibility made me consider Queen Baataania's request with some concern. I was uncomfortable with the idea of appearing before her nude. But I did not think I had much choice. Queen Baataania did not seem to be a person who took kindly to being disobeyed. So, with much reluctance, I readied myself for her reappearance. I consoled myself with the thought that all this was in the interest of science. As soon as this idea crossed my mind, the whole affair did not seem so bad and I began to see why the request might seem more ordinary to the queen.

I undressed and made a bundle of my clothes and put them away in a corner of the hangar. When the queen reentered the hangar, I was ready for her. I was lying flat on my back, as I usually did when the queen arrived to engage in one of her expeditions over my body. My modesty still made me a little uncomfortable until I noticed how businesslike the queen herself was.

As usual, the queen used my arm as a ramp to climb onto my body. With no shirt intervening between us, the pressure of the queen's small feet and cane on my chest as she walked back and forth was peculiarly stimulating. "The whole point of my scientific examinations of your body is to figure out how we can make the human body work more efficiently," she said to me as she paced back and forth over my chest. "As you know, we are very interested in the physical capacity of the human body. The key to human progress is the ability to get more work out of the human body. In your huge size we have a great opportunity to examine this question in detail. In the process, we will also learn exactly how we can maximize the benefit of your size."

So saying, the queen turned and began examining various portions of my body, looking sometimes at small diagrams that she had in her hands and pausing sometimes to consult the large charts that had been set up earlier along the wall. She walked to where my kidney was and poked at it with her cane. The area where my heart was came in for attention too. She tapped a few of my ribs carefully with her cane, taking measurements with various instruments. Standing over my solar plexus, she gently stamped down with her foot, asking me whether I felt anything. When I described to her what I felt, she made a note of it on her pad.

The queen also walked to each of my nipples and measured its circumference and diameter. She was fascinated by the wrinkles on my nipples and spent numerous moments detailing them on her pad. At my right nipple, she bent down, her face screwed up with disgust as she did so, and felt it with her hands, running them over the mound in the middle again and again. At this, a shiver went through my body that the queen seemed to feel. She straightened up quickly and waited intently for the shiver to subside and proceeded to write an account of this too on her pad.

As a consequence of the queen's walking back and forth over my body and examining my nipples so closely, my penis was beginning to grow turgid and rise up. Strange sensations, sensations that I had not felt in months and which I would have been perfectly happy never to have felt again, were beginning to flow through me. The queen did not notice my rearing penis until much later, but it gave me great cause for concern. As the queen went about her work, I secretly regarded my penis, looking past where she was standing at the moment on my chest or stomach. As time went by, and the queen continued to pace here and there over my body and poke at different parts with her cane, my penis only grew harder and longer. Soon, it began to throb, first almost imperceptibly, and then more and more convulsively.

The shameful incident to which I have referred has to do with my pulsating penis. What happened was this. The queen finished looking at my body and decided to shift her attention to my legs. "I will now examine the muscles in your upper legs," the queen informed me, as she made her way toward my thighs.

She had, of course, to pass near my penis to do so. As she came nearer, my penis began to throb with greater force and rose to its full height and stood erect. It sort of threw itself in her way. When it rose up directly in front of her in this sudden manner, the queen jumped back, surprised. She forgot about her intention to examine the muscles in my legs and stopped to observe the throbbing penis. My rebellious body, despite my exerting my mind to the best of my ability to control it, had been aroused and was in turmoil within. The entire energy of my body seemed to be concentrated in my penis.

For a long while now, I had been hoping the queen would discontinue her examination of my body and leave. Instead, when the queen noticed my erect penis, she stopped in wonder to examine it. She went up close to it, so that she was standing up to her knees in the thick undergrowth of my pubic hair. Using her cane, she poked the penis, an expression of wonder and disgust on her face. At the touch of the cane, the penis shuddered and did something that would have seemed impossible to me just a moment before—it rose up even further. The foreskin began peeling back from the head of the penis.

I could hear the queen mumbling to herself in High Lilliputian as she examined my penis. "Interesting," she was saying. "Surely there is great force and energy to be harnessed here. Surely this massive strength can be put to some fruitful work." She poked my penis some more with her stick and made notes on her notepad. She ran her hands up the sides of the penis as far as she could reach, her face screwed up with determination. "Warm," she observed and noted it on her pad.

The queen's attitude toward my penis seemed to be completely scientific and objective—she seemed to be interested in it simply as a function of my body. But all kinds of sensations and emotions were beginning to flow through me. I was having to fight to keep control of the growing rebelliousness of my body and feelings. Any moment, I felt, there would be an explosion, and my body would escape from my control and do something terrible to the queen.

Even as I was thinking these thoughts, in a sudden rush I lost all control. There was an explosion of body fluid from my penis. This turn of events took the queen completely by surprise. She was noting something in her notepad when it happened and looked up to find a fountain of warm, white semen spurting out from the penis.

And then drops of the white body fluid began to rain down around her and some of it began to flow down the side of the penis. She stood aghast for a moment, watching the tower of flesh she had been observing a moment before begin to deflate. Then a scream burst from her throat and the charts and diagrams were falling from her hands and she was scrambling to get off my shaking body. I was in no condition to help her, for my body was undergoing spasms I could not control.

The convulsions made my body an unreliable surface. The queen fell in her hurry to get off my arm and landed on her face on the cement floor of the hangar. She picked herself up and quickly rushed out. I was left alone.

As the convulsions began to subside, I began to worry about what had happened. The unfortunate loss of control on my part left me in considerable fear. I was not certain what the consequences would be. It was obvious to me why this had happened. It was months since I had had any kind of sex. Sex was hardly a possibility in my strange circumstances and I have never learned how to masturbate. I hoped the Mildendans would understand.

I wiped myself with a shirt that needed washing and began putting on my clothes as rapidly as I could in the cramped confines of the hangar. I was in the process of pulling on my underwear when the Alando Leed rushed in with what seemed like a whole regiment of Lilliputian soldiers. They were preceded by four trakas. The soldiers surrounded me.

"I mean no harm," I cried. "What happened was my body's

fault, not mine. Do not punish me! Please listen to what I have to say, I beg you! Listen to what I have to say!"

The Alando Leed did not heed my words. "Fire!" he instructed his soldiers and they pointed the guns in their hands at me. I felt sharp pain in various parts of my body. A few moments later, I was unconscious.

Chapter 13

What a horrible way to die! Stabbed in the stomach and chest more than thirty times. There was blood everywhere, even in the hair, which had come loose and fallen on the shoulders. Her spectacles lay by her head, one lens smashed to bits. Her saree had been pushed up above her knees, revealing her thighs. In the bright lights of the police jeep, the body appeared small and shrunken, as if life were some material substance that had been scraped out from this bag of skin in death. The body looked so small, so broken.

And to think I had slept through it all. Shanthamma was being killed less than a hundred yards away, behind the Ganapathy temple across the street, and I was in my bed, sleeping. Shanthamma might have shouted out or screamed and I had not heard her.

It seems so hard to believe she's gone. And nothing can bring her back. This seems so hard to believe.

I was among the very first to learn of Shanthamma's death. A sound of commotion in the street woke me before day had broken. My mother was standing at the window in my room, looking into the street below.

"What is it?" I said to her from my bed.

"Something is happening down there," she said, without turning around. "I think somebody's been killed."

I went to the window and looked out. It was almost dawn. A faint color was beginning to seep into the fabric of the night. I leaned forward to see properly. There was a small cluster of people by the Ganapathy temple. A few policemen with sticks in their hands had sealed off the space behind the temple. To one side, under the tree, stood a police jeep, its bright lights pointing behind the policemen. A police officer in khaki was standing by the jeep, nodding his head as he listened to someone in plain clothes. From my vantage point, I could not see what was behind the temple.

"How do you know someone's been killed?" I asked my mother.

"I heard someone shout something to someone."

I began putting on my shirt and trousers. My mother turned around to frown at me disapprovingly. She didn't think I should go running down in the middle of the night to the scene of a murder and said so. "I'll be back soon," I said to her. "I just want to see what's going on."

And thus, in the street below, I learned of Shanthamma's death. The group of people that had collected by the temple had grown a little bigger by the time I had descended from my room to the street. As I crossed the street to join the group, I heard one man tell another, "Union leader Shanthamma has been killed." It took me a few moments to absorb the words. I had to make sure I had heard right. "What did you say?" I said to the man who was speaking. "Who did you say has been killed?"

"Shanthamma," the man repeated. "Union leader. Don't you know her? She was standing for election from here. See!" He pointed to a poster of Shanthamma that had been pasted to the wall of the temple. Shanthamma's face looked back at us gravely. I had seen her in person only two or three days earlier.

An urgency to make certain for myself overtook me. I tried to get closer to where the body was supposed to be lying behind the temple. One of the constables stuck a stick in my way. "No, sir," he said. "Not allowed."

"I think I know her," I said. "I want to make sure."

"Not allowed," he said again patiently. He was a small elderly man, with a graying mustache. He wore his hair pulled back in an attempt to cover a balding spot.

"Is it union leader Shanthamma?" I asked.

"You will read everything in the newspaper," he said. He seemed patient for a constable.

I twisted my neck to look around him.

It was indeed Shanthamma. I was immediately sure of it. Because the lights of the police jeep were pointing toward the body, I could make things out quite clearly. At the moment of her death, she had been wearing a sari that I had seen her wear before. It was a white cotton sari printed with a blue pattern. Her spectacles were lying by her side, but the wide mouth and sharp nose were unmistakable. Mercifully, her eyes were closed. An old concrete trash bin that was usually overflowing stood behind the temple. Shanthamma's body was lying half in the rubbish that surrounded the bin. It looked as if the killer had tried to throw the body into the bin, but had given up the attempt on realizing that the bin was full. Two men were leaning over the body. Even as I watched, they spread a sheet over it.

Another police jeep drove up through Ganapathy Kovil Street and came to a halt by the temple. In Anand Vilas across the street, I noticed, lights were appearing in a few windows in response to the activity around the temple. Heads at windows were trying to see what was going on.

I went over to the police officers to try to talk to them. They would not listen to me. "I know her. Don't you understand?" I said to them.

"The family has been informed," one of them replied. I could not get anything else out of them.

Too many people were accumulating at the scene. The constables started moving them along. A scooter came down the street with a man and a woman on it and stopped by the temple. They looked like journalists. The man had a camera slung over one shoulder. The two of them went over to talk to the police officers.

The place to go to, I knew, was Chandran's house. When I reached it about an hour later, a number of people were already gathered there. Selvi was there and so was Vasanthi, Shanthamma's friend and companion, who had also been a key adviser to Shanthamma. Vasanthi, who stayed with Shanthamma and her mother in their house in Krantinagar, had brought Shanthamma's mother to Chandran's house as soon as the news had reached her.

Chandran was sitting alone on the balcony when I reached his house. Selvi and Vasanthi were with Shanthamma's mother, who was resting in one of the rooms inside. I was glad I did not have to meet Shanthamma's mother right then. When I went up to the balcony, Chandran looked up at me and said, "Shanthamma is dead. Some bastard of Sethuraman's killed her last night." He spoke in English, which was already out of the ordinary for him, for he always insisted on speaking in Tamil to me. He was sitting in an armchair, still wearing the veshti he had slept in. His legs were resting on a stool he had pulled up in front of the armchair.

"I know, Uncle," I said. "I saw the body. She was killed in front of Anand Vilas. I saw the body lying behind the temple."

"You saw the body?" he asked. His fingers stopped their uncontrollable drumming on the arms of the chair. "What did the body . . . What did she look like?"

I could not look at him as I described to him what I had seen. I knew that he and Shanthamma went back many, many years. I looked down into the street and watched a newspaper boy come up on his bicycle as I spoke. He flung the day's edition onto Chandran's balcony with a precision born of practice. It landed behind me with a loud thump. When I had finished speaking, Chandran said, "Have you had your bath?"

I shook my head.

"Shanthamma was like a daughter to me," he said. "She was family." He was silent for some time, thinking about something. At last he came out of his reverie. "I have not lost such a close friend since your father died," he said. "Now all who matter are passing on and I am left." He stopped. I could not find anything to say. "I have not had my bath yet either. I think I will go and have it now. You should go home and have your bath too. And remember to change into fresh clothes. Shanthamma may not have been related to me but I consider this a house of bereavement." He rose painfully out of the armchair, smiling at the effort he had to make. "I have been sitting here a long time now," he said. He disappeared into his study but was back in a moment for the newspaper.

"My son has gone to find out more about this thing from the police," he said as he picked up the newspaper from where it was lying between two potted plants. "A number of people have to be informed. Vasanthi has made up a list. Will you go with her to the post office when you come back? We have been trying to reach Shanthamma's daughter in the U.S. by phone. We haven't been able to get through yet. We should send her a telegram just in case. Vasanthi will have an address. Go have your bath and hurry back soon. There is much to be done." He paused. "And get rid of the election posters in my study, will you? Throw them away or put them away where I can't see them." He disappeared into the study with the newspaper under his arm.

Thus began a time of uncertainty and sadness for those of us who had gathered around Shanthamma in her attempt to get elected. I am surprised at how much sorrow I feel at Shanthamma's death. I had not realized how important she had become to me. Psychologically, I thought I had situated myself at the margins of the group around Shanthamma. I had been at loose ends for some weeks, the campaign was something worthy I could relate to, it made sense to get involved in it. This is the way I thought of my work in the campaign. I was in it as much for Chandran as for Shanthamma. But this sense of loss I feel at Shanthamma's death tells me there was more going on. I feel more than anger. I feel the loss of someone close, someone who is important to me in ways I have not understood.

I have been going through this journal to see if there are any clues to why I feel the way I do—not only why I feel as sad as I do, but also why my sorrow is such a surprise to me. The journal has not helped. I have written about all kinds of things in this journal in the past few weeks. I have detailed things carefully, described people's expressions, tried to recapture exactly the way conversations went. I have spent endless time on it. But how selective all my entries have been. At this very moment, I can think of all kinds of important incidents and people that are not in the journal.

It is strange, for example, how little the most important person in my life, my mother, appears in this journal. It would be impossible for me, I think, to write about my mother in any great detail here. When I write in my journal, it is as if I am writing about people in a book. There is a distance between the people and things I write about and me. In my journal, I'm a person standing apart, looking in. I often miss the ways in which I am a part of what is happening and what is happening is a part of me. This seems so difficult for me to capture in my writing. In my journal, sometimes, I feel like a stranger in a strange land, drifting through events and noting some of the details of their unfolding.

The newspapers have been full of the murder of Shanthamma for the past few days. I have been saving clippings from the newspapers. This is something that Chandran has asked me to do. The repeated question in all of them is why? why? why? "Why was Shanthamma killed?" report after report asks, as if the answer were not self-evident.

Some of the answers to the question have been completely absurd. One, by T. Sivarajan, suggests that Shanthamma was "done in by people around her" in a "power struggle." It's a little chilling to think that he could mean people like me. Other reports have tried to find personal motives for the murder. They have gone off to investigate Shanthamma's personal background. Was there a secret lover? they have gravely asked and fabricated some story about a man from Kerala who had stayed with Shanthamma two or three times about five years ago. They have failed to mention that the man was an old friend of her husband's who was suffering from heart disease and had come to Madras for treatment. He is now dead. This small detail of his death is missing from the news reports. Some newspapers have even gone as far back as the financial scandal surrounding her husband to rake up muck. These are the reports in the newspapers and magazines that are clearly in the pockets of Sethuraman, his supporters like Bhimanbhai Dwarkanath, and the Congress (R).

Most newspapers and magazines have not been so ridiculous. They have tried to maintain a pretense of objectivity and neutrality in covering the murder. But with these publications too there is a coyness about investigating Sethuraman and Bhimanbhai Dwarkanath that is suspicious. Those two surely have something to do with the murder of Shanthamma. Yet, most newspapers have taken a hands-off attitude toward them. They have faithfully repeated "allegations" and "rumors," but they have not assigned reporters to look into Sethuraman and Dwarkanath and their activities more closely. If they have, I have not seen the stories. Isn't it ridiculous not to look into the activities of the people with the clearest motive to murder Shanthamma?

This bias in reporting is surely linked to Sethuraman's quiet attempt to trivialize Shanthamma's campaign now that she is dead. Through well-placed journalists, who speak for him, Sethuraman has made it a point to ignore all the evidence of growing support for Shanthamma among the voters of Krantinagar and Kuppancherry. He has tried to make her into just another candidate who had run against him for frivolous reasons and posed no challenge to him in the constituency. Therefore, he means to imply, he could not have anything to do with the killing. It is, however, well known that out of his five opponents in West Madras constituency, only Shanthamma had any real chance of beating him. The others hardly even campaigned. Sethuraman's position was by no means secure against Shanthamma. That is ample motive for murder.

Since an election is automatically postponed on the death of a candidate, the situation in West Madras constituency is now quite complex. With Shanthamma safely out of the way, Sethuraman is positioning himself for victory whenever an election is called again. It is therefore vital to him that the death of Shanthamma should not be associated with him in any way. He is distancing himself from the affair by ignoring the murder, pretending that it has nothing whatsoever to do with him. He is letting journalists he has bought off with Dwarkanath's money do the talking for him. All he has done is issue a statement condemning the murder of Shanthamma and condoling with the family.

But Sethuraman and Dwarkanath will not get away with things so easily. Chandran is bringing out a special issue of *Achamillai!* devoted to the murder of Shanthamma. It will be in the stands tomorrow. Among other things, there will be detailed stories (with dates and figures) examining the connections of Sethuraman and the Congress (R) to Bhimanbhai Dwarkanath and Dwarkanath's links with criminal elements in West Madras through his involvement in the liquor business. It is well known that most of the thugs in Kuppancherry are ultimately on Dwarkanath's payroll. Dwarkanath is heavily into the moneylending racket as well, which gives him effective control over many of the small businesses in the area. Dwarkanath does the dirty work of Congress (R) in West Madras. There is motive and there is ability. This should be sufficient grounds for a police investigation. Even I, who am no criminologist, know that much.

The police, however, think otherwise. While they were cooperative enough in promptly turning over Shanthamma's body to us for cremation once they were done with it, things have been quite different in the investigation of the murder itself. The election may have been automatically postponed and Sethuraman may have successfully avoided the possibility of defeat for the moment, but the stakes are still quite high. The election will be held some time, sooner or later. Sethuraman will certainly stand for election then. He must protect himself in the meantime from any suspicion of guilt in the murder of Shanthamma. To this end, I'm sure, Sethuraman and his friends are exerting all their influence on the police. Actually, I wouldn't be surprised if the police were themselves involved in the murder. Dwarkanath must have his errand boys in the police too.

The whole world seems to have been bought off by some Dwarkanath or the other. It's enough to make anyone cynical.

In the mornings, Carol usually sits in a cane chair in Chandran's garden with her papers and notes around her. She is now organizing and collating the results of her research over the last few weeks. She saw me as I was going into Chandran's house today and called out, "I'm leaving for the U.S. in a couple of weeks." I nodded and did not say anything. She has tried to talk to me a couple of times before. I have not been very receptive to her. I have usually made some inane comment and passed on.

She did not let me off so easily this time. "I would like to talk to you before I leave," she said. I wanted to refuse, but Chandran's daughter-in-law, nosy woman that she is (I don't like her), was watching us curiously from the living-room window. Already, she has noticed the coolness between Carol and me and asked me one or two probing questions.

I stopped and said, "Okay. When?"

Carol thought for a moment. "How about Saturday afternoon? Four o'clock. I'll order out for some idlies and coffee from Ruchi Bhavan. We can have tiffin in my room. How about that?"

I did not want to meet Carol in her room. She noticed the hesitation in my face and quickly said, "Or we can go somewhere else. That's okay with me too. Would you rather that we went out to Ruchi Bhavan instead of ordering out from there? Would you like that better?" And then of course I had no choice but to insist that it was okay, it was fine, I would come to her room on Saturday. I wasn't going to let her think I was afraid to meet her in her room.

I wonder what she wants with me. I hope this isn't about what happened in Mahabalipuram.

The knife with which Shanthamma was killed has been found. It had been hidden in Mohan's cart—the cart he uses when he is ironing clothes and that stands under the tree. The police found the knife many days ago, soon after the murder of Shanthamma, but did not release the information to the press. It took a leak from one of Chandran's contacts in the police for the information to come out and the police to admit that they had the knife.

The police claim that the discovery of the knife was not publicized in order to keep the investigation from being jeopardized. Nobody believes the police. It is many days since the murder and they still haven't been able to arrest Mohan, who has absconded. He could be anywhere in India by now. The real reason for their reluctance to release the information is obvious. The discovery of the knife in Mohan's cart clearly indicates the involvement of Sethuraman and Bhimanbhai Dwarkanath in the murder of Shanthamma. Mohan is Dwarkanath's man. Always has been. The police are trying to protect Sethuraman, the Congress (R), and Dwarkanath.

Mohan's guilt in this matter is beyond dispute. It is true the discovery of the knife in his cart does not automatically mean he is guilty. Somebody else might have hidden the knife there after the murder, as some people have been overeager to point out. After all, the cart is not under lock and key or anything. But not only was the knife found in his cart, it has been identified as his knife, a knife that he has been seen using. Delaying the release of the information allowed Dwarkanath to spirit Mohan away. If Mohan is not caught, there is no one to put on trial and no way of actually proving the involvement of Sethuraman and Dwarkanath. This is the idea. This is the reason the chief minister has personally intervened to put a hand-picked officer, who can be trusted to drag his feet, in charge of the investigation.

But now that the news of the knife being discovered in Mohan's cart is out, things don't look so good for Sethuraman and the Congress (R). Not just *Achamillai!* but even mainstream newspapers have begun to ask questions that he must find uncomfortable. They have started digging into Dwarkanath's unappetizing past, and Sethuraman's connection with Dwarkanath is so well known that this cannot but hurt him. Dwarkanath's money and the Congress (R)'s political clout may still be able to save him, but the right questions are being asked now. We'll see what happens.

To think Shanthamma was killed with a common kitchen knife late one night in a deserted street by a ruffian like Mohan. What a terrible, terrible way to go.

Carol's room is reached by going around to the back of Chandran's house. It has an attached bathroom and a separate entrance from the back garden, so that it is essentially independent. It is on the second floor and looks onto the garden, from which steps lead up to the room. The room is pleasantly dark most of the time because of a huge mango tree that stands in the garden. The branches extend right to the windows of the room. I know this room well. This is where we stayed whenever we came to Madras from Bangalore for visits, before we moved here permanently. How many years ago that was!

Inside Carol's room is a desk and a chair, a bed, a single sofa, a small table with a table fan on it, a wall shelf on which Carol has arranged some of her books, and a black-and-white television on a stool. There are also pictures on the wall shelf—of her family and friends, of the Virgin Mary holding Jesus as a child, of Shiva with Parvati, of the Buddha. In front of the pictures is a small leather pouch with feathers attached to it. I recognized it as a Native American medicine pouch. I think I too bought one like it on a visit to a reservation, but I lost it a long time ago. Some of the furniture in the room came with it, some of it Carol has acquired during her stay in Madras. Because the room is large, all this furniture does not seem excessive.

When I arrived at the door of Carol's room, she was at the desk, laboriously typing away on one of Chandran's old typewriters. The door was open. I knocked on the door and stepped in.

She turned around from the desk and put on her brightest voice. "Come on in. Take the sofa," she said.

All through the day, I had had half a mind to cancel the meeting by giving some reason or the other. The only thing that had stopped me was my certainty that she would have immediately recognized it as an excuse. I did not feel like giving her that satisfaction. Now that I was in the room, I felt curious to see what, if anything, would happen.

I settled myself on the sofa and permitted myself an Americanism. "How is it going?"

She thought I meant her typing and said, "Slow and tedious. Computers have spoiled me. I can't use these typewriters anymore." She turned back to her desk and rummaged under books, paper, and index cards, saying, "Here, I have something to show you." She does not seem to be a very tidy person. At last she came up with a few sheets of paper stapled together and handed them to me.

"This is a very rough draft of a paper that I'm writing," she said. "I want you to read it and tell me what you think. Can you do that? Don't mind the typos. There are simply millions of them. There are three typos right in the title. I refuse to do anything about them. I won't deal with this typewriter any more than I have to."

The title of the paper read "Politicl Mobilization and Clasz-Consciousness among Female Domesti Workers in Krantinagar and Kuppancherry in Madras: A Case Study."

"Look at the first footnote," she said, leaning over me to point at it with her finger. A faint smell of sweat rose from her.

She had acknowledged my help in the footnote. "This paper would not have been possible without the help of the following people" the footnote said, and then my name was listed among others.

"You didn't need to do that," I said out of politeness. It didn't matter to me much whether she acknowledged me or not.

"You did help, you know," she told me. "I mean what I say in the footnote. This paper would not have been possible without your help."

"Well, thanks for remembering. And, yes, I will read this paper and get back to you." I put the paper away in my bag.

"I'm going to have to rewrite the last portions of it," Carol said. "You'll see that. I drafted it before Shanthamma was . . . Before she died. It will probably end up being a completely different paper, but I want you to give me your opinion on it anyway. The paper is about what all of you are doing here. I want to see if you all agree with what I say."

I see, I thought. Mischief stirred within me. "Have you shown it to Selvi?" I said, wearing an innocent expression. Selvi is also one of those acknowledged in the footnote.

Carol didn't seem to notice the mischief in my voice. "Selvi doesn't read English," she said. "That's a problem. But I'm having someone summarize the gist of the paper to her. She's such an important part of the paper. I really want to hear what she has to say. I did show it to Shanthamma before she died." I felt both annoyed that Carol had not noticed my maliciousness and ashamed at myself for feeling malicious.

Carol and Selvi have struck up a strange friendship in the last few days. Carol found out somehow that Selvi was religious and they have had long conversations about God and religion with the help of Carol's assistant, who acts as an interpreter. Ostensibly, these conversations are somehow relevant to Carol's research. I have not been present at any of these conversations, but they have become something of a friendly joke among us all. Chandran teases Carol about trying to convert Selvi to Christianity. Carol complains that it is she who is being converted to Hinduism. The picture of Shiva with Parvati on Carol's shelf is a gift from Selvi.

There was a long silence. We seemed to have said whatever we had wanted to say. There seemed to be nothing more to add. This was not the way I remembered other conversations between us.

"Isn't it terrible about Shanthamma?" she said at last. She tried without much success to make the question seem natural.

I nodded and kept quiet.

"What will happen now? I mean, now that the knife has been found in that man's cart?"

"Well, we hope the police will find Mohan and arrest him of course." I allowed my tone to imply surprise at the question.

"I know," Carol said patiently. "But what are you going to do about it? Are you just going to wait for the police to do something?"

"There is going to be a demonstration on Monday. To demand the prompt arrest of Mohan and the investigation of who he is working for. It's going to be held in front of the Krantinagar police station."

"Maybe I'll come too," Carol said. "It might be an interesting thing to go to."

Another silence.

Carol frowned at the watch on her wrist. "I don't know why the idlies haven't come yet. They should have been here by now."

"I can't stay much longer," I lied. "I have some things to do for the meeting on Monday."

Carol looked at me speculatively. "You are not comfortable, are you?" she said.

"Why do you say that?" I said, without looking at her. I was taken aback by the directness of the question.

"You think I screwed you over in Mahabalipuram." She was not being ironic.

I considered my response for a moment. "I think you didn't behave well," I said.

"Why?"

"You have to admit it. You didn't behave properly."

"Why do you say that?"

"I don't want to talk about this."

"Why. I asked you why you think I behaved badly." Carol spoke very carefully. Her voice had grown hard with anger.

"I don't want to talk about this," I repeated.

"You think I fucked you and discarded you like an old shoe. And now your manly pride is hurt. Is that right? Is that what it is? Or are you in love with me and don't want to admit it? Is that it? Is that it? Why can't you tell me?" There was hurt mixed with mockery in Carol's voice. "Indian men hit on me all the time. In buses, in trains, in hotels. All the time. They think every white woman wants to get laid. You think I like that? How do you think that makes me feel?"

I wasn't sure what this had to do with me. Anger had made Carol's face red. She was speaking in a loud whisper, as if she were performing a role in some sinister drama. Her right hand was gripping her left hand, hard. I sat on the sofa and watched her with a detached calmness. I pretended I was surprised at the anger.

"I think I should go," I said, getting to my feet and speaking carefully. "But I just want you to know, I'm not in love with you. And my pride is not hurt because you fucked me and threw me over. I'm angry, and hurt I might add, because of how you behaved toward me the next morning. You thought it okay just to walk up and announce your decision as if I were some child who needed to be told things in that firm voice. Otherwise I would be really out of control, and that would be really, really bad. Wouldn't it? Do you understand what I'm saying? So don't go imagining ridiculous things about my being in love or hurt in my manliness or things like that."

And then I turned around and quietly walked out of the room.

A boy was coming up the steps with a flask in one hand and a food carrier in the other. That was the tiffin. But I was not going to stay for it.

I wish I had never gone to Mahabalipuram. I hope Carol doesn't get it in her mind to say something about all this to Chandran or someone. That would be terrible.

Chapter 14

For some days now, I have not been feeling well. Every time I go to sleep I have nightmares, and when I wake up in the morning I don't feel rested at all. I am afraid to go out because of all the giant people out there, these huge monsters that walk the streets of this city day and night. I hear rumors of violence everywhere and this scares me.

Earlier, I used to force myself to go out, something I have been very particular about since my return to Madras. I must begin to do this again. Otherwise, I might as well commit suicide. Unfortunately, it is from the detestable animals out there that I must buy the things that keep me alive. There is still hope that I might be able to return to Blefuscu and escape from these monsters. I must keep alive for this purpose.

Today is the first time in days I have felt able to sit at my desk again. I have eaten a little bit of lunch and now I must continue with my memoirs. Maybe the nightmares of horror and killing will cease now. This work of writing must proceed as swiftly as before.

And so, to pick up my narrative where I had left off:

When I came to, I was lying in the hangar, in complete darkness. There was only a faint light from the end of the hangar where the doors were located. Sunlight was struggling in through the crack between the doors. It was daylight outside. I remembered with dismay the tragic outcome of Queen Baataania's last visit to my hangar. I did not know how long I had been lying unconscious. When I tried to crawl to the doors, I found that I could not move. I was chained to the walls of the hangar and my hands and feet had been shackled. All this was not a portent of good things. It had been a long time since I had last been shackled or chained. Weeks earlier, the Alando Leed had decided to dispense with this precaution as well.

Even as I was considering my next course of action, the doors to the hangar were thrown open and the Alando Leed entered, accompanied by countless soldiers with their weapons at the ready and preceded by three trakas, which positioned themselves in front of me. My eyes took time to adjust to the sudden brightness that filled the hangar.

"O Alando Leed," I said, when I could see where he was standing, between two trakas and surrounded by soldiers. "Why am I chained and shackled? What have I done to deserve this? I can explain what happened with Queen Baataania. That was not my fault at all. It was my body's fault. You know I would never do anything to harm the queen."

"I bring you tidings of sorrow, bandur," the Alando Leed said in reply to my words. "The queen is very ill. Ever since your vile behavior with her, she has been delirious and running a high temperature that will not come down. Her son, Prince Angleinhand, is ruling in her stead. We hope and pray daily that the queen has a speedy recovery."

I was stunned. "I am very sorry to hear this," I said to the Alando Leed. "I too hope for the queen's quick recovery. May Yaaga take good care of his favorite child."

The Alando Leed looked at me, his eyes so full of hate that I could feel their force palpably. "You mock us, bandur. You are the one who caused this," he said. "How could you do such a thing to us? We trusted you and helped you. I personally arranged for everything that you might need, from your education to your daily requirements. When others were for sending you back, I insisted that we should keep you. I believed you when you told me you wanted nothing more than to stay here. And this is how you repay us."

"I did not mean this to happen," I said weakly. "It was my body's fault." There was nothing else to say to the Alando Leed. How could I deny what my body had done to the queen? I could say nothing to challenge the great truth of the Alando Leed's words.

The Alando Leed turned to leave the hangar. "It is still being considered what to do with you," he said. "Until a decision is made, you will be confined to this hangar." Before he had reached the doors of the hangar, however, he seemed to think of something and came back. "If the queen dies, I will personally make sure that you are executed," he said. "And the execution will be as slow and painful as I can make it."

I remained chained and shackled in my hangar for many days following this interview with the Alando Leed. The Mildendans added some drug to my food, so that I was sedated most of the time. I slept a great deal and could not keep track of the passage of time. Innumerable days seemed to pass like this, but perhaps that is only my imagination. The hangar was little better than a coffin to me. My brief periods outside the hangar during the daily trips into the desert for my toilet were something I looked forward to with great eagerness.

When I was conscious, I went over what had happened in my mind and considered my future. I anxiously listened to any news from the outside, especially news of the queen's condition. I prayed fervently for the queen's recovery, not only because I genuinely wished her well, but because I remembered the Alando Leed's promise that he would have me executed if the queen died. I did not wish to die. I was genuinely ashamed and contrite for what I had done, or rather, what my body had done, but I had no desire to give up my life to make amends. I did not see what such an event would achieve.

News of happenings outside was not easy to get. I had been placed in complete isolation and all my daily tasks and occupations discontinued with immediate effect. The few Mildendans that I saw seemed to have been given express instructions not to talk to me. I could find out nothing from them. I did, however, manage to overhear a few sentences here and there and learned that there was great turmoil all over the land. There seemed to be all kinds of agitations in different parts of the kingdom. Violence was breaking out everywhere. Of what kind and why I could not discover. All this made me despondent and the only specific bit of information I could learn only made me more so. The dam I had been helping to construct before the terrible accident with Queen Baataania had been blown up by some arsonists. I felt very bad about this. It was as if everything that I had been involved in was going badly for the Mildendans. Although I had nothing to do with these troubles, I somehow felt personally responsible.

Then, one day, the Alando Leed brought Nat Vathesims, the Blefuscudian high official who had come to see me once earlier, to my hangar. Nat Vathesims had a proposal for me. If I consented, Blefuscu was prepared to take me from the Mildendans. The Blefuscudians had thought of uses for me. Compared to my present situation, my transfer to Blefuscu would mean freedom. In Blefuscu, my movements would still be restricted. I could never again expect the same kind of mobility I had had earlier in Mildendo, but I would not be confined as I was now. The alternative was for me to remain imprisoned in the hangar until the Mildendans permitted me to return to the bandur lands from which I had come or some other event came to pass. The choice was mine.

I first wanted to know how the queen was doing.

"Queen Baataania," Nat Vathesims told me, "is not fully recovered. But she is better. Her fever has come down."

"I'm glad to hear it," I said. "The condition of the queen has concerned me greatly, O Nat Vathesims. I must have you know that I regret deeply what happened and blame it all on my body. I myself would never do anything to harm the queen, who has been nothing but a good friend since the day I arrived in Mildendo. It is important to me that you understand this, for your offer is a generous one and shows that you trust me. I want you to know that your trust is not misplaced."

Nat Vathesims smiled when he heard my words. He looked very handsome in his gorgeous robe, despite his advanced age. His blue hair was turning white in parts. It gave him a distinguished look. "Generosity has little to do with it, bandur," he said. "We will find uses for you. Let us consider this a three-way business transaction—you will no longer be confined as you are now, we Blefuscudians get you and the use of your services, the Mildendans are rid of you. All three parties benefit."

"Even so I find your offer quite generous," I insisted to Nat Vathesims.

"There is one more condition that I have not yet mentioned. You may not find my offer so generous, once you know what it is. You have mentioned the incident with the queen that has placed you in this predicament. The organs that were the culprits in that tragic incident must be detached from your body before you can be permitted to leave Mildendo. This is something that Mildendo has demanded and Blefuscu has acceded to. Without this condition there is no deal. Are you amenable to this condition?"

The condition that Nat Vathesims was laying down, to put it bluntly, was my castration. I considered it for a minute.

"Will it be painful?" I asked Nat Vathesims.

"No," he replied. "You will be unconscious throughout the procedure and will feel nothing."

At once the decision became a simple one for me. The loss of my penis and testicles seemed to be a small price to pay for what I was being offered in return. In fact, their removal would keep me from worrying that the tragedy that had happened with the queen could recur. I said as much to Nat Vathesims. "I gladly make this atonement for my body's misbehavior," I said.

"Very well," Nat Vathesims said. "Arrangements will be made for the operation and for your journey to Blefuscu. The journey will be short, only two days, but you might find it quite strenuous. We will therefore leave when you are fully recovered from the operation."

The Alando Leed, who had not spoken a word throughout this exchange between Nat Vathesims and me, now spoke up. "The Blefuscudians are indeed generous, bandur," he said. "You are getting off very lightly indeed, considering the enormity of what you have done. Do not betray the trust they have placed in you, as you betrayed ours."

"We will watch him carefully," Nat Vathesims said. "We will not take any chances. I do not mind saying this in front of the bandur. I'm sure he realizes our need to be cautious."

And this is how I came to leave Mildendo for Blefuscu—not immediately, but a few days later, after the operation. Many readers who read these lines might wonder at the readiness with which

I consented to what was, after all, castration. Others might be wondering about the details of the procedure and the condition. But I must insist that I will not discuss this matter any further. Only a prurient mind would dwell on such subjects. Let me simply reiterate that the loss of my penis and testicles was a small price to pay for the goodwill of the Mildendans and the Blefuscudians. In fact, their removal achieved the desired effect. I have had perfect control over my body ever since and never has any incident similar to that which happened with the queen recurred, either in Lilliput or since my return.

The operation for the removal of my penis and testicles was performed right in the hangar. I was asked to undress completely, and then two or three trakas carrying the necessary equipment were brought into the hangar. One traka, with a cranelike contraption on its back, was positioned near the mid-section of my body. Something that was long and flat and sharp extended from the end of the crane, but a black cloth had been draped over it and I could not tell what it was. Bright, blinding lights lit up the whole scene. Mildendan surgeons and engineers dressed in white arrived to conduct the operation. Nat Vathesims was with them. I felt better when I saw him there. I was given something to eat which made me unconscious. I remember thinking as I was going under of the last time I was naked in this fashion. At that time, Queen Baataania was surveying my body with her instruments. That episode had ended tragically.

When I became conscious many hours after the operation, I was still naked in my hangar. The hangar was dark again, except for a light at each end. In the dim light of the bulbs, I could see a large white bandage covering the middle section of my body like a diaper. Between my legs I was numb. I tried moving my legs. I could not move them.

"It will take some time for the drug to wear off, bandur," a voice said. It was Nat Vathesims. He had been sitting in a chair that had been placed against the wall and now walked up to me out of the shadows. I tilted my head to the left so that I could see him more clearly. He was alone. There was no one in the hangar but the two of us. "The doctors say you will be ready for the trip to Blefuscu within a week."

I did not say anything. I was feeling sad and frightened.

"You now regret the operation," Nat Vathesims observed.

I denied it.

"Then you must tell me what you are feeling. I have taken personal responsibility for your journey to Blefuscu. I must know everything that you are thinking and feeling."

"I am sad at leaving Mildendo. I have been happy here. The Mildendans have been good to me."

"I am glad you feel such gratitude. The Mildendans, however, have no love for you anymore. Their kingdom is in great trouble. There is dissension and revolt everywhere. Dams are being blown up. Transportways are being blockaded. They have no time for you. They will be glad when you are gone. Your departure will free up troops which are urgently needed elsewhere. Even today, in the city of Puur, thousands of men, women, and children flooded the streets and occupied the administrative buildings. They had not one weapon among them and yet the Mildendans could not control them. Such an event is unthinkable in Blefuscu. The Mildendans have lost what it takes to hold and exercise power. Their great days are behind them."

"I am sorry to hear of their troubles. Is there nothing I could do to help them?"

Nat Vathesims laughed. "Oh no! Be assured of that. Many Mildendans feel you are responsible for the troubles. They do not think of you as the solution. Do not worry about the Mildendans. They will be fine. They have requested help from Blefuscu. Within hours, Blefuscudian troops will be here. And then you will see how soon things return to normal."

Nat Vathesims was right. In a matter of days, the Blefuscudian troops had brought life to order in Mildendo. Most of the chief instigators were caught and jailed. The common people who had been duped into participating in the revolt were persuaded to return to their jobs and everyday lives. By the time the day of my departure from Mildendo came around, the Mildendans were talking of the troubles as something in the past.

I was kept updated about these ongoing events in Mildendo by Nat Vathesims, whom I saw daily between my operation and my departure from Mildendo. The main purpose of his visits was to prepare me for my life in Blefuscu. In Blefuscu, I learned, I was to be placed in the takalat of Wachicork, which is the chief city of Blefuscu, so that the work of examining my body could be continued. In the Wachicork takalat, researchers were going to take forward the work of Queen Baataania in a far more professional and scientific manner. A research team had already been put together and was awaiting my arrival. The enormous size of my body represented an undreamed of opportunity, both for research as well as for more utilitarian purposes. The Blefuscudians were determined to make use of the opportunity to the fullest.

I was, however, full of misgivings at this prospect of renewed meddling with my body. When Nat Vathesims saw this, he put forward arguments to allay my fears. He gave me to understand that the experience would be quite different from anything that I had thus far been through with Queen Baataania. Proper precautions would be taken to ensure that contact between me and the researchers was maintained at a clinical level of professionalism. Procedures had already been worked out so that no Lilliputian would ever come in contact with my naked body. For the first few days, at any rate, the research team was mainly going to go over Queen Baataania's copious notes, copies of which were being taken to Blefuscu, and interview me on various topics. Thus, I would have time to adjust to the idea of once again having my body examined. Also, the operation that had just been done on me rendered the occurrence of any uncontrollable accident less likely. These were the arguments put forward by Nat Vathesims to reassure me about what awaited me in Blefuscu. As it happened, a tragic incident precipitated my sudden departure from Blefuscu and I never had to undergo a physical examination by the Wachicork takalat research team.

I was also told by Nat Vathesims that Vico Karunar, sycodent of Blefuscu, had a special assignment for me. "The sycodent," Nat Vathesims said to me, "is standing for reelection this year. I must tell you things do not look too good for him. The crowds have not been turning out to hear him speak or watch him perform on the tarunol, which, as you may be aware, is a musical instrument very important to the political process of Blefuscu. There is great apathy among the people. They do not seem to feel that voting in elections makes any difference to their lives. They are right of course, but they must not be allowed to understand that. They must be cajoled to vote and to vote for Vico Karunar. This is where you come in, bandur. The people, who are not very intelligent and are easily given to sensationalism, will certainly turn out in great numbers to see you. You are therefore to accompany the sycodent on his campaigning. Your time will be very full in Blefuscu, bandur. You had better get used to being busy. You should take all this very seriously. This is how you are going to earn your keep in Blefuscu."

In my many conversations with Nat Vathesims, I found him to be a very blunt man. He had an unromantic view of the world, almost to the extent of being a cynic. He said as much to me one day in Blefuscu, when I knew him much better. "I have no illusions about the world," he said. "I know very well whose side I'm on and what that side stands for. I simply do my best for my side, for if my side wins, I win. I look out only for myself. If you press me on this point, I will admit that there are sound philosophical reasons for arranging the world in this fashion. But I am a practical man. I have nothing to do with philosophy." He had a reputation for being ruthless and was fiercely loyal to Vico Karunar, for he understood that if the sycodent prospered, he prospered. There are many in Blefuscu who think as he does. I wonder if he is not right and if his way of organizing the world is not really the most efficient and the best. In his dealings with me, not only was he certain that I would benefit from being in Blefuscu but he was also clear that he and Blefuscu would benefit from my presence there. This attitude gave the interaction between us the cleanness of a mutually beneficial business transaction.

On the day of my departure from Mildendo, I was up at the first light of dawn. My bag of things had been brought to me the evening before and the documents the Mildendans had confiscated on my arrival were returned. I had asked to see the Alando Leed before I left so that I could say goodbye to my first Lilliputian friend properly, but he refused to see me. I would also have liked to see Queen Baataania, but I did not think asking to see her would have been taken well by the Mildendans.

The convoy from Blefuscu that was to accompany me on my journey arrived right on time. My chains were removed, I had a hurried breakfast, and, with my bag slung from my shoulder, I set out with the convoy in the direction of Blefuscu. I was glad that I was not being kept shackled during the journey. Apparently, Nat Vathesims, who had gone ahead to make arrangements for my arrival in Blefuscu, had decided it would slow the convoy down unnecessarily. The convoy was an impressive affair, with many trakas and chochos in it.

Soon after we began the journey to Blefuscu, my spirits began to revive. We were going through country that I had never seen before. We passed many small towns and villages in the distance. Our route had been charted in such a manner that we would be out of the densely inhabited regions of Mildendo within the hour. Blefuscu lies to the east of Mildendo and is separated from it by the sea. Before the morning was gone, we would arrive at the seacoast that faces Blefuscu, and on crossing the water, we would be in that great country (some said the greatest in the world). My sense of adventure returned. I looked forward expectantly to the end of the journey, but it would be late the next day before we reached Wachicork, Blefuscu's chief city.

On the eastern coast of Mildendo, at the point where we were to enter the sea, ships from Blefuscu were waiting for us. Surrounded by this naval accompaniment, I set out into the sea, with my bag on my shoulder to keep it from getting wet. Most of the way the water was shallow enough for me to wade through, though this made the going very slow. At times, when the water was too deep for me to handle, ten of the Blefuscudian chochos lowered cables with hooks at their ends and carried me through the air for a distance. But the wear and tear of this on the chochos was tremendous and this expedient was used only as a last resort. The crossing of the sea between Blefuscu and Mildendo took a few hours and a number of times I had to rest by sitting down in the water in a shallow part of the sea. I was very wet and tired by the time we reached the Blefuscudian coast.

Nat Vathesims was waiting to receive me on the Blefuscudian beach when we arrived. He had a team of doctors with him, who examined me to make sure that I was not injured in any way because of the crossing. After I had changed into dry clothes, Nat Vathesims came up to me and handed me documents (tiny specks that I could not read) permitting me to enter and reside in Blefuscu. "Welcome to Blefuscu," he said, as he handed me the documents. "You know I like plain speaking, so I will be straight with you. You and Blefuscu have a deal. You keep up your part of the bargain and I'll make sure Blefuscu keeps up its."

I put the documents away safely in my bag and settled down between trakas for the night, for we were to stop here on the coast before proceeding on to Wachicork the next morning. As I lay there under the open night sky, with the lights of patrolling chochos appearing and disappearing overhead, I could not help remembering another night many, many months before, when I had fallen from the sky into Mildendo. So much had happened in the meantime. I had paid little attention to the passage of time. During the trek to Blefuscu, however, I had realized how much colder the weather seemed to have suddenly become. Winter was coming on rapidly. I was wearing two shirts and an undershirt and I was still feeling cold. More than nine months had passed since I had jumped out of a plane to discover Lilliput. Many things had happened to me during that time. I am producing a broad outline of my experiences here, but I will produce a much more detailed account at some future date.

The next morning, we set out without much delay for Wachicork, because we wanted to make sure that we reached it the same day. Blefuscu is a vast country, much larger in size than Mildendo.

In Lilliput, it is considered a country of continental proportions. My journey from the coast to Wachicork, which consumed all of one day, took us through mainly agricultural districts containing immense farms, which stretched endlessly in all directions across the flat land. We passed field after field with crops neatly arranged in rows up to the horizon. When I pulled out one tiny plant (with the permission of Nat Vathesims), I discovered the fields had been planted with corn. I tucked away this miniature plant in my shirt pocket. Its dried remains are still with me. I am, in fact, looking at them even as I write these lines.

The country that we went through was lonely. I saw very few Blefuscudians. At long intervals, a harvesting machine (similar to the one that had been applied to my hair) would be visible in the middle of a field. Sometimes, a Blefuscudian the length of a finger would be standing by its side, watching this strange convoy with a monstrous and abnormal creature in its midst pass on its way to Wachicork. We arrived at Wachicork a little before sunset.

Wachicork is a great metropolis, the greatest that I have ever seen. The buildings of this city are taller, larger, more beautiful than those of even Mildendo City. The tallest buildings of Wachicork stand many, many times higher than even I do, so you can imagine how wonderful these buildings are in relation to the size of the Lilliputians. Many transportways swing high above. It is as if a white web lies over the city. This web is constantly shifting and changing as some transportways withdraw and others dart out in different directions.

The city itself is organized in a manner similar to that of Mildendo City, with the tallest buildings in the center. Gardenlike residential areas surround these buildings. At the very center of Wachicork, in the place occupied by Queen Baataania's palace in Mildendo City, is the tallest building of them all—the Administrative Tower. During the time that I was in Blefuscu, Sycodent Vico Karunar had his office at the very top of this building and from this vast structure all of Blefuscu and its far-flung interests were administered. Nat Vathesims also had his office in this building, only two floors below that of the sycodent.

In some ways, Wachicork is not as impressive a sight as Mildendo City, for there is no great black cloud hanging over it. That black cloud gives Mildendo City a somber but distinctive look. Wachicork, on the other hand, is all brightness and order. There are no chimneys nearby spewing smoke into the sky. The streets are wide and beautiful. Some of them are so wide that even I could walk through them. There are countless parks and fountains throughout the city. Wachicork is what Mildendo City should look like once the beautification program has been completed. Mildendo City might be more impressive, but Wachicork is more beautiful.

The Wachicork takalat, where I was to take up residence, is situated a little outside the city, and this is where Nat Vathesims led me after he had permitted me some time to survey the great towers and transportways of Wachicork. I should explain here in greater detail what a takalat is, though that is no easy matter. I have noted somewhere above that takalat means "institution of higher learning" in High Lilliputian. A more literal translation of takalat might be "large pits of knowledge," which explains the etymology of the word, as will become clear when I describe what a takalat looks like.

A Blefuscudian takalat (there are many of them all over Lilliput) typically consists of a number of very large pits surrounded by large service and residential buildings. The pits extend deep into the ground and are very elaborate affairs. They descend in steps to a large central area called the Herding-Place. Here there is a podium and a kind of arena with seats and benches laid out in intricate patterns indicating proper hierarchy. Each pit has a number of regular members, who may only sit in their appointed places. The scholars assigned to each pit are required to come together in the Herding-Place of the pit for a number of hours daily. Reaching the Herding-Place of a pit is not an easy matter, for the paths are laid out in the form of cunning mazes which are changed and rearranged at regular intervals, and it is not uncommon to hear of even an experienced member of a pit getting lost in a maze for days, only to emerge exhausted and delirious to face the derision of his colleagues. For every meeting in the Herding-Place, the members must make their way through the maze to the center of the pit.

Each pit of a takalat is a place where scholars interested in similar ideas and issues gather for discussions; for example, a takalat might have a Pit of Physical Science, and a Pit of Geography, and a Pit of Lilliputian History. When the scholars gather in the Herding-Place, they are duty-bound to talk. Each scholar has to say at least three things in a week. It does not matter what the scholars speak, but speak they must. This is the law of every takalat. It is believed that if only the scholars are required to speak, they will say something worthwhile.

Those scholars who fail to heed the laws of the pit to which they belong are banished from the takalat and left to work in the outside world. This is the worst thing possible for a scholar who has spent any time within the takalat, for the scholar has by now grown so used to walking on the elaborate steps and paths which make up each pit that it is difficult to walk on level ground outside the protected environment of the takalat.

The paths laid out in the pits are deliberately made to be treacherous and convoluted, and the scholars have to walk with their eyes on the ground to negotiate their way through the pit and to look out for other members of the pit who may try to trip them up or otherwise show up their clumsiness and ignorance—for a scholar's position in the hierarchy of a pit is decided not only by the value of what is spoken but also by how well the member performs on the paths of the pit. Indeed, tradition has shown that there is a direct correlation between these two activities. Hence the emphasis that is placed on the proper negotiation of the paths of the pits by the members of the takalat.

The habit of walking with eyes on the ground is a hard one to break for a scholar of a takalat. When the scholars are banished from the takalat, therefore, they are prone to getting into accidents, which often prove fatal. Even during the few days that I spent in Blefuscu there were two cases of scholars, who had been banished from a takalat being run down by fast-moving trakas in the streets of Wachicork. Active members of a takalat rarely leave it to go out into the outside world. When they do, they are accompanied by servants whose job is to make sure that no accident befalls their masters.

This is then a brief description of what a takalat looks like. The takalat as an institution emerged in certain parts of Lilliput many centuries ago and evolved slowly to its present levels of complexity and intricate organization. Every element of the takalat is important to its totality. Thus, the elaborate geographical and organizational structure provides a competitive framework in which the scholars are required to perform their work with maximum effectiveness. Without such a framework, the takalats would decline into inactivity and fall apart in no time at all. The truth of this is proven by the success with which the takalats have performed their social function over the centuries.

In the takalats of Blefuscu (and Mildendo and Karamany and Faaranaaser) are gathered together the best minds of Lilliput. They are given every privilege that society can offer them and devote their lives to the pursuit of knowledge. No topic is too trivial for the attention of some scholar or other. In this fashion, all of existence is being rapidly catalogued and codified in the takalats of Southern Lilliput. This organization of knowledge then becomes the basis for the most wonderful discoveries and inventions known to living beings—discoveries and inventions that help enrich the lives of all Lilliputians, but especially those of the Southern Lilliputians.

In addition to this invaluable work which is performed by takalats, the brightest young people of Southern Lilliput—things are different in Northern Lilliput, which is still at deplorable levels of savagery—are given over to their care for certain years of their lives. In the takalats, the young people are equipped with all the skills and knowledge necessary to manage the interests of their countries in such a manner that the success attained by them is not eroded and is in fact further developed. The readiness with which parents turn over their children to the takalats is proof of the great trust in which takalats are held. All in all, the takalats of Southern

Lilliput are glorious institutions indeed. So great is the reputation of these takalats that even a few Northern Lilliputian parents send their children there. The Southern Lilliputians graciously allow them to do this.

I, therefore, consider it something of a distinction that the Blefuscudian government had decided to place me in Wachicork takalat, perhaps the greatest takalat in all of Lilliput, for the duration of my stay in Blefuscu. The research team which had been put together to examine me had been assigned to hold its meetings in the Pit of Northern Lilliputian Affairs of that takalat. When I properly understood the great distinction of the research scholars who had been brought together in this pit, I began to be reconciled to the idea of my body being examined by them.

For my residence, a building large enough for my needs had been set aside in Wachicork takalat before my arrival. This was a large warehouse in which chemicals for use by the scholars of the Pit of Chemical Sciences had formerly been stored. A faint pungent smell still hung in the air of the warehouse for the first few days of my stay, but otherwise it was quite comfortable. This building was much larger than the hangar in which I had lived in Mildendo and I could sit up with comfort in it, though the lowness of the door meant that I still had to crawl to get into it.

The warehouse was a little separate from the other buildings of the takalat so that it was convenient both for me and for the scholars of the takalat. For my toilet needs, a modern facility had been constructed at the back of the warehouse. The construction of this the Blefuscudians had accomplished in the few days since the decision to bring me to Blefuscu had been made, and it never ceased to amaze me, every time I used it, how quickly they had set up an elaborate system to dispose of what must after all be for them an immense amount of bodily waste.

After he had shown me to the warehouse which was to be my residence and made sure that I was properly secured for the night (chained and with a traka on guard outside), Nat Vathesims left me. The next day had been put aside for my rest, so that I might recuperate from the arduous trip that I had just made. Only a few minor details were to be taken care of—I was to be shown how to use the scinca pads with which my warehouse had been specially provided and measurements for some winter clothing Nat Vathesims had decided I needed were to be taken. The following day, Nat Vathesims had informed me, my activities and engagements would start in full earnest.

After Nat Vathesims' departure, I prepared myself with great eagerness for the night. There were many things to be done—journal entries to be made, incidents during the trip that I had just concluded to be thought about, the scinca pads (soft white objects attached to cables extending from a wall, two for my eyes and two for my ears) to be examined. But I planned only to unpack my bag before stretching out for sleep on the rough floor of the warehouse. Everything else I was going to leave for the next day. The scinca pads were very tempting indeed, as I had heard so much about scinca, but I resolutely decided to ignore them for the time being. I was very tired and looked forward to a good night's rest. Though the night was quite cold outside, it was cosy and warm inside the warehouse. I remembered with gratitude Nat Vathesims' concern for my lack of winter clothing. I had not said anything to him about my inadequacy in this matter. He had noted the fact and made the necessary arrangements himself.

Wanting to be done with my unpacking as quickly as possible, I picked up my bag from where I had flung it and turned it over to dump all its contents on the floor. Along with the objects I had packed in the bag, out tumbled Lar Prent and Fargo Withrun. I looked at them in astonishment. I had no idea how they had gotten into my bag. I remembered that once when I had put my hand into the bag during my journey from Mildendo, I had felt something move. At that time, I had dismissed it as my imagination.

Lar Prent and Fargo Withrun both looked very unwell. Lar Prent looked so ill that his green skin had turned almost yellow. Fargo Withrun lay coughing and shivering on the floor of the warehouse for a long time before she felt better and was able to sit up. If they have traveled from Mildendo in my bag, I thought to myself, I am not surprised at how they look.

Lar Prent was the first to recover. On tumbling out of the bag, he had fallen on a rolled up pair of socks and lain there in exhaustion. Now he slid off the ball of socks and looked over to where I was sitting cross-legged, still inarticulate because of my surprise. His clothes were wet and sagged in damp folds from his body. I remembered that a couple of times while crossing the sea, water had splashed on the bag and soaked it. I had congratulated myself at that time for my foresight in wrapping all things that could be damaged by water in protective plastic sheets that I had brought with me from India.

"At last you are alone," Lar Prent said. "We were about to come out ourselves."

"You two did not travel all the way from Mildendo in my bag?" I said incredulously, at last finding some words to speak.

"We did," he replied. His voice was hoarse. He seemed to be catching a cold. He shivered and ran his fingers through his blue hair, which was limp and plastered against his cheeks because of the wet.

"How did you get into my bag?" I wanted to know. "I was in confinement. No one was allowed to come near me."

"There are ways," Lar Prent said. "We have friends."

"But why in my bag?" I asked. "Surely there are easier ways to travel."

Lar Prent did not answer. He did not seem to be particularly interested in clarifying things at that very moment. He walked over to Fargo Withrun and helped her up. She stood unsteadily, holding on to his arm. It suddenly occurred to me that the two of them might have been trying to sneak into Blefuscu. They might have realized that the chances of my bag not being searched on entry into Blefuscu were quite high indeed. After all, the Blefuscudians had searched the bag in Mildendo the day before the journey. That might explain the strange and dangerous mode of travel that Lar Prent and Fargo Withrun had adopted.

"Do the Blefuscudians know that you are here?" I asked them.

It annoyed me when neither of them bothered to answer the question. "I will have to inform the Blefuscudians of your presence here," I added. That got Lar Prent's attention. He walked over and stood in front of me. He looked at me severely, with a petulant frown on his face. He did not seem to be in the best of spirits. Well, I thought to myself, you have only yourself to blame if you choose to do such sneaky things as travel secretly in my bag and enter a country without permission.

"I wouldn't do that, if I were you," Lar Prent responded to my threat. "You might have to explain how we got here. They might believe you and then again they might not. They might think you helped us escape and then turned against us because of some quarrel. That's what I'll tell them, if you turn us in. I don't think you want to take the risk of their not believing you right now, so soon after that incident with the queen." He gestured to the chains that secured me to the wall of the warehouse and added, "The Blefuscudians already have you in shackles, don't they?"

When I thought about what Lar Prent had said, I had to admit he had a point. Even the suspicion of any association with Lar Prent and Fargo Withrun was to be avoided. The two of them could not be up to any good, if they had sneaked into Blefuscu in this fashion. It suddenly dawned on me that they were probably associated with the troubles in Mildendo. Something I had overheard when I was in confinement in my hangar, following the incident with the queen, came back to me.

"You two are the ones that blew up the dam in Mildendo," I gasped. Things suddenly fell into place. They had lied to me when I had had that long conversation with them at the dam site about being tired of leading the life they had led and wanting to reform themselves. Their whole purpose in working on the dam had been to blow it up. They had always been part of the conspiracy to disrupt normal life in Mildendo. I was appalled at the viciousness and audacity of their criminal bent.

"You lied to me," I said to Lar Prent and Fargo Withrun. "You lied to the authorities in Mildendo. You never wanted to change yourselves and learn to be good citizens. How could you do such a deceitful thing? Have you no sense of honor?"

While I had been turning over these thoughts in my mind, Lar

Prent and Fargo Withrun had taken off their clothes and were wringing them out. Now they stood before me, quite shamelessly naked. Lar Prent was at least a man, but even Fargo Withrun seemed to feel nothing about appearing without clothes in front of me. It was left to me to avert my eyes from their shameless nudity. I remembered what my tutor in Mildendo had told me once about the licentiousness of the lives led by Lar Prent and Fargo Withrun and their friends. Apparently, some of them were even fiderent, a High Lilliputian word which means "homosexual." I was not surprised at the behavior of these two at that moment in Blefuscu.

"You have been here a long time now, bandur," Fargo Withrun said to me. "You can no longer plead lack of knowledge. Can you not see things around you? You say you are shocked at our lying. You must either be very unperceptive or you are mocking us. Have you no interest in the reasons why millions of people have risen up in Mildendo? Do you not know how many people have been killed in Mildendo by the Peeg Immeegar and the Peeg Pleesa in the last few weeks?"

"You who blew up a dam should not sound so self-righteous," I told her.

"But we killed no one," Lar Prent interjected. His voice sounded tired and irritable. He came around and stood in front of me so that I was forced to look down at his naked body. I admit I felt a twitch of curiosity. This was the first time that I had had the opportunity to see a Lilliputian naked. "Not a life was lost. We carry no weapons. We do not believe in taking life."

"So you say," I said. "You have already lied to me. Why should I believe you?"

"Do not believe us, bandur," Fargo Withrun said. "Believe whatever you like."

The two of them began putting on their wrung-out clothes, which were now slightly drier. When they were done, they looked a little more relaxed and composed. They had, I noticed, torn pieces out of one of my undershirts some time during the trip to use as blankets. They now stood before me, wrapped in these pieces of my clothing. I was very annoyed that they had destroyed one of my undershirts in this fashion and did not offer so much as an apology, but I did not say anything. I wanted them out of my warehouse as quickly as possible. The consequences might be terrible if one of the guards posted outside heard our voices and decided to come in to investigate. It would not redound to my credit that I was engaged in conversation with two saboteurs.

"And don't meddle in my affairs anymore," I said to them. "By hiding yourself in my bag without my permission, you placed me unfairly at risk. I have nothing to do with your kind. I will not jeopardize my position here because of you." I was, I think, quite justifiably angry. I found it preposterous that my relationship with the Blefuscudians might be spoiled by the repeated meddling of these two malcontents in my affairs.

"Well, goodbye then, bandur," Lar Prent said. He was smiling and seemed calmer and ready to be on his way. Fargo Withrun too seemed to have recovered some of her composure. The two of them were standing in front of my crossed legs. Lar Prent stretched out and patted my shin, where the ring of one of the chains was attached. "You will not see me again if I can help it. I hope your stay in Blefuscu is more successful than your stay in Mildendo." He thought about that for a moment and added, "Well, I don't really mean that, but, anyway, goodbye."

I was curious.

"Where will you go now?" I asked them.

"Don't worry about us," Lar Prent said. "We have friends in Wachicork. There are more of us around than you think—in all the mean and dirty streets of the city that your Blefuscudian friends would not even dream of walking through. They probably will not even admit that such streets exist. Besides, Wachicork is my hometown. This is where I was born."

Before they left, Fargo Withrun said, "You don't happen to have any food, do you? I haven't eaten in two days."

I replied in the negative. I did, in fact, have some pieces of bread left over from my dinner in my trouser pockets, more than enough for the two of them, but I was not feeling particularly friendly toward either of them at that very moment.

There was a door at the back of the warehouse. Lar Prent opened it and cautiously peered out to check if it was safe. Since the door was much too small for me, the Blefuscudians had not bothered to place a guard on it. The traka and the guards were stationed on the front side of the warehouse.

Lar Prent and Fargo Withrun exited through this back door and shut the door behind them. I wanted to make sure they made it away safely. I put my eye to one of the round windows high up in the wall of the warehouse. It was a cloudy night and quite dark outside. There was some open space behind the warehouse and then some trees beyond. Lar Prent and Fargo Withrun were wearing dark clothing and so were not easily visible in the blackness of the night, but I thought I saw two figures wrapped in the off-white of my undershirt disappear into the trees.

And then, at last, after I had flipped the tiny light switch to the off position with a pin, I stretched out on the floor of the warehouse for some much-needed rest. I had pushed the things from my bag into a corner. It was now too late to arrange them neatly along one wall as I had had them in Mildendo. Before I fell asleep, I thought about the way in which Lar Prent and Fargo Withrun kept coming back into my life. I hoped that I would never have to see those two again.

Chapter 15

Carol is in the hospital with a dislocated shoulder, two broken fingers, and three broken ribs. Chandran is at home with a fractured arm. For a man his age, that is not a trivial injury. I have some scrapes and cuts. Miraculously, Selvi, who was speaking when the violence happened, is unhurt. So is Kulan, though one or two of his fellow cycle-rickshaw wallahs, I'm told, are hurt quite seriously. They took the brunt of the attack from Sethuraman's thugs.

In retrospect, it is amazing that we did not consider the possibility of Sethuraman's Congress (R) goondas disrupting the demonstration in front of Krantinagar police station. Even though the immediate aim of the demonstration was getting the police to act in earnest in apprehending Mohan, the ultimate target was always Sethuraman and the Congress (R). We should certainly have expected him to prepare something for us. Yet no one brought up the possibility when the demonstration was being planned. Perhaps nobody expected even Dwarkanath and Sethuraman to be so barefaced as to attack a meeting in front of a police station, with police watching and journalists present.

Despite the terrible way in which it ended, the meeting was a success as a show of strength. There was a fair-sized crowd assembled, even though the meeting was held at such short notice. Selvi and Kulan worked indefatigably over the last two days to achieve this. They had bills announcing the meeting posted all over Kuppancherry and Krantinagar. Bills were also passed out to commuters at Krantinagar railway station and Madras Central. The sensation of the murder has heightened interest in Shanthamma. Many people on their way home from the Krantinagar railway station stopped at the meeting out of curiosity, with their plastic briefcases or cloth bags in their hands. Some of them had umbrellas, since it is supposed to rain soon. We were worried that the meeting would be rained out, but it wasn't.

Things were going along quite well. Chandran spoke to the crowd to tell them why this demonstration had been organized. After him and Selvi, P. Sivakumar and Sharada Varadaraj, two prominent city politicians who were sympathetic to us, were to speak. They had called up and asked to be part of the event. I have never seen Chandran speak at a public gathering before. He spoke with great effectiveness. He demanded that the police get serious in their investigation of the murder. There would be no letup in pressure until proper actions were taken, he promised. He demanded the arrest of Mohan and the investigation of links between Sethuraman, the Congress (R), Dwarkanath, and criminal elements in West Madras. It was a hard-hitting speech. He was brief. He was direct. He did not hesitate to name names. After him, Selvi went up to the microphone to speak. She began hesitantly. She does not have experience in public speaking. And then, even before she could get properly started, from the direction of Krantinagar railway station came a large group of Sethuraman's Congress (R) men, carrying banners and shouting slogans against us. Suddenly the atmosphere became charged. The crowd in front of the platform grew apprehensive.

Sethuraman's supporters stopped a little down the road. They had a van with speakers atop it and they used it to amplify their slogan shouting, so that Selvi's speech was drowned out. Hypocritically, their slogans too asked for the murderers of Shanthamma to be caught, but declared that Shanthamma had been deceived and done in by her own people. The slogan shouting was being led by a small man in a red shirt, who seemed to be in charge. I have seen him often at Joseph's stall. He was known to be one of Dwarkanath's key men. Selvi stopped and looked helplessly at the crowd. Two rickshaw-wallahs whom Kulan had enlisted to help with organizing the demonstration went over to Sethuraman's supporters to talk to them.

From where I was positioned by the side of the platform, I saw some of what happened. The leader of Sethuraman's goondas, the man in the red shirt, confronted the two rickshaw-wallahs with a smirk on his face. Behind him, his men kept up their shouting. The crowd in front of the stage became more restive. Some of the people detached themselves from the crowd and walked away down the street, hurrying but throwing curious glances behind them as they went. The discussion between the rickshaw-wallahs and Sethuraman's goondas was quickly becoming a quarrel. The man in the red shirt was shouting loudly at his two antagonists. His men had begun to move into the crowd. They were encouraging the crowd to disperse with threatening glances and words. But they too were confronted by some of Kulan's men. And then someone pushed someone and, before Kulan or anyone else could do anything, violence had erupted and the ground in front of the police station was a confusion of people rushing here and there.

This was just what Sethuraman's men had been pushing for. Cycle chains and sticks appeared suddenly among them. In a moment, a riot was in progress. Sethuraman's men quickly spread out into the crowd gathered in front of the platform, swinging their sticks and chains indiscriminately. Some of Kulan's men responded. Some of them too produced sticks and chains. Perhaps everybody had not come to the meeting unprepared for trouble. Scuffles developed here and there. The narrow street between the ground and the police station was suddenly filled with people trying to get away. A man rushed past me with blood pouring down from his face. To one side, a woman was on the ground. A bag was lying by her side, trampled by the people rushing past her. Once or twice she tried to get up and then lay still, using her arms to protect her head from the feet of the people around her.

The policemen across the street stood quietly and watched and did not intervene in what was happening in front of them for quite some time. They were present in strength. Jeeps and policemen filled the yard of the police station and the street in front. Khaki uniforms were everywhere. Yet they stood by and watched while Sethuraman's paid thugs pulled out sticks and chains and went at the gathered crowd. I suppose they have no reason to love us. After all, we were there to point fingers at them.

For the first few moments, I stood by the platform and watched the rioting helplessly. I noticed Carol, who was positioned far back in the crowd, along one edge of it. She had not come with us to the demonstration but had arrived later. She was down on the ground. She seemed to be hurt. I could see her trying to get up and then a stick caught her in the side and she went down again. Stones were flying about. Sethuraman's thugs were throwing them at the stage. A couple of the thugs had come up to the stage and were thumping hard on the boards. They threw threatening glances at those who were still on the stage. Some of them began to pull the stage apart. One of them rushed up to me and grabbed me by my shirt. He pulled me close to him. I could smell the liquor on his breath. "Go away," he hissed at me. "Go away now." Fear made my tongue feel heavy. I could not say anything to him. He pushed me away and began to help his companions take down the stage. Two of Kulan's friends joined me and we wanted to stop them, but we were badly outnumbered.

Chandran, Selvi, and the two city politicians hurried down from the stage. Chandran was clutching his left arm. A stone had struck him. He looked weak. Selvi was holding him up.

"We have to get him away," Selvi said. "We must get him to the car." Chandran's car was parked a little down the street. I had driven him to the demonstration. We hurried to the car with Chandran between us. P. Sivakumar and Sharada Varadaraj made for Sivakumar's car, which was parked next to Chandran's. I kept looking for Carol but I could not see her anywhere.

"I saw Carol go down," I said as I started up the car. "She may be hurt."

"Do you see her now?" Chandran asked. He was sitting in the back with Selvi, holding his left arm with his right hand. His face was small with pain and covered with sweat. "See if you can find her."

I quickly scanned the scene before me. The police were beginning to move in to control the situation. Both the van and the man in the red shirt were gone. Most of the crowd that had been gathered had melted away, but there was still some scuffling going on. The men who had been dismantling the stage had disappeared. The stage sagged down on one side, where they had managed to remove a few supports and boards. The microphone was lying on its side. I could not see Carol anywhere. "I hope she got away," I said.

As we went down the street, I saw Kulan on his rickshaw. Carol was lying in the backseat, crumpled like a ball of paper. I stopped the car. "Get her in here," I said to Kulan. Kulan and I moved Carol into the car. She was chalk-white and barely conscious. Two fingers in one hand were hanging limp in a strange way. She whimpered in pain as we put her in the backseat with Chandran. Selvi had moved to the front seat. "Poor Carol Carby," Chandran said, looking down at her head which was lying in his lap. "What a way to research India."

Kulan turned his rickshaw back toward the police station and the open ground in front of it. "Come with us. Aren't you going to come with us?" I said, as I got back behind the steering wheel.

"I'm going back to see what's happening," Kulan said. He looked up the street. "I think it's beginning to quiet down. I'm going to see if anybody else is hurt."

The whole disruption of the demonstration by Sethuraman's men took only a few minutes.

I went to see Carol at the hospital. She is in a private nursing home in Mandaveli. Dr. Gopalan, who is an old friend of Chandran's, is one of the consultants there. Carol has a room on the third floor with wide windows and air conditioning. The air conditioning was switched off and the windows were open when I arrived. Outside the windows was a gray sky. It has been building up to rain for the past few days. They keep announcing the possibility of rain. It hasn't rained yet, but it will soon.

Carol was lying in bed, staring out the window. "Hello," I said, knocking on the door, which was open. "Hello," she said, slowly turning her head in my direction. A shadow of pain passed over her face. "I wasn't sleeping. I was looking out the window."

"Yes. I noticed. How are you doing? How are your ribs?"

"They are mending. I still can't move easily, though. I won't be leaving for Texas as planned. It is a long trip there. A day and a half, two days, in airplanes and airports."

I was standing by the bed looking down at her. She had tied her hair back with a ribbon. Two of the fingers on her right hand were encased in white. Beneath the sheet, her torso bulged abnormally. She looked pale.

"I don't know if it will make you feel any better," I said, "but Joseph's been arrested. The police have been picking up known criminal elements for questioning ever since the demonstration. Joseph was picked up then. He's confessed to being a part of a plan to kill Shanthamma. So maybe the demonstration achieved something."

"Who is Joseph?" Carol asked, frowning in that typical way of hers. "Should I know him?"

"You remember that tea and coffee stall in front of my apartment building? I think we stopped there once. Long back. That's his. He is the one who is usually sitting in the stall. A stocky man with curly hair."

"I think I remember him."

"I didn't know this, but apparently he has a criminal record. Involvement in a murder long back. He was one of Velan's men then. Velan looks after Dwarkanath's liquor interests in Kuppancherry. Anyway, Velan talked to him a few weeks ago about a plan to kill Shanthamma if things got out of hand."

There was a chair on the other side of the bed. I walked around to it and sat down.

"Do we have the murderer at last?" Carol asked.

"Perhaps not. Joseph insists he didn't kill Shanthamma. He says he doesn't know who did. Who knows what the truth is? Apparently his fingerprints are not on the knife. He has an alibi. He claims only the plan was laid. In case it was necessary. And then the next thing he knew Shanthamma was dead. He claims he had nothing to do with that."

"So it's still not over. Sounds really complicated." She paused to think for a minute. "I have been reading this stuff about Shanthamma meeting with Sethuraman and Dwarkanath a number of times in the last few weeks. Do you know anything about that? I mean, that is a strange thing for her to do, isn't it?"

I shrugged. I had seen those reports too. I didn't know what to make of them. There was probably a perfectly innocent explanation for it all. Shanthamma, who could have given us that explanation, is dead. It makes sense to suspend speculation. I said as much to Carol.

"Poor Shanthamma," Carol said. She looked at me. "All this is so complicated."

"It is, isn't it? There are so many interests at work here. But, as Chandran says, at least Dwarkanath and Sethuraman have been clearly indicted by Joseph's confession. If the right people are not brought to justice, things could get really nasty now. There is tremendous sympathy for Shanthamma out there in the streets. Even the chief minister can't do anything to protect Sethuraman and Dwarkanath. If he isn't careful, he could be pulled into the whole mess himself. Politically, that is of immense importance."

Carol nodded. "I suppose so. Do you think the right murderer will be caught? Ever?"

"I hope so. The police just have to catch Mohan. He is still free. I bet he is really right here in Madras someplace, hidden away by Dwarkanath's men. I'm certain he is the murderer."

"We don't know that for sure, do we? Why would he hide the knife he used to kill Shanthamma in his own cart? That is very stupid, isn't it?"

"There could be all kinds of reasons."

"Like what?"

"That is why we have to catch him."

Carol nodded and did not say anything.

"I brought your paper back," I said, taking out the paper she had given me to look at from my bag. She took it with her good hand.

"What did you think? How did you find it?"

"Pretty good. I suppose you will work on it some more still. But I agree with everything you say."

"Everything?" Her tone was teasing. The paper had made a long argument about religion and mass mobilization.

"I brought you something to read too," I said, giving her a copy of "A Map of Where I Live." I have decided to distribute copies of it to people to see what they think.

"What is it?"

"It's just something I wrote. You can call it a short story if you like. I had this dream a few days ago that I remembered really clearly the next morning. I wrote it up in story form. It's not exactly the dream, of course. But it has its origins there."

Carol read the first few lines. "Sounds quite interesting," she said.

"You don't have to read it now," I responded.

She put it away on her bedside table.

"About the other day," I said, taking the plunge. "Your feelings were right. I wasn't behaving well toward you. I'm sorry."

"We have been at each other a lot, haven't we?"

I nodded. "I don't know why. Because I do like you," I said, speaking quickly. This wasn't easy for me. "I think you are okay. On the whole. You could change some things, but maybe that doesn't matter so much." I smiled to indicate I was joking. I did not want to be misunderstood.

Carol smiled back. "I've been thinking too," she said. "Maybe you are right. Maybe I didn't talk to you the right way that morning in Mahabalipuram. I wasn't very happy with myself for what I had done, you know. For my own reasons, which have nothing to do with you, I wasn't very proud of myself. And I just rushed out in the morning and said a bunch of things. It didn't help that you are so much younger than I am." She hesitated, as if she wanted to say something more, but then she didn't.

"Not so much," I said. "Anyway, it's all quite trivial."

"Is it? I don't know. I was going to write you a note before I left. It's much better to do this face to face."

I nodded.

"Here we are," I said, suddenly, "saying all the right things."

"I suppose that's good."

"I suppose."

There was a long silence.

"I should go," I said, getting up. "Let me know if you need anything. I'll probably see you before you leave. Chandran is planning a send-off party for you. Now that we are friends again I'll come." I smiled.

Carol smiled back. "Will you ever be in the U.S. again?" she asked.

"I don't know. Maybe. I want to see how things go here first. My mother is here."

"Well, look me up if you ever are. I would love to hear from you."

"And you should come back to Madras."

"I will. Of that I'm sure."

"We'll try to keep you out of riots the next time," I said.

"And I'm looking forward to reading your story," she said.

I took her good hand. "'Bye, Carol," I said.

"'Bye, Aziz," she said.

"Aziz? Who's that?"

"It's nothing. It's just a private joke I have."

"I like jokes. What's the joke? Why did you call me Aziz?"

Carol laughed. "I'm not going to tell you. Let's call it a puzzle. You try to figure out what I mean."

I think I've figured out what she means. I have to ask her the next time I see her if I'm right.

It looks as if things are finally over. Chandran told me this afternoon that Mohan had been apprehended in one of Velan's hideouts in Kuppancherry. He had just received the news when I arrived to see how his arm was doing. He was sitting by the phone in the living room when I walked in through the open front door.

"I was just on the phone," he said. "The police have caught Mohan. He was in a hideout in Kuppancherry. His fingerprints match with the prints on the knife. He's been charged with the murder. Let's see Sethuraman try to get out of this one."

"Has Mohan confessed to the murder?" I asked.

"Of course not. He claims he had nothing to do with it. But what else do you expect? He says the fingerprints match because it's his knife. If somebody else used the knife, why are his prints on it and not theirs? Only his prints are on the knife. He can't explain that. He insists the only reason he went into hiding was because he knew he would be accused of the murder. He gave the police an alibi but it turned out to be a lie."

"It would still help if he confessed," I noted.

"Would it?" Chandran rose carefully to his feet, nursing his arm, which was in a cast. "Come into the kitchen and make me some coffee," he said. "They have all left me alone at home today and gone off. You have come at a very opportune time. You shall make me coffee."

In the kitchen, Chandran sat down at the table while I heated the water, milk, and coffee decoction. "You'll find sugar on the shelf above you," Chandran said. "I take one spoon."

"No, you don't, Uncle," I said. "You needn't try to deceive me. I know you are not allowed to have sugar." Chandran did not contest my admonition. He was thinking of what we had been talking about earlier.

"Mohan is small fry. It doesn't matter if he is innocent of this crime or not. He isn't. But that doesn't matter anyway. You see, the people we need to hurt are Sethuraman and Dwarkanath and the Congress (R) party. We need to keep Mohan on the hook because that's the way you keep the others on the hook. It's not often you manage to get at people like Sethuraman. With Mohan being charged for the murder of Shanthamma, Sethuraman's political career, at least here in West Madras, is over. That's what charging Mohan with the murder is all about."

Chandran stopped and fell silent, lost in some thought of his own.

"Do you think Selvi would make a good candidate for political office?" he said suddenly.

I had not considered the possibility.

"I think she's interested in a political career," Chandran said. "I think she's been giving me some indications. But it's hard to tell."

"She doesn't have Shanthamma's experience, does she?" I asked.

"She has a long way to go before she will be a Shanthamma."

When the coffee was ready, I took it over to the table in two steel tumblers. The coffee was so hot that I had to hold the tumblers by the rims.

The table was by a window which looked out onto the back garden of the house. Through the branches of the mango tree, I could see a gray sky full of clouds. A brisk wind was about, shaking the branches of the tree vigorously. Dry leaves made a complaining noise on the hard ground as they were hustled and bustled from one end of the garden to the other by the wind. A squirrel appeared on the windowsill, looking for shelter. Clothes hanging on the line fluttered and waved frantically, begging to be brought indoors.

"It's going to rain quite hard," I said.

Chandran looked out the window. "About time," he said. "We need some rain. It hasn't rained for some time." He noticed the clothes on the line. "The clothes. They'll get wet. Can you bring them in?"

I brought the clothes in and left soon after. I did not stay longer because I wanted to reach home before it started to rain. I left a copy of my story "A Map of Where I Live" with Chandran. I would like his opinion of it. I would also like to translate it (or have it translated) into Tamil if he thinks it's any good. He has told me he will be able to get to it quite soon, since he spends all his time at home because of his arm. His arm is going to take time to heal, but otherwise it's fine.

Now I'm sitting here, writing in my journal. My mother's in the kitchen, getting dinner ready. The smell of cooking rice fills the apartment. It's evening and it's raining outside. Hard. I love the smell and sound of rain. It's nice when it's raining and you are inside by an open window. Some of the water is falling in. My arms and the desk and the pages of the journal are slightly damp, but I do not want to shut the window. I like to watch the rain falling over the maidan, the temple, the gates to the building, Joseph's stall. Occasionally, some poor soul hurries down the street under an umbrella. White-Beard Grandfather went by just a few minutes ago. I haven't seen him around for a few days. He had no umbrella and was soaked through and through. He did not seem to mind it.

Am I visible from the street? Do these people eager to get home ever look up and see me at my desk, in the light of my lamp?

I wonder what, if anything, will happen to Joseph's stall now.

I wonder what Shanthamma was doing out that late at night in this street. Maybe she was out for a walk. She was religious. Maybe she came to the temple. The strange thing is she lives on the other side of Krantinagar. It's a long walk from there to here. Strange, especially after midnight.

We'll probably never know the real reason. Whatever it was that brought her here did her no good.

Even as I write these words, I feel a sense of finality. I feel as if something has come to an end. Something *has* come to an end. Shanthamma is dead and her killer has been caught. I feel pessimistic and sad when I think of this. About Shanthamma being dead, I mean.

I wonder what my entries in this journal will now concern themselves with. So much of the journal has been about Shanthamma and her campaign. What will I write about now?

I don't know. But I have decided to add my story "A Map of Where I Live" to the journal. I feel it belongs here. After all, Shanthamma does appear in it. Other than me, she is the one character with a name in the story.

Be kind to the story, whoever reads it.

A Map of Where I Live

I was alone at home, waiting. I was going to make a map of where I live, as they had taught us once in primary school, many, many years ago. Five people were going to help me. I was waiting for them to arrive, but I could not remember who they were. I kept thinking and thinking, trying to figure out who my expected visitors were. I could see them in my mind but I could not make out their faces or remember their names.

On the dining table, in the kitchen, I had piled up dosas that I had just made, because I expected my visitors to be hungry. The aroma of the hot dosas filled the apartment. The dosas were standing in a corner of the table, most of which was taken up by a huge sheet of paper. The paper was for the map I was going to make. I had placed four black stones on the corners of the sheet to hold it down. In the center of the sheet I had already made a dot, which was me, and drawn a square around it. Against this I had written "RK in his apartment." Once my visitors had arrived, we were going to fill in the rest of the paper. I was very excited about this map we were going to make.

I went into my bedroom to put on my shirt because it was almost time for my visitors to arrive. This took me only a few moments, but when I went back into the kitchen with my shirt on, a dog was at the dining table, with its mouth in the pile of dosas and a dirty paw on the clean sheet of paper. "What are you doing here, dog?" I said with surprise. "How did you get in here?" The dog looked at me quietly out of its big brown eyes. I went to the front door to check if it was open, but no, it was locked and chained, as it always is.

I was walking back to the kitchen, thinking about this strange happening and wanting to take a look at the dog again to see if I knew it from somewhere or something, when the doorbell rang. When I opened the door, a man was standing there with a leash in his hand. "You have my dog," he said to me without preamble.

"Is it your dog?" I asked him with relief.

"You have stolen my dog," he said. "I'm going to have to report you to the police." I know he had a severe face, even though I could not see it.

"What do you mean?" I said with some annoyance. "I haven't stolen any dog of yours. I don't even know how the dog got here. If it's your dog, *you* tell *me* how it got into my apartment."

"You'll be hearing from the police about this attempt to steal my dog," he said and stretched out his hand (with many gold rings on it) to the dog, which had come into the living room. The dog ran to him as if it knew him.

After the dog and the man had left, I shut and locked the door and went into the kitchen to assess the damage. There were dirty paw marks all over the sheet of paper and half the pile of dosas was lying on the floor. I wrapped up the dosas in an old newspaper and put them away in a corner. The paw marks I tried to remove with a wet piece of cloth but they left smudges behind on the sheet of paper.

I was in the bathroom after doing all this when the doorbell rang again. That must be one of the people I'm waiting for, I thought, and I rushed out to open the door. Someone, a woman, was standing at the door. I knew who she was and I knew she had come to help me make my map, but I could not remember her name or make out her face. "Come in! Come in!" I cried to her. "Everything is ready. Come in!" She smiled and nodded and stepped into the living room. I shut the door and locked it and put the chain back on, for this world is a very dangerous place and I like to be sure everything is secure.

"I was just washing my hands," I said to the woman, showing her my wet hands. "I'll be back in a moment." The woman nodded understandingly and sat down on the sofa to wait. In the bathroom, as I was drying my hands, I ran through names I knew one by one, hoping to hit on her name. I did not.

When I went back into the living room, the woman was gone and a dog was sitting on the sofa. "Hello, where did you come from?" I said to the dog. The dog looked at me out of its big brown eyes and panted in reply. I went into the kitchen to see if the woman was there. The kitchen was empty. The dosas and the sheet of paper were as I had left them. I went into the bedroom. The bedroom too was empty. And so was the bathroom, from which I had just come anyway. I went to check the front door. The door was just as I had left it only minutes before, locked and chained. Where could the woman have gone?

All this was very strange.

"Hello, woman who just came," I shouted, standing by the door. "Are you there? Where are you?" The dog turned its black muzzle toward me and barked in reply from the sofa. I looked at the dog closely.

Was it possible? Could it be?

I had to make sure. I waited for a moment, till the dog was looking away somewhere else, and said, "Hello, woman," tentatively. At once the dog looked at me and barked inquiringly. Its big brown eyes watched to see what I would do. Maybe it was . . . How could it be?

At this very moment, the doorbell rang. I undid the chain and opened the door. The same man as before was standing there, in a silk kurta and with gold rings on his fingers.

"You have stolen my dog," he said, pushing me out of the way. "You'll hear from the police." He took out a leash from his pocket and beckoned to the dog with a finger. "Come here, doggie. Now be a good doggie and come here," he said. The dog jumped off the sofa and went over to him and they left.

I shut the door behind them and made sure I put the chain back on. All kinds of strange things were happening and I wanted to make sure things were as secure as I could make them. Dogs and women were appearing and disappearing through locked and chained doors. I live in a third-floor apartment with bars on the windows. I could not understand how all this was possible. Were things normal? Was the world as usual? Had the sky turned green or something? I went over to the window to see.

The sky was blue, or rather whitish because of the bright sunshine. The leaves of trees were green. People were as usual. Things were normal. I took note of the normality of things with relief. As I was doing this, I saw down in the street the man who had just been in my apartment to repossess his dog. He was with a woman, the same woman who had come to my apartment. I suddenly recognized her. It was Shanthamma! What was she doing with this man? Wasn't she supposed to be up here with me? How strange that she would go off hand in hand with this man when she had an appointment with me.

"Shanthamma!" I shouted, opening the window. "Shanthamma! Shanthamma! Come back here! Where are you going?" But the two of them had turned a corner and disappeared out of sight.

I shut the window and went back into the living room, feeling anxious and frightened. What was happening? What would happen next? Who was this man who came to my apartment and took away dogs that came from I don't know where? Why didn't the other people I was waiting for arrive?

I was turning all these questions over in my mind when the doorbell rang yet again. Maybe that's one of them, I thought with relief, maybe that's one of the people who are going to help me make a map of where I live. It couldn't be the man who kept coming back for his dog because there wasn't one in my apartment. I looked around to make sure. No, there was no dog in my apartment.

When I opened the door, the man was standing there with a leash in his hand. "You have my dog," he said.

"No, I don't," I said, quite confident of myself this time and angry with him because of it. "No dog here. There is no dog in my apartment." I spoke clearly so that he would understand.

"Yes, there is, you liar," the man said and began attaching the leash to my neck.

"You can't do that," I shouted. "Stop. I'm not a dog."

But the man did not listen to me. He made sure the leash was properly attached and led me away down the corridor to the stairwell.

I watched with helpless anger as he led me away. I was too frightened and confused to chase after him and stop him. There I was, being led down the corridor by this man, and I could not stop him. I shut and bolted the door, put the chain back on and brought in a chair from the kitchen to wedge it under the handle of the door. I wanted to make sure nothing could get in without my letting it in. And perhaps I would never let anything in again.

When I had done all this, I walked over to the window, musing over all the strange things that were happening. Down below in the street, the man in the silk kurta who had just been at my apartment door was disappearing round the corner with a dog on a leash.

Now I am just standing by the window, not knowing what to do. I want to open the window to let in some fresh air but I'm too frightened. Now I'm just waiting here, standing and waiting to see what will happen next.

Chapter 16

On the morning of my second day in the Wachicork takalat, I met Gar Elon, who was to play a brief but important part in my life in the future. Gar Elon arrived with the tailors who had been engaged to produce the overcoat. He was a member of the research team that had been entrusted with the task of examining me. When he had heard of the proposed visit of the tailors from Nat Vathesims, Gar Elon had volunteered to bring them. He was a young Blefuscudian with fine green skin and an eager face. He was excited about meeting me and wanted to see me as soon after my arrival in Blefuscu as possible. I felt very flattered by this brilliant young Blefuscudian's interest.

Gar Elon's main field of research was Northern Lilliputian history. The research team that had been given the task of examining me consisted, Gar Elon said, of scholars from a wide variety of disciplines—not only surgeons and scientists, but also others, such as linguists and even geographers. The research team was not only to examine my body physically but also to engage in conversations aimed at eliciting information from me. My presence in Blefuscu was regarded by the administration as an unheard of opportunity for accumulating knowledge.

When Gar Elon had warmly welcomed me to Blefuscu on behalf of the research team and informed me of his personal excitement at my presence there, he introduced the tailors with whom he had come. There were five of them, dressed in the distinctive blue colors that tailors wear in most Lilliputian countries. They were at first transfixed by my monstrous size and could not say a word. Lilliputian media had been full of news of me ever since my arrival. But the tailors obviously found the real thing beyond any descriptions they had read or pictures they had seen. Perhaps they were also thinking of the lewd stories about me that were being carried by the Lilliputian media after the unfortunate incident with Queen Baataania had happened. In Blefuscu, I was often questioned (never by truly cultivated people) about that incident. I always politely refused to discuss it. Apart from wanting to protect my own privacy, I thought it was the least I could do to safeguard the dignity of Queen Baataania.

My abnormal size made the tailors cluck their tongues in amazement as they began taking the necessary measurements of my body. The special requirements of my size raised the difficult question of the material out of which my overcoat was to be made. Even the thickest Lilliputian cloth, the tailors were certain, would prove too thin and delicate to be of any use for my overcoat. They considered material after material and finally discarded each one of them as unsuitable. I began to feel, with alarm, as if there was no way to produce my overcoat. The cold outside the warehouse was becoming quite unbearable. I wished I had had the presence of mind to bring some winter clothing with me to Lilliput.

At this time, Gar Elon, who had been listening intently to the discussion of the tailors, had a moment of inspiration. He suggested that they try out the material used to make the artificial turf with which the Lilliputians cover their playing fields. As an avid sportsman, Gar Elon was well aware of the many properties of this artificial turf. He knew, he said, that the thick fabric used for the playing fields was a wonderful insulator. At first the tailors were skeptical of Gar Elon's strange suggestion, but since no better alternative offered itself to them, they decided to go with his idea. And this material was what was used for my overcoat. The overcoat made from this artificial turf turned out to be both soft and comfortable. I still have the overcoat. It is hanging even this moment from a hook in the wall, over my cot.

My overcoat was produced by a team set up for that specific purpose. Tailors, engineers, and curators of playing fields were brought in and supplied with as much of the fabric as they needed. For all of three successive evenings they worked on and around my prostrate body, taking measurements and drawing up designs. Two days after these preliminary activities, an enormous overcoat, more than sufficient for my needs, was brought to me in a large traka. Nat Vathesims presented it to me with the team of engineers, tailors, and curators standing behind him. Embossed on the back of the overcoat was the name of Nat Vathesims' explos (corporation), which had paid for the coat.

The overcoat was in the Blefuscudian style and in the characteristic bright green color of the playing fields. This proved to be a source of great amusement to the Blefuscudians when I started using the overcoat and walked through the grounds of the takalat all covered in green. I soon came to be referred to by the Lilliputians as "the walking playing field." The overcoat was ready for me just in time, for it suddenly grew much colder and the first flurries of snow began to fall.

For the first few days of my stay in Blefuscu, I was engaged in conversations with members of the research team. The chief of the team, Pamp Pusass, was always present at these conversations. And so was Gar Elon, who had taken a special liking to me. These conversations usually consisted of questions about the bandur lands that I came from or my opinions on various subjects. My answers were duly recorded in machines that the researchers had with them and taken away for analysis.

When I had free time, I went for walks in the takalat and its environs, which was mostly open countryside. Sometimes Gar Elon would accompany me and I would carry him in the pocket of my overcoat. Gar Elon was actually a good walker. He was one of those rare members of a takalat who was a sportsman and quite at ease in walking around outside the takalat. But I carried him in my pocket because it was more convenient.

During my walks, I was often able to see Wachicork not too far in the distance. The vegetation of the countryside was, as elsewhere in Lilliput, miniature in size, appropriate to the measurements of the Lilliputians. The tallest of the trees in this area rose only up to my knees usually. A traka accompanied me on these excursions and I sometimes glimpsed a chocho circling high above me in the sky. When Gar Elon was with me, the security was usually less strict. The members of the research team, who had been put through the highest security screening, had been permitted special access to me. Gar Elon was often able to instruct the accompanying traka to keep at a distance. At such times, we would have pleasant conversations to which close surveillance was not conducive.

However, these walks were not very frequent. Between the interviews with the members of the research team and scinca, there was not much time for anything else.

Scinca took up most of the evenings. Scinca in High Lilliputian means "down on all fours." Scinca is something like our television. To watch scinca, you typically have to get down on all fours (which is the best possible position) and attach two pads to your open eyes and two pads to your ears. These pads are connected to cables through which flow images and sounds that are sent out electronically by the generating posts of the Blefuscu Scinca Explos, the corporation (owned by Nat Vathesims) that provides most of the scinca services in Blefuscu and, indeed, Lilliput. These images and sounds flow into the eyes and ears with a strength that is unmatchable. There are buttons on the pads to switch them on or off. When all four pads are switched on, you are watching scinca; and when only the ear pads are switched on, you are listening to trinka. Dials on the pads allow you to choose different sequences of images and sounds.

Watching scinca, or more idiomatically "eating scinca" as the Lilliputians say, is a favorite pastime among the people of Blefuscu. They spend many, many hours a week doing this. Each resident of Blefuscu, including babies, has personal scinca pads. Every home has special pieces of furniture that allow the Blefuscudians to get down on all fours and stay in that position for hours with little discomfort. For many people, life is a commute between work and the scinca.

Nat Vathesims went over the process of eating scinca on the second day of my stay in Blefuscu. He had come personally to make sure I understood everything about scinca. He considered it an important part of my daily routine during my stay in Blefuscu. "Scinca is very addictive," he said to me, when he had finished explaining how to use it, "but it is also very good for you. We would like you to eat lots and lots of scinca. Scinca has a very soothing effect on the people who eat it. We both know how important it is to keep your body soothed, don't we? Only make sure that you don't get so addicted to it that you can't perform the tasks that you are assigned. There is always a danger of that happening."

With Nat Vathesims watching me, I got down on all fours and attached the pads to my eyes and ears. At first there was a burst of different colors and noises, and then a cool sensation ran through my body, beginning with my eyes and ears. Images and sounds began to form in my mind. Lilliputians were talking in rooms. Lilliputians were dancing joyously to music. I played with the dials. New pictures and sounds flowed through the pads. Two Lilliputian women were crying in a small room. They went out into the street and they were attacked by men with sticks. I played with the dials some more. Northern Lilliputians were running here and there, shouting. Great chochos flew above them and dropped things that made loud noises. There were more cries and screams and the ground opened so that the Northern Lilliputians fell into holes and disappeared. And then, quite suddenly, the picture of two Southern Lilliputians drinking something and looking happy appeared. Their faces, which were enormous, began to dissolve and the name of the beverage that they were drinking formed in the pads.

These images and sounds flowed ceaselessly through the pads, repeating over and over again with small but fascinating changes every time I played with the dials. When at last I disconnected the pads from my eyes and ears, I found that Nat Vathesims had long since departed, having left word with the guards outside. Four hours had passed and I had not noticed it. It was evening outside, whereas it had been afternoon when I had begun to eat scinca. I felt completely drained and peaceful within, as if I had spent the whole afternoon masturbating (which of course is something I have never done in my life, I simply use the metaphor that suggested itself to me that day and which I noted in my diary). All the tensions that had been building up in my body seemed to have disappeared. My body was at peace with itself. All I wanted to do was sleep.

The next day I ate some more scinca. And in the days following, even more. Two or three times, Pamp Pusass had to have the guards disconnect the scinca pads before he could get through to me. He was not pleased about this. I secretly made arrangements with the guards to be warned at the approach of anyone to the warehouse. Whenever someone came to visit me, the guards would automatically disconnect the scinca pads, which they could do from their traka. This was their signal to me that someone was approaching. I later found out that Nat Vathesims had approved of this arrangement I had with the guards.

Aside from being interviewed by the research team, I was to perform other tasks in Blefuscu. Nat Vathesims had already told me that I would have to make public appearances in the company of the sycodent of Blefuscu, Vico Karunar. I left Blefuscu suddenly in the evening of the only day I made such an appearance. To this day, I am ashamed that I was not better able to perform this task that I had had assigned to me.

Blefuscu, unlike Mildendo, is a republic. The sycodent, the chief ruler of Blefuscu, is selected every few years from the greatest tarunol players of the richest and most powerful families of Blefuscu. There is no official law that the sycodent be only a great tarunol player from a rich family, but this is how it works out in practice. It has been so for centuries now and it has become something of a sacred custom. Since tarunol playing requires great ingenuity, imagination, and skill, such a process of selecting the sycodent is also quite effective. For many centuries now, the tarunol has been an integral part of the political process in Blefuscu. Blefuscudians love tarunol music so much that they will vote for any candidate who is able to move them with his team's tarunol playing.

Vico Karunar, a stern and imposing man to whom I was introduced (only very briefly) on that final day I spent with the Blefuscudians, is regarded as one of the great tarunol players of all time. The moment he climbed onto a tarunol, he would undergo a personality transformation and seem to lose all his sternness. However, the crowds had been especially uninterested in his performances recently, and Nat Vathesims had come up with the idea of including me in the performances as a way of drawing the crowds back. I was to be on all fours, bearing the tarunol on my back, while the sycodent and his team performed on it. This novel twist, Nat Vathesims felt, would have the desired effect on the people of Blefuscu.

Nat Vathesims was right. The crowd that came out to watch Vico Karunar perform was three times as large as usual. Not just Nat Vathesims' Blefuscu Scinca Explos, but also many other scinca exploses sent out their chochos to record and transmit images of Vico Karunar's tarunol playing on that day. Even the sycodent, who has the reputation of a man who keeps himself aloof, was so pleased by the turnout and the scinca coverage that he came up to me after the performance was over and made a present of the tarunol shoes (these are special shoes) that he had performed in. This was a great honor indeed and indicated a special mark of favor. I consider it one of the great disappointments of my life that I was able to return this favor only by abruptly running away from Blefuscu and placing the sycodent and especially Nat Vathesims in an awkward position.

Before I recount the manner of my departure from Blefuscu and ultimately Lilliput, there is one other experience I had at Blefuscu that I must describe. A few days after my arrival at the Wachicork takalat, Maku Vait, a famous inventor and businessman of Blefuscu, approached me through Nat Vathesims with an idea. He had perfected, he said, a chemical process through which large living beings could be reduced to a smaller size. He had secretly tried this process out on a Lilliputian elephant and had found it to work. He offered now to repeat the process on me for free, if I was willing.

You can imagine how excited I was when I heard about Maku Vait's chemical process—especially after I saw the miniaturized elephant he brought with him to show me. The elephant had been reduced to about a tenth of its former size and appeared perfectly healthy. This animal, which would formerly have risen a third of the way to my knees, now fit on my thumb.

The process, Maku Vait warned me many times, was long and painful. This, however, did not bother me. The benefits of the process were too great for me to worry about a little pain. I was for trying out the process on myself immediately and Maku Vait was prepared to do it, but both Nat Vathesims and Pamp Pusass were absolutely against it. They both admitted that one day Maku Vait's chemical process might offer an admirable solution to what to do with me. For the moment, they felt, it was better to keep me the size I was. This is the one act of Nat Vathesims that I have not been able to understand. He who was so reasonable, straightforward, and just in all his other actions would not, for some reason best known to him, consent to having the process applied to me right then.

Maku Vait and I were, however, able to convince Nat Vathesims and Pamp Pusass to consent to an experimental application to my left hand of an ointment that Maku Vait had prepared. If a certain temporary and harmless change took place in the hand, Maku Vait said, it would mean that the process was feasible. I could be reduced to a size almost that of a Lilliputian.

After consulting with Pamp Pusass, who was a chemical scientist, Nat Vathesims finally agreed to this limited experiment. The ointment was applied to my left hand on the morning of my last day with the Blefuscudians. There was a brief sharp pain at the moment of application, as Maku Vait rubbed the ointment onto my hand with a mop. Nothing happened. My hand remained as it was. Maku Vait was not surprised at this, for he did not expect any results for many days.

The precipitate events that overtook me that same day did not allow me to check the status of my hand until many days later, when I was back in India. I found then that my hand had begun to grow smaller and all the lines and fingerprints on the hand were beginning to fade. Now my hand has shrunk to a size slightly smaller than before and the lines and fingerprints have disappeared so that the front of my hand is completely white and without mark. I do not know if this is the temporary and harmless change that Maku Vait was speaking of but it is how my hand has remained to date. I offer it for inspection as one more proof of the veracity of the account of Lilliput I am putting down here. It is well known that there is no process known to bandur which can cause such a change in a hand.

And now I come to the final pages of the narrative of my journey to Lilliput. I must now note down how I came to leave Blefuscu and the sorrowful events that followed it. Two promising things had happened to me on the same day. I had earned the goodwill of the sycodent and Maku Vait's process had been tested on my left hand. A day that had proven so full of possibilities was to turn out disastrous in the evening.

When I returned from the sycodent's tarunol playing, I was very tired. I took a moment to inspect my left hand to see if Maku Vait's chemical preparation had had any effect. At that time, my hand did not yet show any changes. A little disappointed, despite Maku Vait's warning not to expect any changes for some days, I immediately turned to the scinca to relax and get my mind off my treated hand.

Some time later—how much later I cannot say, since I was eating scinca—the scinca was suddenly disconnected. This was the signal from the guards that someone was approaching. Suppressing the annoyance that I always felt at any abrupt disruption of my scinca eating, I took off my pads to see who it was. Gar Elon entered the warehouse with someone in a hooded cloak. Through the door of the warehouse, before Gar Elon shut it behind him, I saw that it was night outside.

"I have bad news," Gar Elon said to me, without further ado. "Lar Prent has been caught."

I was surprised at Gar Elon's reason for disturbing me at this late hour. "What does that have to do with me?" I asked. Why was Gar Elon taking so much interest in Lar Prent? I wondered. And then it occurred to me that Lar Prent had indicted me for helping him escape from Mildendo. If that was what had happened, it would indeed be cause for alarm.

Even as I was considering this possibility with a sinking feeling, the figure in the cloak stepped forward and threw the hood back.

"Perhaps that is bad news more for me than for you," said the woman in the cloak. I could not recognize her for a moment because she had tried to disguise herself. And then I saw it was Fargo Withrun.

"Gar Elon," I said, "what are you doing with this woman? Don't you know she is a traitor and a rebel?"

"I have no time to explain," Gar Elon said. "The matter is urgent."

"My bad news is that Lar Prent has been caught," Fargo Withrun said. "Your bad news, bandur, is that Queen Baataania is dead."

"No!" I cried out. "That is not possible." I could not believe that my good friend the queen had returned to Yaaga's dream.

"It happened suddenly," Gar Elon said, speaking rapidly. "And not long ago. Her sickness unexpectedly became worse and she passed away in her sleep. Very few know about it still, but we must act fast, within minutes. Fargo Withrun is on her way to Northern Lilliput. The Blefuscu Peeg Pleesa is on her tracks even this second. You also need to escape, because you will certainly be blamed for the queen's death. If both of you go together, you can help each other. You, bandur, can travel much faster than she can and she knows the way and you don't. Traveling together, you will be in Akalan, the nearest Northern Lilliputian country, within hours, perhaps before the night is over. This is the plan. Are you willing, bandur?"

"Gar Elon," I said, "I am surprised to hear you, in whom the Blefuscudian administration places so much trust, speak in this fashion. Do you not know that what you are proposing is the highest treason?"

Gar Elon's face grew angry. "I am well aware of what I am proposing, bandur," he said. "I am risking everything in coming here. It is absolutely crucial that Fargo Withrun escape. I am a friend of Fargo Withrun's and no enemy of yours. That's the only thing which brings me here."

"I have nothing to fear," I said. "I will have nothing to do with your plan. I do not need it."

"Bandur," Fargo Withrun said calmly, "even as we speak the Mildendans are demanding that the Blefuscudians turn you over for execution. There is a clause in the deal that the Blefuscudians made with the Mildendans for your transfer to Blefuscu. That clause says that in the event of anything happening to Queen Baataania, you will be immediately returned to the Mildendans for execution. I'm surprised that Nat Vathesims is not already here with his Peeg Immeegar thugs."

The quiet confidence with which Fargo Withrun spoke stopped me. Perhaps she is correct, I thought. I remembered the Alando Leed's harsh words of threat to me in Mildendo and I panicked. If I could relive that moment, I would not do what I did. Perhaps the Mildendans would indeed have executed me, but I would have taken my chances.

"All right," I said, "I'll go. But from Northern Lilliput, I'll explain everything to Nat Vathesims and then come back to Blefuscu."

"You will be a fool if you do that," Fargo Withrun said.

"No time to discuss all this," Gar Elon said. "Bandur, put only your most important things in your bag quickly and wear it under your overcoat so that it can't be seen. If you wear the coat loosely without buttoning it, the bag won't be more than a slight bulge. It's good that you have not yet been shackled for the night and the chocho that is usually present has gone off duty. For some reason, its substitute has not arrived yet. If the guards ask you anything, we are going for a walk. Let's hope they have not received any instructions regarding Queen Baataania's death yet."

I quickly did as Gar Elon had instructed me. Before exiting the warehouse, I placed Gar Elon and Fargo Withrun in the breast pocket of my overcoat. The pocket was shallow enough for them to stand with their heads peeping out. We left the warehouse and set out into the snow-covered grounds of the takalat, accompanied by the guards who followed a little distance behind in the traka. It was a cold, dark night. It had snowed heavily earlier in the day and a white layer lay over everything.

"How will we get away from the guards in the traka?" I asked.

"You two will get away. I'm going to stay behind. But we must make it look as if I tried to stop you and you escaped despite me," Gar Elon replied. "We are coming up to the Pit of Northern Lilliputian Affairs. The fence of the takalat is just beyond. As soon as you are past the pit, turn sharply to the right so that the trees you see are between you and the traka, throw me down from your pocket and jump over the fence. Then you must run as fast as you can. The traka will be past the trees within moments."

"You may be killed if I throw you out from such a height," I warned.

"Be gentle. There is snow which will cushion my fall. Some injuries will only make it seem more believable."

"How will you explain her and her escape with me?" I asked. "You did bring her to see me."

"Everything's been planned already. He will tell them I forced him," Fargo Withrun said, passing an object I saw was a Lilliputian gun to Gar Elon. "With a gun. I have always had some tendencies toward violence, as the Blefuscudians know well. He struggles with me to stop me, gets my gun away from me, but in the process falls to the ground. With luck, Gar Elon will get away with this explanation."

"But Nat Vathesims is very clever," Gar Elon added gloomily.

I could not help noting in my mind even at that tense moment the thoroughness with which everything had been planned by Gar Elon and Fargo Withrun. I have fallen in with real desperadoes, I realized with a fainting heart. I wanted to turn back, but it was already too late. We were past the Pit of Northern Lilliputian Affairs. I had turned sharply to the right. I had taken Gar Elon from my pocket and flung him on the snow. The plunge had been taken. With a bound I was over the fence and running madly across the open ground.

"Make for that hill," Fargo Withrun said, leaning out of the pocket. I saw a mound to my left and ran toward it. Things were whizzing past us in the night. Voices rang out in the cold air. There was the scrunch of the traka going over the fence of the takalat and coming after us. "I hope Gar Elon is okay," Fargo Withrun said in an absurd whisper, as if there were some danger of being overheard.

I made it to the mound and was over it in a few strides. To one side of us sprang up the towers of Wachicork, dimly visible in the night. On the other side lay a white plain stretching away into the distance.

"Northeast. That way," Fargo Withrun said, pointing away from Wachicork. Fear drove me onward with all the might I could muster. I realized there was no going back. If I was caught in this situation, I would be killed. It was as simple as that. I had to escape. The thought drove me to lengthen my strides even more. The traka, if it had made it over the mound, seemed to be falling behind.

"The chochos should be out any time now," Fargo Withrun said. "Against the white background of the snow, you are going to show very clearly to them in your green overcoat."

I had not thought about that. Even as I was turning this idea round in my mind, Fargo Withrun shouted out triumphantly. "There it is," she said, pointing to a great dark mass in front of us.

It was a thick forest, with huge trees that stood even taller than me. Refuge! and just in time. I was breathing in great gasps and had slowed down significantly. I came up to the first trees and plunged past them gratefully. The forest got thicker and thicker as I made my way into it and the branches brushed against my shoulders and head. "Stop and rest," Fargo Withrun said after some time. There was a tone of command in her voice, but I was too tired to challenge it. I dropped gratefully to the ground.

As I lay panting on the snow, the lights of three or four chochos moved swiftly across a gap in the thick foliage of the trees overhead. Fargo Withrun crawled out of the pocket of my overcoat and stood on my chest. Ever since I had run out of shaving material, I had been growing a beard. She looked past the beard into my face. I looked back at her. What was left of her disguise was rubbing off. She had grown quite gaunt since I had last seen her. Her cheeks were sunken and her eyes were dark hollows.

"That was good running," she said admiringly. "What strength you have, bandur. Of course, the traka would have caught up with us were it not for the snow. The snow was too deep for it."

"Gar Elon," I said, between deep breaths. "He is one of you."

"All this is confusing, isn't it, bandur?" Fargo Withrun said. "You have real trouble figuring out who is good and who is bad, don't you? Well, I shouldn't expect anything else from someone who consents to participate in the absurd ritual of tarunol playing."

I let the malicious comment pass. It was beginning to snow again. The first flakes drifted slowly to the ground. And then more. And more. It was turning into a storm, but inside the forest it was not so bad.

"Good," Fargo Withrun said. "That should hide our tracks and give us some cover. Let's go, bandur."

I lurched wearily to my feet and set off in the direction she pointed to. It was slow going in the thick forest. I had never seen trees this big in Lilliput before. Most of the trees were many times larger than me. The snow fell without letup. Fargo Withrun was very pleased with it. She did not have any trouble making her way through the forest and seemed to know exactly where she was going. She would only stop now and then to inspect our position carefully. To me, the forest looked the same everywhere. Sometimes she would inspect the bark of a tree closely. She seemed to be looking for some secret directions. As we went deeper and deeper into the forest, the terrain got more and more mountainous. We stopped for a rest every two or three hours. I was glad that all the strenuous exercise in Mildendo had kept me in optimum shape.

"This forest extends all the way to the Akalanian border," Fargo Withrun said. "If this snow keeps up, we may be able to keep moving even after daybreak. The Blefuscudian Peeg Immeegar should have trouble tracking even someone of your size in this storm."

As if the snow had heard her words, it kept falling through the morning and we arrived at the Akalanian border a few hours after daybreak. Fargo Withrun stopped us a little distance from the half-frozen stream that formed the border. We had to leave the cover of the forest to cross the stream. A little distance behind the other bank, the forest rose up again on the Akalanian side.

"We'll rest for a few moments and then cross the river," Fargo Withrun said. "I have an Akalanian friend waiting in the forest on the other side. He is an official in the Akalanian administration, one of the few good ones. Once we are on the other side, we are relatively safe. The Blefuscudians may treat the Akalanians like dirt because they are Northern Lilliputians, but I doubt they will be so brazen as to openly violate Akalanian territory in the presence of an Akalanian official. My friend will show himself if need be."

I did not say anything. During the whole journey, I had not spoken a word to Fargo Withrun. I had quietly followed her instructions and kept moving. My legs were numb from cold and fatigue but I had forced myself to put one foot in front of the other. Sometime during the night, it had occurred to me that Fargo Withrun and Gar Elon might have lied to me about Queen Baataania being dead. I had panicked at that moment, I realized, but there was nothing to be done about it. I felt resigned to my situation. I could not retrace my steps to Wachicork. I did not even know the way back.

"You think Gar Elon and I lied to you about Queen Baataania," Fargo Withrun noted. She could not help noticing how taciturn I was with her. "Once we are in Akalan, you will be able to ascertain whether we told you the truth or not. You will be safe in Akalan for the moment, but you will need to start making plans. My friend is not a high official in the administration. He cannot protect you very much. There are chances that the Akalanians will use you as the Blefuscudians and the Mildendans did. Or else they will give you back to the Blefuscudians, to stay in their good books."

"The Mildendans and the Blefuscudians did not use me," I said. You did, I wanted to continue. I didn't because I didn't want to antagonize her.

"Let's not argue about that," Fargo Withrun said. "I'm just telling you things to warn you. You may do as you please. I will be able to disappear when necessary. My parents originally went to Mildendo from Akalan many years ago. I still have family in Akalan. You can't disappear anywhere. You should think carefully of what you want to do once we are in Akalan."

I did not bother replying to her. She and Lar Prent had used me at every turn and now she was showing mock concern. Why hadn't she told me all these small details about the Akalanians before hustling me out of the warehouse so that I could carry her here? I was amazed at how stupid I had been in dealing with Lar Prent and Fargo Withrun ever since I had met them.

When Fargo Withrun decided the moment was appropriate, we crossed the stream and made it into the forest on the Akalanian side without incident. Fargo Withrun's friend, who met us in a clearing in the forest, was a little brown Lilliputian with a thick moustache. He had small shifty eyes and was constantly smiling. For an official of the Akalanian administration, he was deplorably dressed in crumpled trousers and a loose overcoat that hung shapelessly to his knees like a sack. So low have I fallen, I thought to myself, when I saw him. In Blefuscu, Nat Vathesims himself, one of the most powerful men in all of Lilliput, was my personal friend and liaison. Now I was to be represented and guided by this scruffy Akalanian, who looked like an impoverished peasant.

"This is Vodhavi Kudukaravan," Fargo Withrun said, introducing me to her friend. "He is a goatherd by profession. He is also a deputy-mayor of the border town of Vaasal."

Vodhavi Kudukaravan looked up at me with his mouth open, tilting his head back as far as it would go. Even from my great height I could tell that his teeth were discolored and rotten.

"Well, what do you think of the bandur, Vodhavi?" Fargo Withrun asked him.

"He is even bigger than I imagined," Vodhavi Kudukaravan replied. "It will be hard to hide him even temporarily. I suggest we don't go into Vaasal at all. I have a cabin up in the hills. Let us go there first and decide what to do."

The snow had stopped falling. As we made our way toward Vodhavi Kudukaravan's cabin, the forest began to give way to rocky terrain. We climbed higher up into the hills, picking our way carefully over the snow-covered rocks. The going was slow, as Vodhavi Kudukaravan refused to be carried by me and I had to adjust myself to the pace of his mountain traka, a primitive apology of a machine.

In the valley below us, the town of Vaasal was clearly visible as we climbed into the hills. It was a sprawling, dirty little collection of shacks and badly constructed stone buildings, with no transportways or gardens. There were only two buildings of any size, both of them located a little outside the town. They had chimneys from which smoke rose into the sky. They seemed to be factories. Two or three narrow roads led into the town. Broken-down trakas moved with painful slowness along them. My tutor in Mildendo had shown me pictures of Northern Lilliputian towns. Vaasal seemed even worse than the pictures.

"Vaasal is the fourth largest town in Akalan," Vodhavi Kudukaravan said to me proudly, leaning out of the window of his traka. "I am a deputy-mayor of it." I faked a smile for him. Suddenly, all my interest in Lilliput was disappearing.

As we approached Vodhavi Kudukaravan's cabin, which was up on a hill overlooking Vaasal, two chochos appeared in the gray sky. They circled over us a couple of times, hung in the air for a moment, and then flew back in the direction of Blefuscu.

"We have been spotted," Fargo Withrun said, leaning out of my pocket to look up at the disappearing chochos. "Bandur, you had better decide what to do soon. When night comes I will be gone. And then you will be on your own."

I barely heard what Fargo Withrun had said. A wave of exhaustion was flooding through me. Vodhavi Kudukaravan's cabin was a small wooden box leaning against the rock face of a hill. I dropped myself on the cold ground by the cabin and promptly fell asleep in my overcoat. Fargo Withrun and Vodhavi Kudukaravan were saying something to me but I could not understand their words. I was too exhausted to keep my eyes open.

When I awoke some hours later, I found that it was night. Fargo Withrun and Vodhavi Kudukaravan had been joined by three other Lilliputians, two women and a man. The Lilliputians had started fires all around me to keep me warm. Vodhavi Kudukaravan had boiled three sacks of potatoes and roasted five of his goats to provide me with a small but hot meal.

Fargo Withrun wheeled my meal to me in a large handcart. "Gar Elon is in the hospital," she said to me. "He is badly injured but he'll survive."

I ate my meal sitting up in the center of the circle of fires and looking down at the meager lights of Vaasal, which served to remind me how far I had descended in the space of a few hours.

At the end of my small meal, I felt grateful to the Akalanians, even though I was still hungry. And then Fargo Withrun spoke and destroyed my warm feeling of gratitude. "Bandur, we have a plan which may work," she said. "I'm needed here but I'm prepared to make time to go with you to Rupatchi. Rupatchi, as you may be aware, is a country far to the north. There is no love lost between Rupatchi and the countries of Southern Lilliput. Rupatchi is sure to provide you with the kind of sanctuary that Akalan cannot or will not provide. Now I'll be straight with you. The journey there will be long and hard and very, very dangerous. We may not make it. But if you are willing to try, I'll go with you."

Once again, I realized, Fargo Withrun was scheming to use me. No wonder she had taken such good care of me. She probably had some ulterior motive of her own for going to Rupatchi that she was, as usual, lying about. My tutor in Mildendo, Edu Kator, had told me all about Rupatchi. It was the most savage country of all in Lilliput. It was even poorer than Akalan. It was constantly quarreling with the other countries of Lilliput and secretly funded violent acts against Blefuscu and Mildendo out of an irrational hatred for them. It had a terrible record of violence against its own citizens. For many centuries, both the Mildendans and the Blefuscudians had tried to teach the Rupatchians the most basic norms of civilized behavior. But the Rupatchians had rejected all their help with base ingratitude. I had no intention of traveling to such a country.

"I think I will return to the bandur lands I came from," I said.

"How will you do that, bandur?" Fargo Withrun asked.

I ignored her and spoke to Vodhavi Kudukaravan. "The seacoast is nearby, isn't it?" I said to him.

He nodded and pointed to the north. "Over the hills," he said.

"If you will just give me help in building a raft and providing me with some food, that will be enough," I said to him.

And this was how I came to leave Lilliput. Fargo Withrun tried to object to my plan. She kept trying to get me to travel to Rupatchi with her. She claimed she was trying to repay the favor I had done her by helping her escape from Blefuscu, something she might not have been able to do on her own. She pointed out how cold it was and how I had no idea in which direction to sail. She wanted to know if I had any experience as a seaman. She was correct about the foolhardiness of my plan, but I had no intention of staying to be used by the Northern Lilliputians. I had no reason to believe that they would be any less unscrupulous in their behavior toward me than Lar Prent and Fargo Withrun had been.

My main objective in life was to return to Blefuscu or Mildendo, which were the only places, I had decided, I would be happy to live in. It is only in Southern Lilliput that I would find people who thought like me and were suited to my sensibility. After the manner of my departure from Blefuscu, however, I could not return there immediately. It made sense, therefore, to retire to the bandur lands temporarily. If I could not make it there and died in the open seas, even that was better than being an instrument for the vile plans of the Rupatchians. I had more chances of making my peace with the Blefuscudians and the Mildendans from the bandur lands than from Rupatchi, which was after all their worst enemy.

Having come to this decision, I worked with single-minded purpose with the Akalanians through the night and by morning had a rude raft ready. Vodhavi Kudukaravan had brought in many more of his friends to help us. We built the raft on the beach so that it would be easier to launch it. All of this was done in the greatest secrecy, for officials of the Akalanian government had already arrived in Vaasal to meet me. Vodhavi Kudukaravan was stalling them with excuses about the weather and my exhaustion.

Rumor had it that Blefuscudian officials would arrive in Vaasal within hours. I wondered if Nat Vathesims would be with them. I had half a mind to stay and find out, but did not have the courage. I was certain that the Blefuscudians would not understand the way in which I had left their country. My explanations for my actions would have to be carefully made, in such a manner that the proof for what I claimed was incontrovertible. For this I needed time. I could not put myself in the hands of the Blefuscudians until I was sure that I could convince them. It would be better if I waited until a more opportune moment in the future.

Fargo Withrun, who had delayed her departure from Vaasal apparently in the hope of still persuading me to go with her to Rupatchi, came to see me just as I was loading my bag and some provisions in the raft. It lay drawn up on the beach, just beyond where the gray waves lapped at the land. A rudimentary sail had been fashioned for the raft. I planned to sail north as far and as fast as I could. I had no idea what awaited me in the future. Vodhavi Kudukaravan and his friends could only provide me with some loaves of bread and some sacks of apples. The food would not last me for more than a day or two. Perhaps the Blefuscudians would send out ships to capture me. Perhaps I would be dead in a few days because of the cold. I did not know. I did not really care. Life seemed to have lost all meaning. Returning to the bandur lands was at best the lesser of evils.

"The Blefuscudians have executed Lar Prent," Fargo Withrun said to me. "I just heard the news." She was standing on the beach with the raft towering high over her. I stopped what I was doing and looked down at her.

"Is this another lie?" I asked. "And even if it were true, why would I care?" I went back to loading the raft.

Fargo Withrun did not say anything. She was looking very ill and thin, even in her overcoat. The black skin of her face seemed to have been stretched tight over the bones beneath. She turned around and walked away to where the rest of the Lilliputians, Vodhavi Kudukaravan's friends, were standing by two trakas we had used in constructing the raft. They were watching me prepare to launch the raft. When all my things were in it, I pushed the contraption of wooden logs lashed together with ropes into the sea, sprang in myself, and grabbed a tree that I had prepared for use as an oar. A helpful wind was behind me and swept the raft out to sea. The tiny Lilliputians on the beach rapidly disappeared from view. I set about using the little knowledge of seamanship I had.

I was on the raft for two days, sailing toward what I thought was north. It was bitterly cold, especially because the sea seeped in through cracks in the raft despite the attempts the Lilliputians had made to waterproof it with some resinlike substance they had. Most of the second day I was unconscious with exhaustion, cold, and hunger, so I don't remember when I was picked up by the Indian merchant ship. It was apparently late in the evening. A crewman had spotted me by accident.

When I came to I was in a huge bed in a warm cabin with a monstrous brown face hanging over me. I screamed and screamed and screamed in terror and disgust. The face disappeared in consternation and returned with another one, even more ugly. I shivered with fright at the sight of them. For the first few days no one could get anything out of me. I even had to be force-fed.

I don't want to go into all the dreary details of what happened after that. The captain of the ship thought that I was delirious from my experience on the sea and I let him think that. I had no intention of telling him where I had really been. He had gone through my bag and discovered some of the tiny Lilliputian plants and artifacts and books that I had in there. I explained them away by saying something about inventions and hobbies. The notes of my stay in Lilliput, I said, were ideas for a novel. So incredible is the idea of a land of tiny people that it never occurred to him to disbelieve me. When he saw me updating my journal a few days later, when I was feeling better, he thought I was working on my novel and was pleased.

On our return to Bombay, there were some questions from the

authorities about who I was and where I had been. I made up some story about falling sick in Australia and losing my memory. My disappearance in Australia, nearly ten months earlier, was on record. The real problem in my return to the bandur lands was not making up some story to fool the bandur but keeping my disgust and terror at the sight of them from showing. Every moment, I had to grind my teeth and swallow the nausea that I felt when I saw them.

After the formalities with the authorities were over, I was at a loss to know what to do. One day, I got into a train going from Bombay to Delhi. This became the pretext for traveling by trains all over India for a couple of months. During this time, I lived by pretending to be a beggar. As a beggar, I could travel without attracting too much attention to myself. It was a period of readjustment to life in bandur lands. It took time for me to get used to my disgust at the sight of bandur. I am still not fully reconciled to the sight of them and never will be, but I am more in control of myself now.

I have now returned to Madras, my hometown. I have taken a little room in Ganapathy Kovil Street and am engaged in writing these my memoirs and organizing my notes from the trip to Lilliput. In these memoirs, I have mostly confined myself to a narration of events that happened to me. I have not attempted an exhaustive description of the lands that I visited in Lilliput. Such an ethnographic description of some of the lands of Lilliput is a task I have set myself for the future.

I have also not written about what has happened to me after my return to Madras. The despicable animals who live here are going through one of their meaningless rituals. Something that they call an election has been under way. Predictably enough they have managed to make it into a contemptible and violent affair. The two main sides in this electoral contest were a woman and a man. The idea of the woman running for office is terrifying. Once, she came and confronted me in my room. She was a big ugly thing. She was wearing glasses to make herself look intelligent but the coarseness of her facial features revealed her true status. I have met her opponent too. I used to know him quite well years ago, in the life I have left behind. A few weeks ago, he was passing in a car and recognized me in the street. He stopped the car and called out my name. He was surprised at my state but quite sympathetic. I have met him once or twice since then. Of all the bandur that I have met, he has the most potential. There actually is something approaching dignity and culture about him. I have hinted very broadly to him of some of my experiences in Lilliput. He is a powerful man. It is possible that he will be able to help me in my attempt to get back to Blefuscu. Though he knows nothing about Lilliput, he has promised to help me in my future endeavors in whatever way he can. Of course, as he says, he must first win the election and return to power. That is what needs to be accomplished first.

I plan to return to Lilliput as soon as I can. In the meantime, I live on the little money that I still had when I left India. I'm glad I do not need to work to get by. The thought of working among bandur disgusts me. I would like to know if Queen Baataania is really dead or not. If only I can get a message to the Blefuscudians, explaining exactly what happened, I'm sure they will let me return. Now that so much time has passed, I'm sure they will be able to assess the sincerity of my feelings toward them calmly.

I'm not certain how I'll raise money for my return. Most of my property and earnings from before my trip to Lilliput are gone. Perhaps I will be able to sell or otherwise make use of some of the things that I have brought back from Lilliput. Until now I have kept everything secret. But if need be I can make use of these things. Maybe I will be able to publish this memoir of my trip to Lilliput. Perhaps, if the man returns to power, I will be able to tell him everything. He seems a reasonable man. Ideally, however, I would prefer to wait until the Blefuscudians and Mildendans are themselves ready to publicize the news of their existence. This news is sure to revolutionize the way we think of the world. At that time, if I have not yet managed to return to Lilliput, my services will be invaluable to all bandur and I will be able at last to capitalize on all the information I have. I will be able to move out of the obscurity of an insignificant little room in an insignificant little street (in which I am sitting this very moment with the rain falling outside) and take my rightful place in the world as the first and best friend of the Blefuscudians and Mildendans.

Epilogue

The rain blankets Madras with a torrential flood of water. In homes across the city, windows are being shut, candles are being taken out of drawers and cupboards and readied, anxious telephone calls are being made back and forth. Men and women hurry through the streets with their heads bowed under umbrellas. Some men ride bicycles with an umbrella perched precariously between neck and shoulder. Already in some streets, the water is beginning to collect in dark pools whose surfaces have taken on an oily sheen as they reflect the light of streetlamps. Women who get the hems of their sarees wet as they hurry toward railway stations or bus stops complain under their breaths. In railway stations throughout the city, commuters wait anxiously to find out if trains have been delayed or not.

In the Kuppancherry branch office of the Domestic Workers Union, a light is shining over a number of figures bent over a table. Two of the figures are Kulan and Selvi looking at something, a pamphlet of some kind. They are sitting together at one end of the table. They are consulting about a project they have decided to start. At the other end, two women are discussing something loudly. To a figure outside in the rain, passing along the street under an umbrella, the scene inside the Domestic Workers Union branch office is visible quite clearly. At one end of the table, two figures are engaged in silent appraisal of something that is lying on the table. At the other end, two figures are talking animatedly, their mouths engaged in vigorous but inaudible activity.

Let us leave these figures where they are and move to the dark verandah of the building.

Two beggars have taken over one corner of this verandah to escape from the rain. Now one of the beggars, who has been sleeping, raises himself slowly from the floor of the verandah and looks at the rain from within the matted jungle of hair that frames his face. His yellow eyes gleam in the gray twilight of the rain. He scratches his left armpit and shivers in the cold. The other beggar, who is sitting with his back against the wall, draws a dirty brown cloth around himself. He is younger and has one blind eye, which is permanently shut. He digs out two beedis from a pocket in his vest and passes one to the beggar who has just woken up. They both light their beedis and smoke them, sitting side by side and looking out into the rain in the street.

"This is Shanthamma's place," says the beggar with the one eye to the other one.

"Who is she?" asks the other beggar indifferently.

"Union leader. I saw her killed."

The other beggar's interest is piqued. "Where? What happened?"

The one-eyed beggar's beedi is going out. He pauses to draw deeply on it. The fading end of the beedi bursts into a red glow again. He looks at the tip of the beedi with satisfaction. "Over in Krantinagar. You know that little temple by the maidan? Behind that. It was late at night. Nobody else saw it but me." There is pride in the beggar's voice as he says this. "She was killed with a knife. An old man with long white hair and a white beard killed her. He held her with his right hand and stabbed her again and again with a knife in the left hand. I was sleeping on the other side of the temple. He kept shouting at her in some strange language I could not understand. He kept shouting 'bandur! bandur!' or something like that at her. Shanthamma did not make a sound. I was so frightened."

"How do you know that was Shanthamma?"

"Haven't you seen posters of her? They are everywhere. See!" He points to a poster of Shanthamma on a wall across the street. The poster is peeling off. There is a great hole where the mouth had been.

"Did you tell the police?"

The one-eyed beggar laughs. "Why would I do that?"

The other beggar nods understandingly. The attention of both of them is drawn to a figure.

An old village woman with ears made pendulous by heavy

earrings has stopped in the middle of the street in front of the office of the Domestic Workers Union. She stares out from behind thick glasses at the rain. She has a plastic bag in one hand. Her skin is wrinkled and sagging. A little in front of her is her son, who is hurrying on through the rain. When he notices that she has stopped, he calls to her in annoyance, turning his whole body to address her because of the small metal trunk he is carrying on his head. Neither the beggars nor the two figures in the street know it yet, but the murder of Shanthamma is to have important consequences in their lives in the future. Oblivious, the mother and the son seem to hurry on to this destiny, while the beggars seem to sit silently in the verandah and wait for it.